BLOOD
TIES

ALSO BY RUTH LILLEGRAVEN

Everything Is Mine

Sickle

BLOOD TIES

A NOVEL

A Clara Thriller

RUTH LILLEGRAVEN

TRANSLATED BY DIANE OATLEY

Text copyright © 2021 by Ruth Lillegraven
Translation copyright © 2022 by Diane Oatley
All rights reserved.

Previously published as *Av mitt blod* by Kagge in Norway in 2021. Translated from Norwegian by Diane Oatley. First published in English by Amazon Crossing in 2022.

Published by Amazon Crossing, Seattle

www.apub.com

Amazon, the Amazon logo, and Amazon Crossing are trademarks of Amazon.com, Inc., or its affiliates.

ISBN-13: 9781542025003
ISBN-10: 1542025001

Cover design by Caroline Teagle Johnson

Printed in the United States of America

To Eva Hildrum

PROLOGUE

ANDREAS

October 5

Nikolai is lying beside me in the cramped, dark space. It is so noisy in here. The sounds from the motor, the tires, all of it becomes a rumbling drone that fills my head as we are carried farther and farther from home.

Nikolai and I have slept side by side ever since we were inside Mommy's tummy. I lay head down, prepared to launch, she told us. Nikolai lay above me, waiting for me to lead the way. To this day, he almost always waits for me to sort things out first.

These days, he often leaves his own bedroom and comes into mine at night. There is a mattress on the floor, but he always gets into bed with me, especially after what happened to Dad. He stinks of foot and body odor, but his hair smells good, and he is my brother, my little brother. Yes, we were born at the same time, but I have sort of always been the big brother.

The fact that Nikolai is lying beside me is normal.

Everything else is not.

"Are you okay?" I whisper.

"Yes," he replies, but I know tears are trickling down his cheeks.

"Nikolai. Try to believe that everything will be fine. Then it will be. Okay?"

He sobs, and I can almost smell his tears, even though I don't think tears have a scent.

I am lying in an awkward position and have a cramp in one of my legs. I try to stretch it out. How long have we been here? An hour? Two? Three? It's impossible to say. It's completely dark in here, and for sure, it's dark outside, too. I feel queasy and unwell—maybe we're breathing up all the air in here? But. I. Must. Not. Think. About. It. If I start to panic now, Nikolai will completely lose it, and that won't do.

Mommy must have come home by now. This morning, she said that she hadn't organized a sitter for us, but she assured us she wasn't going to be late. She says that a lot, even though it's not true. But today, it seemed like she meant it a little more than usual.

I can picture her: Clara, Mommy, the minister of justice. She opens the door and wades through all the shoes, the bags, the jackets strewn everywhere. She's always saying how much it irritates her, but she doesn't do anything about it. She notices how quiet it is, and calls our names. Silence. She calls again. Then she understands that something is very wrong.

"Andreas?" Nikolai says. "I'm scared."

Of course he's scared. I'm scared, too, but I can't let him see that. I mustn't become cross with him either, not now.

"It will be fine," I say, and try to talk in a daddy voice.

"Are we going to die?" he squeaks.

"Yes," I say. "But not now. In another eighty years or so."

"How do you know?"

"I just do. Calm down now, please. Think about Daddy."

I immediately understand that was the wrong thing to say. It makes him sniffle and squirm.

The vehicle makes a sharp turn and then another. I can feel something acidic rise in my throat, and I have to swallow. Really. Can't. Throw. Up. Here. Now. I swallow again, swallow it down, but Nikolai is still sniveling and crying.

"Nikolai," I say, and this time I try using a mommy voice. "We have to pull ourselves together."

2

PART 1

THE JOB

CHAPTER 1

CLARA

One month earlier

"We're on," the prime minister whispers into my ear. "Go."

As we walk out onto the Palace Square, I notice them. The raindrops. Hitting my cheek, my hand, my forehead.

The press turnout is huge, even though this time there are only two new cabinet ministers. I look out into the crowd without meeting a single pair of eyes, just a sea of black camera lenses of varying sizes. It's like staring into a throng of pistol barrels.

"Act like it doesn't bother you," the prime minister whispers as the rainfall grows heavier.

She keeps one hand firmly against the small of my back. The other hand rests on the back of the new minister of health. The idea is perhaps to offer support and encouragement, but her hand is clenched into a tiny fist, and as she presses it against the fabric of my expensive jacket, it feels more like a threat than reassurance.

I've played it safe. A black skirt, black jacket, black stilettos. A light-blue blouse that is freshly ironed but rumpling with every falling raindrop.

You look nice, Mommy, Nikolai had said, always more generous with compliments than his brother. Andreas seemed cross; he does not like that I have agreed to do this.

The journalists and the photographers have already pulled their hoods over their heads, opened their umbrellas. I have nowhere to seek shelter, and the water has started trickling down my face now. Still, I keep smiling. That was the last thing the prime minister said to us before we walked out, that she didn't want to see a single photo of us looking glum.

We are supposed to look happy, proactive, and strong, which is also what her fist is communicating. Happy. Proactive. Strong. Happy. Proactive. Strong. Click, click, click.

I stand tall in my stilettos. The soles are so thin that I can feel the gravel against my feet. Carefully, I move an inch or so away from the largest stone.

The Mother of Our Nation, former prime minister Gro Harlem Brundtland, apparently always put a stone in her shoe in situations she thought might make her cry. I suppose it's a good solution for people who cry easily, but I have never been one of those people.

The position of minister of justice was always one of the most coveted in the government. Due to a series of ugly scandals over the past year, all that has changed.

I know that people are whispering about how none of the more obvious candidates wanted the position, and that is why it was offered to me. The prime minister said I was the first person she asked. I don't really care. I want the position regardless. This is my chance; now I can finally accomplish something.

Two groups have gathered, one on either side of the press mob. The largest group appears to be the minister of health's family. An elderly couple, probably his parents; a few friends or maybe brothers. A tiny blonde woman with three children. My boys are at school. Asking them to come did not even occur to me.

My mother- and father-in-law, however, are here. I can see them now. They have aged considerably over the past few months, and they seem to be cloaked in a veil of sadness. Sometimes, I feel a stab of guilt about this. Their son would be here had it not been for me. Other times, their melancholy irritates me.

Today they actually look almost happy, especially my father-in-law, the retired supreme court judge. Henrik always complained about how his father was more interested in me and my achievements as a lawyer than his own son who saved lives every day. Maybe there was some truth to it. My mother-in-law wipes away a few tears as she stands beneath her umbrella. I look straight at them, smile as warmly as I can. Then I see another familiar face beside Åsa, my mother-in-law. He pulls her into a hug, kisses her hair, makes her laugh.

It's Axel, Henrik's best friend. All his life, he has wandered in and out of the Fougner family home, like another son in the household.

I hadn't expected any of them to be here, especially not Axel, though he works just down the street. It's nice that they're here, in a strange way.

My mother-in-law lifts a bouquet, holds it out to me.

"Go over and accept the flowers," the prime minister murmurs. "Quickly. We can't stand here for long."

I walk toward my group. My mother-in-law kisses me on both cheeks; then my father-in-law does the same. Axel hugs me, whispers congratulations. I am unable to hear his words but can feel his warm breath against my ear.

Then it happens. A woman about sixty years old with dark, curly hair, coarse skin, and heavy eyelids behind thick eyeglasses comes rushing toward me. In her hand, like a kind of weapon, is a small bottle.

"Murderer," she screams. "Murderer!"

I stiffen but keep smiling. It feels like a grimace. Instinctively, I raise my arms as if to protect myself. I take two or three steps back, wobbling on my stiletto heels, until I back into someone. He, because I sense it is a man, takes hold of me under my arms, holds me up, keeps me from falling.

"Take it easy," he says softly. "I've got you."

For a second or two, the world freezes right there. Then everything starts moving again.

"Murderer," the woman screams again.

"Go back to the prime minister, behave like nothing happened," my rescuer whispers.

I glance at him. He is tall and lean, with chiseled facial features. Deep-blue eyes. Light-blond hair with a reddish sheen, a beard. The rugged type, no doubt, he looks like a veteran from some battle, reminds me of the kind of men I meet now and then when skiing deep in the forest on the coldest days of January, in places where people rarely venture. The uniform is from the government car service, so he's not a policeman.

We regroup at the front of the crowd, stand posing for a few seconds. The unexpected, overwhelming rain that has stolen all our dignity, combined with the unexpected attack on me, has the press photographers snickering in a mixture of compassion and malicious glee.

"Keep smiling," the prime minister whispers.

CHAPTER 2

—

LEIF

My first thought when I wake up in the morning is that today my daughter will become Norway's minister of justice.

I swing my legs across the bed and onto the floor, using my hands to push myself away from the edge in an effort to compensate for the early morning stiffness in my ankles and knees. It always gets better after I have been up and about for a while.

Finally, I am standing solidly on my feet. I turn around and tug the wrinkles out of the sheet, making the bed as best I can. I look forward to going upstairs to a cold bedroom in the evenings, lying down on the tucked-in flat sheet under the duvet, as much as I also look forward to getting up in the morning, making the coffee, pouring the first cup.

In the kitchen, I make two pieces of toast, one with Gouda cheese and one with jam; fill my cup with coffee; and pour the rest into the old thermos that has been here since my mother was alive.

Next, I go outside to see to the chickens. They are clucking and carrying on when I enter with their pellets. I bend down. One egg. Two. Three. They are still warm in my hand as I tiptoe out of the henhouse, head inside, and place the eggs on the kitchen counter before going back out to the barn and the sheep. It smells of wool and warm animals. The sheep bleat. Everything is the same, yet also different.

After finishing up in the barn, I go outside to work on my new project. I am going to put in a new fence on the top of the hill, facing the woods. The sheep can pasture there after the lambing in the spring.

For a long time, I have been working out a method to secure the fence, something I can do myself. Now I have developed a new system using a crowbar, loading straps, and a tractor.

It works so well I wonder why I haven't done it like this before.

I stop, place one foot on a rock, and rest my elbows upon my knee, gazing into the distance. First the hills, then the forest, the orange blaze of foliage. Behind it is a belt of dark spruce forest. I can't see it from here, I just know it's there. The spruce belt is on a steep hill that continues down to the highway. I can't see the highway from here either.

What I can see is the fjord. On a windless, sunny autumn day like this, it gets a kind of glossy surface. It lies far below, shining, reflecting the light from the huge sky, all the way up to me.

Still, after an entire life here, the sight knocks the breath out of me.

I live here; this is where I will live as long as there is life left in me, and a more beautiful place doesn't exist.

Back inside, I pour myself another cup of coffee. On the table beside my chair, in front of the window, is the book I'm reading. It is almost one thousand pages long, about WWII, like many of the books I read. Usually, I would read for a half hour now; today, I will watch television instead.

Afterward, I will go back to working on the fence and doing other things, but tonight, after dinner, I will pour myself a drink from the bottle in the corner cupboard, sit down in my chair by the window, turn on the reading lamp, listen to the crackling of the woodstove, and disappear into the book until my eyelids grow so heavy that I will have to turn in.

I enjoy those hours. I like my life. For so many years, I have been filled with uneasiness. After my time in Lebanon, it was bad, but the worst period was after Lars died. Years and years of different kinds of anxieties have piled up, like layer upon layer of different sediments in the ground.

Lately, though, it's as if everything is just fine. Maybe I've gotten too old, maybe I just can't be bothered to worry anymore.

I settle down in front of the television set. Clara called me yesterday evening, as she does every day, but yesterday, she had something out of the ordinary to tell me.

I can't believe it. My Clara, the daughter of a poor farmer. In spite of everything that happened to us, in spite of her useless mother and our losing Lars, she has done well. Now she will have a seat at the king's table.

I hardly recognize her when I see her on the television screen, all made up and stylish, in a suit and blouse and high heels. She looks like a stranger, like a city person. For the first time, I think that she resembles her mother, Agnes, the way she used to be. Regal. Elegant. Dignified.

The television commentator says that Lofthus is a refreshing and unexpected choice, not least because her sole political experience is just a few months as a state secretary. Lofthus has lived in Oslo for many years but is originally from a small village up north in Western Norway. She was recently widowed under tragic circumstances when her husband drowned in a lake in the mountains of Western Norway. Now she is alone with her twin sons. Her personal life does not make the appointment any less controversial.

It starts raining. The prime minister and the new minister of health shift back and forth uneasily, even though they keep smiling. Clara stands tall, undaunted. Henrik's parents are there. Axel, too, I see. For a moment, I am a bit envious; it would have been nice to attend.

A woman approaches Clara; she shouts, waving something. What's going on? Everything stops for a few seconds. Then Clara walks back to the prime minister, her smile now slightly strained. She is a head taller than her boss and also taller than the male minister standing opposite.

She thought she could get a lot accomplished to help children. That's what she said to me on the phone yesterday. That's probably true. I am more doubtful about whether this job will be good for her own children, for Andreas and Nikolai. Had she asked me, I would have told her so, but she didn't ask. For many years Clara always asked my advice about everything. Not anymore. That is both right and wrong. But that gleam she has in her eyes is rarely a good sign. Then I pick up the remote, turn off the television, get to my feet.

At the supermarket, several people come over and congratulate me.

"You must be so proud," the woman at the cash register says.

I simply nod before going back to the car.

Strangely enough, I like driving the stretch from town out along the fjord, the narrow, curving road with a steep rock face on the left-hand side. In the summer and autumn, sometimes stones will tumble down; in the wintertime, often blocks of ice. On the right-hand side is a drop-off, descending straight into the fjord. The landscape opens up, offering an expansive view. The mountains, the fjord, the sky. The hills are aflame with fiery orange foliage. There was an early frost this year, the earliest on record; the autumn colors followed close behind.

A few miles ahead lies the road leading to the mountain ledge where I live. On the way there, I pass Storagjelet, where Clara and her stepfather drove off the road all those years ago. I am used to it. Every time I have been to town to shop or run other errands for the last thirty years, I have had to pass by here. It causes me no sorrow.

Magne died, as he deserved. Clara survived. She escaped from the car and made it out of the fjord, against all odds.

Actually, driving past Storagjelet has always made me feel grateful. Had something happened to Clara on that day, I would never have survived. She was all I had left.

Late last summer, divers found Magne's car two hundred yards down. Still, I wasn't prepared for the sight of the car itself, nor the distress it would cause me. In one way or another, maybe I imagined that the car disintegrated and disappeared, even though I know that's impossible.

As I approach Storagjelet, I see a crowd of people gathered at the rest stop that was put in there. After the accident, they blasted the rock face on the other side of the road and moved the turn a bit farther into the mountainside. Nothing looks like it did before, except there is a rock face on one side and the fjord on the other, and it's still a long way down to the water.

I stop the car, get out, and walk hesitantly over to the crowd.

Frank Birger, people call him Buzz, raises his hand. He walks toward me. Now I mostly just want to go back to the car and drive home.

"Good morning," he says, laying a fist on my shoulder. "I was sure you were in Oslo celebrating your daughter's appointment."

Unkempt and overweight, his trousers sagging low on his butt, Buzz looks like one of those huge plastic trolls outside tourist shops, his dirty hair sticking up every which way. He spends a lot of time sitting at the Grill Bar, stuffing his face with mega burgers and french fries. Given all the hours he has spent there and his many years as a bus driver for schoolchildren living on the most remote-lying farms, Buzz knows everything that is happening in the village. He considers it his responsibility to pass this news on to everyone, whether they want to hear about it or not.

Now he points at the flatbed of a tow truck a few yards away. There I see the rusted skeleton of a car that was once owned and driven by the man who destroyed my family. It has now been hauled out into the light of day, covered with mud and algae.

It all comes flooding back at the sight of that car shimmering past me.

They were my flock. Agnes and Clara and Lars. My flock, those whom I was always supposed to look after. I failed.

Little Lars covered with bruises, Lars cold and blue on a hospital bed, Clara in the police car after the car accident, Agnes at the front door in the rain.

All of this which will never go away, which will never again be quite right.

More than anything, I can see my tall, thin daughter with her arm around her brother's headstone, as if the stone were Lars. Her eyes, so sorrowful yet simultaneously proud because she had done what needed to be done. I'd understood and I'd promised myself that nobody would ever find out anything about it. That was thirty years ago. Nobody found out, and nobody must find out now either.

Buzz just keeps talking, while I can't stop myself from turning away.

"Hard to believe that they hauled the car out after all these years. Poor Magne, he must have been fish food a long time ago. Good thing Clara was able to get out. A tough one, your daughter, even back then. Minister of justice, wow."

He laughs, braying, and leans toward me, close enough that I can smell the stench of fried food, old sweat, unwashed hair, and cigarettes.

"You see the guy with the camera?" he whispers. "Do you know who he is?"

I shake my head. There's something familiar about the guy he's nodding toward, a tall, broad-shouldered man with a piercing gaze and one of those silly little beards on the end of his chin, but I am unable to place him.

"Kjellaug Haugo's boy," Buzz says in a suitably dramatic tone.

Kjellaug was the femme fatale of the village, slender limbed with long, flowing hair, uninhibited. As beautiful as Agnes but lacking the style and elegance my wife possessed. She was the village bicycle for a few years, until she gave birth to a boy she named Halvor. Nobody knew who the father was. Kjellaug turned over a new leaf, bought a house, got a job as a nurse's aide, never showed her face at a party again.

While the other boys in the neighborhood rode their bikes to soccer practice and played on the team, Kjellaug's big son sat in the cellar with the curtains drawn and played on his computer, night and day, long before all the young people were doing this.

I haven't seen him since he was a teenager, a flabby, pimply young boy with man boobs, but for the past year, he has been writing for the newspaper. So he hadn't gone to the dogs after all. On the contrary, he has clearly been working out. Now he's a huge hulk of a man, looks muscular and strong.

"He's onto something," Buzz whispers through his bad breath.

Someone must have pointed me out to Halvor Haugo. He is making his way steadily through the crowd, headed straight for me.

No. Clara as minister of justice. Magne's wrecked car hauled up from the bottom of the fjord. That's more than enough to take in for one day, I don't need to be talking to a journalist as well.

I turn on my heel, walk toward the car, jump in. Then I start the engine and, with a wrench of the steering wheel, pull out onto the road.

CHAPTER 3

SABIYA

"Hello," says Magnus Due-Salomonsson or whatever his name is. He offers me his hand. I rise halfway from my seat to take it in my own. His handshake is as listless and limp as the man himself. I don't trust him. A proper lawyer wouldn't have let me sit here rotting away in a damn jail cell while my life slips further and further out of sight.

"So," he says once he has sat down on the chair by the desk. I am sitting on the bed. "Do you have any news for me, Sabiya?"

I hate the way he says my name, as if he were making an effort to mispronounce it. I have pointed this out to him, several times. Now I have given up.

"Do *I* have any news?" I say. "I thought *you* would have some news for me?"

"Sabiya," he says, and rubs his face a bit before continuing.

He hasn't shaved today, but his suit is expensive, his haircut, too. A spoiled bougie, one of those we despised twenty years ago when I used to hang out with my crew in the city.

I fold my hands and grind the knuckles of my thumbs against each other, a bad habit I have developed recently. The skin is already sore. My elbows rest on my sweatpants-clad knees, which are bobbing up and down. I am like this all the time, unable to sit still. It gets on his nerves, I can see it, which actually gives me a perverse form of pleasure.

It astonishes me. All these years I've spent constructing a new Sabiya, and apparently it never came to anything more than a thin shell, which is now cracking, quickly and brutally. With every passing day, it's as if I can feel the black angel I once was, the actual, real me, emerging with increasing force and clarity.

Would Henrik have liked this version of me, or would it just have frightened him? I will never know.

"Listen," the lawyer continues. "It will make my job easier if you're honest with me. And in return, I will be honest with you . . ."

"Really?" I say. "Shoot. You first."

"Well, the amount of evidence is overwhelming. You will be convicted. The best we can hope for is to avoid prison time, but to achieve that you *must* cooperate. You must put your cards on the table. Do you understand?"

"Avoid prison time? I haven't committed a crime, dammit."

"Of course not," he replies, though the expression in his eyes contradicts his words.

He always speaks in this overbearing, disrespectful tone, as if he were speaking to a teenager, not an upstanding resident physician at one of Oslo's leading hospitals, not a mother of three who attends PTA meetings and performs all manner of soccer-mom duties.

I have worked so hard to become a good Norwegian citizen, and here I am in custody. There is no justice. I used to say it to Henrik: There is no justice. He would always protest, say that I was every bit as misanthropic as his wife. We have something in common there, Clara and I—the wife and the mistress—while otherwise we couldn't be more different.

Clara. It all comes back to Clara.

"Have you talked to anyone about Clara Lofthus?" I say now.

My lawyer leans back, looks up at the ceiling, and exhales a bit before sitting up straight and looking me in the eyes. Is that a glimmer of malicious joy I detect in his pale gaze?

"Clara Lofthus, yes," he says. "Clara Lofthus . . ."

"Yes?" I say in anticipation since it seems he might actually be leading up to something.

He stops, laughs brusquely.

"Well?" I say impatiently.

"Today Clara Lofthus was appointed Norway's new minister of justice."

"What?" I say. My bouncing knees, the thumb rubbing, it all stops.

Clara held an upper-management position at the ministry before all of this happened. That was bad enough, but minister?

"You're lying," I say.

"No," he says, shaking his head. "It's the truth."

Deep down, I know it's true. I should have seen this coming.

Afterward, I lie on the bed. Neither my lawyer nor my family believe me. Nobody believes me. Officially, I am on compassionate leave from my job. Unofficially, I am out, for good. There is nothing to suggest that I will ever get out of here. Premeditated triple homicide means prison time, which can be extended indefinitely. And today Clara Lofthus has been appointed minister of justice.

CHAPTER 4
CLARA

I am greeted in reception by Vigdis, the minister of justice's secretary. She has been one of my closest colleagues since I was made a state secretary early last summer, but this is the first time she has met me here. Although I have a key card and have been entering and exiting this building for fifteen years, today everything is supposed to follow protocol.

Vigdis is on the staff of permanent officials, a subordinate but nonetheless an invaluable colleague. For my own part, I am now a politician. Both of us are cogs in the same system, after all, the powerful machinery that constitutes a ministry, even though from the outside it may appear to move slowly.

"Poor thing, you're all wet," she says. "Unusual weather for this time of year."

"Yes, Western Norwegian weather," I say and try to shake out the fabric of the formerly proud and unwrinkled blouse to prevent it from sticking to my body.

"And you're under attack already? Do they know who she is?"

"No," I say, shaking my head. I can still hear the woman shouting murderer over and over again.

I feel as if I have seen the woman before. Should I know who she is? Or is she just one of those crazy people I've seen downtown in the many years I have lived in this city? Could she be the one who used to stand shouting outside the shopping center on Brugata Street, an area now associated mainly with hardcore junkies? Her voice was just as loud and shrill.

Outside the glass doors leading into the political section, I am met by Secretary General Mona Falkum. For many years, Mona has been my boss. Now I will be her boss. She has welcomed a number of new cabinet ministers—the turnover rate has been high recently.

The scheduled time for the handing over of the keys is dictated by the prime minister's office, and the camera mafia is ready and waiting. Mona smiles, but I notice a difference. The change that has occurred between the two of us began back in the spring when I made the virtually unheard-of transition from executive officer to state secretary. Now there is also something cool and calculating in her eyes.

"Welcome," she says, squeezing my hand. "Well, you're no stranger here."

"No, I'm not," I say. The photographers laugh.

We walk together to the anteroom and beyond it into the minister's office. The spacious room feels cramped today. The conference table and chairs have been pushed closer to the windows to make room for all the journalists and photographers. The political leadership is standing lined up against the opposite wall, dressed in their more-or-less appropriately dull suits. Half of them are from Munch's gang. Since I don't know anyone in the party, they have been assigned to me by the prime minister's office. I will have to vet these people down the road.

Now there is just one man I must concentrate on: the soon-to-be former cabinet minister Anton Munch. He is standing in front of his desk, which is now my desk, cleared of all his possessions.

Munch has made a name for himself as being dynamic and aggressive. He has had high visibility and scored well in media ratings. He was the one who stopped my bill, the bill I spent my best years as an executive officer writing, the bill that would provide vulnerable children with far better protection from abuse and violence. Nonetheless, I said yes when, out of the blue, he subsequently offered me a position on his team as a state secretary. Ignoring all the naysayers and my lack of experience in the party, against my better judgment, I said yes.

A few months later, he hung himself with his own political noose, and here I am.

"Welcome, Minister," he says with a kind of grin.

He takes hold of my right hand with his own, slaps his left hand on top of it for good measure so my hand is trapped between them, and shakes it. I look into his eyes and realize that Mona was not looking at me coolly a few minutes ago. This, on the other hand, is an ice-cold gaze.

"How does it feel to see your own state secretary sail past you in this way, Munch?" a journalist asks.

"I could not be more pleased," Munch says. "I am proud of having discovered Clara's talent. In fact, I want to say that I take credit for the fact that today we are welcoming a young female cabinet minister with a somewhat . . . unusual background . . . here."

Spontaneous applause. What the hell was that? Did he just insult me?

Then he places one hand warmly and paternalistically against the back of my head, knowing full well that this will make for a good visual, before pressing his mouth against my ear.

"Kudos to you," he whispers. "Good luck, bitch. You're in for a rough ride."

He positions me squarely in front of him, one hand on each of my shoulders, with the same false, fatherly smile on his face. Then he gives me a gentle shake before pressing a bouquet of flowers into my arms. I glance down.

White lilies. Flowers more suited for a funeral.

The key card is handed over along with the official bouquet of flowers from the ministry—gaudy, conventional, boring. Fortunately, somebody has remembered to order two bouquets this time, one for each cabinet minister. They've messed that up several times, ordering just one. Then Munch is led away. I greet the state secretaries and the political adviser, taking note of the adviser's limp handshake and the eldest state secretary's blank gaze.

The members of the press corps ask about my vision. Mona has always said that cabinet ministers who can't communicate in a few clear sentences how they plan to spend their time have already proven their worthlessness. I have written down a few statements, drilled them, rehearsed. Now I look into the barrels of their guns and say, truthfully, that my primary goal is to make sure that the ministry and legal system function effectively in terms of providing protection for the most vulnerable in society, specifically, children. That is more important than everything else.

When the people from the media finally file out, I am left standing alone with Mona.

"Sometimes I slip out to accompany those stepping down," she says. "They always look so lonely as they wander away, out of the lime-light, when everything is over. Once, I followed one of them all the way down to the bar Stop the Press and had a glass of wine with him. Do you have a minute to come into my office?"

I nod, registering that we will be speaking in her office, not mine. It is a deliberate demonstration of power. For her, I am still a state secretary, actually an executive officer, as I have been for the better part of the time we've known one another. And she is still the boss.

"You'll be drilled on this soon enough, but let me give you a briefing on the most important items," she says. "First of all, where is your cell phone?"

"I don't know . . . In my purse, I think."

"In your purse, you *think*? That won't do," she says in that slightly irritated, authoritarian tone of hers. "You must always, and I mean always, have your cell phone with you, no matter where you go, no matter what you do. It must be switched on and the battery charged. The prime minister's office and the Police Security Service must be able to reach you at all times, around the clock. You thought perhaps it was demanding to be on call as a state secretary? That's child's play compared to a cabinet minister."

"Okay," I say.

"You will also receive an encrypted cell phone. You must always carry that with you, in addition to your work phone, and that is the phone you must use for all communication of a sensitive nature. You are never to bring either of these phones to nations with which Norway has no national security cooperation. We would prefer that you not use your private cell phone, and neither are you to make public appearances as a private person. Secondly . . ."

She stops, as if to emphasize how important it is, what she is about to say. I feel dizzy and nauseated, I haven't eaten since 5:30 a.m.

"You will receive alerts and you will receive them often. Be prepared to report to the situation room under Akershus Fortress on short notice. You must report there immediately. It will be inconvenient, it will be tedious, you will feel as though you are wasting precious time, it will almost always turn out to be a false alarm, but you have no choice. Do you understand?"

I nod even though I could do without her patronizing tone.

"Thirdly . . . you can't trust anyone, not me, not the prime minister, not your colleagues in government, and especially not the rest of the political leadership. Listen to people, but the only person you are to trust is yourself. Okay?"

I nod, realizing that I have always lived by this rule.

"When a critical situation arises, you can't tell anyone about it. Not your children, not your father. That is the case even if some of them have planned to land at Oslo Airport on that very day and we have received a specific threat at that location."

I nod. The sun filters through the venetian blinds, hitting her in the eyes. She squints slightly. With her left hand, she straightens her bee-shaped brooch. Is it a queen bee? I wonder.

"Putting a single mother in the chair of a cabinet minister is no everyday decision, with all the pressure it involves. I must say it's a bold move on the prime minister's part."

"Honestly," I protest. "It can't be all that unusual, really."

"Oh yes, it is," she insists. "Remember that the majority of those who have held this position have been men like Munch, with wives who have functioned like single mothers, or people with grown children. You're going to have a tough time, for a number of reasons. Today's episode was just a taste of what's to come. If you ask me, you should find yourself a nanny posthaste."

"A nanny is out of the question," I say. "I'll manage."

We sit there for a moment in silence, looking at each other.

"I guess you'll be wanting to get settled into your new office?" she says finally.

I nod. As I stand up and the low beam of sunlight that was just shining on Mona falls across my face, something happens.

I no longer feel dizzy and faint. I feel ready, ready for the full weight of the responsibility now resting squarely on my shoulders. The woman I was no longer exists. Now I am simply Clara Lofthus, minister of justice.

Yes, I think. Let's do this.

CHAPTER 5

HALVOR

From the outside, the garage looks pretty run of the mill, until you walk around the building and see all the derelict cars parked on the hill descending to the river. Then the entire circus is revealed in its colorful, motley, somewhat-battered glory. At the moment, it's enshrouded in the autumn darkness. The floodlights that Geir the car mechanic has set up nonetheless bathe everything in a kind of golden sheen, including the black river flowing past. In Geir's yard are not only other people's junk automobiles but all manner of vehicles that he has personally collected over the years. Bulldozers and mini diggers, potato planters, potato pickers, lawnmowers . . .

I walk across the yard and into the repair shop located behind the garage itself. Geir is screwing something onto a little red sports car.

"Well, look who's here," he says, stretching out his small, gnarled, bony body. Geir has some kind of advanced form of arthritis. It's a wonder he is even still able to work on these cars.

"You started with race cars, Geir?" I ask.

"Yeah, you know . . . ," he says with a crooked grin that reveals a glimpse of brown teeth.

That's how most people talk around here, without really saying anything. Geir can keep spinning his wheels in the mud like this all day long. I don't have time for that.

"That wreck they pulled out of the fjord today, it's here, right?"

"Hmm, dunno," he says.

"Yeah, you do," I say. "Come on."

I can see that he's thinking, conferring with himself. He has probably been told in no uncertain terms not to talk to anyone about this.

"I know the car's here, Geir."

Then it's as if he surrenders, jerking his head to one side, indicating that I should follow him into the garage.

Six years ago, I met Yvonne, Geir's daughter, at an after-party. We danced to Gasolin' and Kim Larsen's "This Is My Life." Afterward, she came home with me. She must have gotten pregnant that first night, a feat I was pretty proud of at the time.

The child arrived, and suddenly, I was no longer good enough, without really understanding why. I didn't like it, of course, but my mind was made up that the girl was to be every bit as much mine anyway. She was to be spared growing up without a father the way I had. I would be there for her.

Suddenly, Yvonne decided to move up to Kirkenes and take Lisa with her. Her mother had left Geir and found herself a man up there in the north, and Yvonne wanted to live close to her now that she had a child. What about being close to the child's father? I asked. By law, she wasn't allowed to just take off like this.

It will only be for a while, she said, but of course it wasn't long before she also met a local guy and had two more children. I began to realize that she was never going to move back, that I would have to take her to court to make that happen. You can move up there, people said. They don't understand. I've never been to Northern Norway. It's probably nice up there, but I could just as well move to Turkey, that's how foreign it is to me. I have never lived anywhere else but here, I can't move to Kirkenes.

We shoulder aside a plastic curtain and enter a small side room I can't remember ever having seen before. There's something about a dirty plastic curtain like this that always makes me shudder and think of a slaughterhouse, but strictly speaking, this is more of a hospital for cars.

I pictured a car every bit as dripping wet as earlier in the day, but already it's as if it has shrunk. Someone has scraped kelp and seaweed and shells off the wreck. Now it's just a sad, rusty skeleton of the car Magne Lia was so proud of back in the day. This car, this wreck, is in a way a symbol of everything in my life that has gone wrong.

Geir pulls out the butt of a rolled cigarette and holds it between yellow fingers as he lights it.

"This car has a whole lot of history," I say.

"I don't know about that," he says.

"What is it you don't know?"

He takes a hit, hesitates.

"Cars are pulled up out of the fjord all the time, you know, mostly insurance scams, but they aren't as old as this one and never hauled up from such depths. By the way, I discovered something funny that I thought I ought to share with the police."

"That right?" I say, cautiously, mustn't spook him so he stops talking.

Now I can feel that familiar tingling in my scalp, the one that means I've definitely found a lead.

"Look here," he says, and opens the door on the driver's side. "Here on the inside, there was a cover once, it's been long since eaten by fish. But look at this. This was, once upon a time, a crank to roll down the window . . ."

Geir maybe looks shabby, *is* shabby, but he's an artist of distinction in his field. After floundering a bit, he continues.

"That there window crank was history before the car flew out into the water. If you look at the metal edge here, where it's broken, you can see clearly that it's been filed off. Not so strange that the driver drowned, if you ask me."

I stand completely still for a few seconds. My heart is pounding, and I can feel goose bumps rising on the flesh of my arms and on my scalp.

"Can I take a picture?" I ask as calmly as I can, taking out my phone.

"Guess so, if you aren't going to put it in the newspaper," he says.

Now we're getting somewhere. Finally.

"Geir," I say. "You trust me, right?"

He looks at me, slightly ill at ease.

"Yeah, sure . . . How so?"

Geir is a simple man, but a good man. I know he's ashamed of Yvonne's behavior, that he's always liked me, feels bad for me. When I tried to object to her moving, Yvonne went on the warpath and told all kinds of lies to child services about me getting high and domestic violence and shit. They believed her, perhaps also because I often got pretty worked up when I tried to talk to them. I think the ladies who work at the child services office always side with the mother, regardless.

Lisa is now five years old. Last time I saw her, she was four. I don't really know her. In that sense, it would have been better if she had never been born.

Geir is the only one in the family who doesn't hate me. Maybe because we are actually two abandoned men in the same car wreck.

"Could you hold off on telling the police about this?" I say now.

He raises a blackened hand with yellow fingers and bitten-down nails, brushes a lock of hair out of his face.

"Well, I can't say . . . Why?"

"Because this could be big, and important," I say. "I can't explain it now. You'll just have to trust me. And believe me, the police have *no* interest in finding out that this window crank was perhaps filed down thirty years ago."

"No, that's probably true," he says.

I have to make a conscious effort to refrain from grinning too broadly. It upset me to see the wreck both earlier today and now. Upset me, but also got me excited.

In the car, I call Leif Lofthus. As expected, he doesn't pick up.

Then I call the Ministry of Justice, explain that I would like to speak with the cabinet minister, to hear whether she would like to comment on the recovery of a wrecked car from the fjord in her home-town, a wrecked car with ties to an accident the cabinet minister was involved in when she was twelve years old. I ask that she call me at her convenience.

Afterward, I go home. It's still strange that I live alone here. Even though it was only Mother and me when I was a child, she wanted at all costs to have a house. In one way or another, she managed to secure a mortgage that was far too big, and she worked several jobs for years to pay it off. The day-care center in the daytime, cleaning the school in the evenings, night shifts at the nursing home. It was important for her to make sure her son grew up in a proper house, she said. So I grew up in a house, with a mother who was always at work.

I've heard people say that she was fond of partying when she was young, that she was always so full of life. It was feasibly the same energy that she channeled into all her work. She often came home at eleven in the evening, did the dishes, did the laundry, and folded clothes, cooked for the next day, went to bed at two in the morning, and got up again four hours later. She kept a box of cheap red wine in a cupboard in the pine sideboard in the living room. On Fridays and Saturdays, she poured herself two glasses while she watched television, never more, never less. This was her only indulgence; otherwise, she scrimped and saved on everything. It was all about duty and discipline. That my mother had, once upon a time, supposedly staggered from party to party, from man to man, was hard to imagine.

When she was forty-nine years old, she developed breast cancer. She would be fine, they said, but before long, the cancer had spread to every part of her body. Two days before her fiftieth birthday, she died, without our ever having spoken about my father. I tried several times, but it was impossible. She didn't know that I knew who he was.

Now I sit down in my chair in the living room and watch the video clip of the official announcement of Clara Lofthus's appointment from earlier that day.

After a while, a message pops in from a communications adviser at the Ministry of Justice. He thanks me for my inquiry but informs me that the cabinet minister does not have any comment. That's as expected. I don't reply.

Instead, I download one of those apps you can use to pay at a charging station, since the newspaper insists that we should all be driving around in electric cars. The idiots in charge think it's environmentally friendly and sustainable, since they aren't smart enough to calculate all the energy it takes to make such cars and what will happen when everyone tries to heat their homes and charge their cars with electricity at the same time. The power grid will collapse, there's no doubt about that.

Electric car or not, I am going to make my way to Oslo, but first I'm going to pay Leif Lofthus a call.

CHAPTER 6

CLARA

Ever since the accident, I've hated being a passenger, but this evening, I am driven home by Stian. He is my new, permanent chauffeur, I've been told. Once in a while, there is a replacement, but Stian is, for the most part, my guy and will drive me back and forth to work every day.

The man is my age, maybe a few years older. I sit behind him on the right, where I have been ordered to sit, and from there, I have a good view of his profile. His hair is short around his ears and neck, longer up top, and is a somewhat unusual strawberry blond color. His skin is tanned and his gaze a penetrating blue. It actually resembles my own, although this does not soften my attitude toward him.

Stian is also the same man who saved me, earlier today. I didn't know at the time that he was my new driver. I still don't understand why he was there, out on the Palace Square, but he handled the situation well. He is without a doubt also a good driver.

I have said that I like riding my bike, that I like walking, that I don't like being dependent on others. It makes no difference. I can't refuse the car service. Apparently, they would prefer to give me bodyguards as well, but I have no intention of accepting that, at the very least.

Before 2011, in Norway, only the prime minister had bodyguards. After the terrorist attack of July 22 that year, a number of cabinet ministers were assigned such security details, including the minister of justice. Since then, the individuals who are assigned security have varied. Most of the ministers of justice have, in fact, not had it, I think, so I hold some good cards. Personally, I can't imagine anything worse than being followed and controlled around the clock, losing all my privacy.

Today, I've become one of the most powerful people in Norway, but in my daily life, I feel already like I have been placed under guardianship. From now on, somebody will decide my daily schedule and have complete access to my life. Somebody will write what I am supposed to say, line by line. Somebody will compose my letters to the editor and my op-eds. Somebody will fill every hour of my calendar. Somebody will drive me to the door and pick me up there. Somebody will deliver freshly pressed suits to my office, put food in front of me, retrieve the plate afterward.

Everything I say and do will be judged and evaluated and rated.

People will recognize me in the store, at soccer games, in the forest.

It will be an arranged, comfortable, and extremely unfree life, a life in which others will have control and oversight of what I do at all times.

Even though I have taken this on voluntarily, already I feel trapped, and that is a feeling that I have never handled particularly well.

Stian tried asking a few questions about my day, but I simply ignored him, and he took the hint, stopped asking. I should probably thank him for his help earlier today, but I don't. Yes, he saved me from something that was probably completely harmless, but it is his job, and not a reason to become friends.

I bet people usually try to kiss up to him, to demonstrate to both him and themselves that they are just common folk.

I am of the common folk; I *am* common folk. I don't need to pretend.

It helps a bit that he isn't especially servile and subservient, although he is ever so polite. The man is used to being around high-profile politicians and diplomats, so he is not bothered by an ill-tempered minister.

"Good night," he says when we've arrived and he has opened the car door for me.

At first, I tried telling him that I would at the very least do *that* for myself but gave up when I was told that it put me at risk.

"I'll be here at 6:50 tomorrow morning," he adds.

He waits beside the car, watching me, until I reach the front door. That is probably included in his official instructions.

Axel appears in the hallway as soon as I walk in the door.

"Hush, the boys fell asleep, finally," he says with a little smile.

"Good," I say. "I would have liked to have seen them, but it got so incredibly late . . ."

"They were tired," Axel says. "We saw you on television. They thought you looked pretty."

"Ha ha," I say, kicking off my shoes and hanging up my jacket. "I didn't mean to keep you here all evening . . ."

"My pleasure," he says, running his hands through his brown, curly hair.

He is shorter than Henrik was, but they resemble one another, as if they were real brothers, not just brothers in spirit. He also has the same tousled hair and taste in clothing, and there is something relaxed, jovial, warm about him, which I have always liked. Besides, he is fond of my children; otherwise, I could never have brought myself to ask him.

I have never been good at asking for help, but since Henrik died, I've sort of had no choice. Already several people besides Mona have suggested a nanny, but never in the world would I allow a stranger to live here. I will manage to take care of my children by myself.

"It's a pleasure for me to borrow some children while my own are traveling with their mother," he says. "We made pizza and played *FIFA* . . ."

"Ah, good . . . They haven't played PlayStation since Henrik . . ."

I stop myself.

Henrik is dead. Everyone around me views me as a grieving widow, even those who know us well enough to know that our marriage was not an especially happy one. In reality, it is the others who are mourning.

The boys, Henrik's parents, Axel. I am not, and that's something I can't tell anyone.

Neither can I tell the truth about our swim last summer, how it came about, how I led us toward the area where the currents are strongest, how I dove under, swimming along the bottom, and saw how the current propelled Henrik toward the place where the lake becomes a waterfall. Nobody can find out about this, ever. Maybe that's why I feel incapable of saying his name out loud.

"No, they said so," Axel says now, with a wistful little smile. "They did their homework, too. Math and Norwegian, completed and delivered." He stops, looks at me inquisitively. "That driver of yours? He looks sort of . . . unreal?"

"Unreal?" I say. "How so?"

"Like elite soldier meets park ranger. Are you sure he's legit?"

"Good Lord, he's not that amazing, is he?"

"Hmm, he suits you, at least," Axel says as he leans forward and kisses me on the cheek.

I stiffen slightly, although Axel is among those with whom I feel most comfortable having physical contact. He stands without moving for a second or two, as if hesitating, before walking down the stairs without looking back. I lock the door behind him. Now I need a joint on the veranda before I get started on the pile of documents I brought home with me. First of all, I want to take off this damn costume.

I trot up the steps to the second floor and into my closet, take off my cabinet minister attire, and pull on a pair of jeans and a T-shirt. Then I nod curtly at Edith, the sewing mannequin. She's named after Henrik's grandmother, the woman who, in her day, played matchmaker for Henrik and me and who, half a century before that, brought a sewing mannequin with her from Paris. The mannequin has stood in the corner of the room ever since old Edith died and we emptied her house down the street. Henrik and I used to joke about how the headless, slender, and elegant Edith torso had us under surveillance.

From Andreas's room, where both of the boys sleep, an enervating, spinning sound can be heard. It's the damn hamsters.

The boys wanted hamsters for years. They really wanted a dog, but they knew that was out of the question. In a moment of weakness after Henrik's death, I promised them that we could get hamsters. They reminded me of it constantly. Soon, I said, without meaning it. Yesterday, in an attempt to compensate for my most recent promotion, on an impulse, I popped into a pet store and grabbed two hamsters, two cages, and two overpriced feeding dishes.

The boys weren't as pleased as I thought they would be. Of course, they would have preferred to come along and choose their own hamsters, they pointed out. Still, they had cuddled and played with the balls of fur for the rest of the evening and scarcely batted an eye when I said I would be getting a new job the next day. They argued about who would get to call their hamster van Dijk, their favorite soccer player. A compromise was reached: Virgil van Dijk's name was divided in two, and both boys were satisfied.

It was after they fell asleep last night that the hullabaloo really commenced.

Two fucking hamsters running around and around in their respective rattling, squeaking wheels, as if they were competing over who could make the most noise. The only reason the boys were sleeping was that they could sleep through anything. For my own part, I heard the noise clearly through the thin adjoining wall of my bedroom.

"Good God," I mumble as I walk out into the hallway, and push the half-open door of the boys' room shut. Then I go into my room.

The noise is every bit as intense. I take out my telephone, google "hamster" and "noise," look through the first hits, and click one of them open. There is something called a "silent wheel"; maybe I should try to get hold of one.

Now I'm going down to the veranda to smoke, just want to wash off the final vestiges of the cabinet minister first. I go into my bathroom, turn on the faucet, work the hand soap into a lather, rub it against my face, collect water in my hands, rinse, grab the towel, and dry.

It's after I've hung up the hand towel that I see it in the mirror, the sight that makes me shudder.

Her cheekbones, under my skin.

She's also looking at me with my own eyes.

My mother. The one who blew up our family into tiny pieces.

CHAPTER 7

AXEL

I end up sitting on the steps outside Clara's house, listening to a podcast on my earbuds.

These days, it's *When We Were Kings*, featuring the Swedish soccer journalist Erik Niva, who tells stories of big teams and important seasons. Rosenborg 1996, Denmark 1992, FC Porto 2003–04, FC Anzhi Makhachkala 2011–12 . . . The list is endless. Niva's didactic dialect from Norrbotten in the north of Sweden is hypnotic; he is absolutely brilliant.

I would have loved to have shared this with Henrik, discussed how Nils Arne Eggen's social democratic leadership philosophy was critical for Rosenborg's success in 1996, or how José Mourinho's déclassé upper-crust background explains his mixture of arrogance and hostility. Caro never understood how much love there was in the way Henrik and I could talk about such things.

Feelings, on the other hand, were a topic we seldom talked about. One of the exceptions was the last time we were in Kilsund, when Henrik told me about his affair with that Pakistani doctor at work, Sabiya or whatever her name was. I remember that I thought this would be trouble, I said as much, too. Now I wish I hadn't been right.

The double episode about Maradona in 1986, which I just finished listening to, Henrik really should have heard it. The day Maradona died, I actually cried. My tears weren't for a fat, sixty-year-old, multiple drug abuser calling it a day. That was no surprise. No, I cried about how the men we once were, Henrik and I, no longer existed. When Maradona died, this became abundantly clear to me. I cried over my childhood that would never return, over the days when we were ten years old and stayed outside playing soccer until the sun went down, the time when we were kings.

When we were a little older, we used to smoke out here when Henrik's parents weren't home. Over the years, we gave up smoking completely. Eventually, Henrik was the one living in the house. Sometimes we took beers outside with us. We needed something to hold on to while we sat and chatted.

We were brothers who weren't brothers, two only children who grew up together. All of these pictures inside my head: soccer trips to Liverpool. Pub evenings. High school graduation. Taking paternity leave together. Jogging together. Trips to the cottage. Dinners. The World Cup on television in the evenings. Diving off the boat. Evening swims in Southern Norway.

What I can see with the greatest clarity is Henrik as a little boy, how we walked to school and back together, every single day. Henrik with that stupid cap he always wore. The knapsack he was so proud of, the way he dribbled a ball, the songs he used to hum, everything filtered through a glow of sepia light. I thought he would always be there, that we would become old men together, like our fathers.

It wasn't true that I had to go home and work, but I thought that Clara must certainly be exhausted and probably needed to get a good night's sleep. I couldn't bear the thought of our sitting there and talking while she really just wanted me to leave. I've known Clara for many years, I know she doesn't like wasting time on unnecessary chitchat. Besides, she was appointed minister of justice today and no doubt has enough on her mind.

At the same time, there's nothing I would like more than to spend some time with her here.

The first time I met Clara was in the back garden of the bar Justisen in Oslo, on a warm spring day, when Clara and Henrik had just become a couple. Henrik had stumbled over her in the garden of his legendary grandmother, where Clara had had some kind of strange au pair role at the time. After that, he didn't talk about anything else but this mysterious Western Norwegian wood nymph with the long hair.

Caroline and I had already been together for a year or two. We sat chatting over our beers while we waited for them, and it was suitably uninteresting, a preview of how fatally dull our life together would later become.

Caro decided that we were going to buy an apartment. We had just started looking, and this was what she was talking about now. Floor plans, kitchen cupboards, wall-mounted toilets, all that kind of stuff. Caro checked craigslist at all hours of the day, shopped the windows of real estate agents, organized an advance on her inheritance. Her enthusiasm was sort of always a bit over the top. Yeah, sure, it was wonderful that she took care of everything, but it was like being wrapped up in invisible plastic wrap from which I would never be unwrapped again.

Deep down I knew even then that Caro wasn't right for me. I just couldn't bear all the effort of untangling myself from the plastic wrap. It took three kids for me to become desperate enough to try. By then it had become virtually impossible, with all the real estate, finances, children, joint insurance policies, and pictures we had, as inextricably entangled as we were in everything but love.

Now I can hear Clara running up the stairs to the second floor. The front door is thin and old and not exactly soundproof; it should be replaced with something more solid.

It was a nice evening with the boys, but it's strange to be with them, in this house, without Henrik. Here it's so obvious that he's gone and is never coming back.

Clara is taking it admirably well, I think. She really has an extraordinary psyche. I haven't seen her cry, not *once*, not even at the funeral. She stood there stoically, arms crooked around the boys, one on each side.

While Henrik obstinately claimed that Clara had no knowledge of his infidelity, I always thought that she would have to be blind, deaf, and dumb, and she was none of these things. She must have known, and if so, her feelings for Henrik must be more ambivalent than my own.

There are so many suppressed expectations and disappointments, so much bitterness and ambivalence between parents and children. Between the members of a couple who have been together for a while, there are often layers upon layers of spiderwebs forming a dark, impenetrably dense blanket.

Between really good friends, on the other hand, there is something real, uncomplicated.

It looked almost comical when Henrik and Clara came walking hand in hand into Justisen that day. She was so tall and slender and seemed reluctant. I never saw them walking hand in hand again either. Henrik told me later, with a snicker, that Clara had implemented a veto on handholding. But there and then, on their way into Justisen to meet us, she had gone along with it.

Clara was fashion-model attractive in a cool and distant manner, her coloring as fair as Henrik's was dark, in a way the opposite of their personalities. Compared to her, Caro looked ordinary and dull. Maybe she saw it herself? Maybe that was why she became sulky and cross in that subtly off-putting way she has?

Clara's handshake was surprisingly firm for such a slim hand. When she looked me in the eyes, I understood it, with an overwhelming feeling of delight mixed with terror and a kind of recognition at the same time. There you are. I love you.

I was on the verge of blurting it out, and I almost wish that I had. Those are still the words that surge through me every time Clara and I meet, and that's how it's always been.

I love you.

If a long time has passed since we last saw one another, I can almost make myself believe that it's all just something I've imagined. Then we meet and it's all there. Just as strong, just as tacit, just as useless. That's how it's always been, how it will always be.

Of course, I didn't say anything that time at Justisen, just mumbled my name. Then we sat there, me blushing and flustered, Caro sulky and cross, and Clara slightly uncomfortable, the way I would later discover she always is when she meets new people. The only one at the top of his game was Henrik, newly in love and high on life.

Of course, trying to steal Henrik's new love was out of the question. And I wouldn't have had a chance had I decided to try either. Henrik always controlled his women with an iron fist, even Clara, who at least never left him, even though she had good reason to do so.

Although Clara didn't cry at the funeral, I sure did. I wept, snorted, sniveled—my father had to put his arm around me and comfort me, both ashamed and compassionate, I think. He had also known Henrik since the day he was born and had a lot of contact with him recently, because of the murder case. His eyes were shiny, especially when he hugged Henrik's parents.

I get to my feet and start walking down the little path leading to the front gate. I need to go straight to bed when I get home and not sit there zapping through the channels or stay up playing Fantasy Premier League. That's how most of my evenings end, especially when the children aren't home. It's still difficult to get used to their not living with me all the time, that they spend just as much time with Caro's doltish new fellow as they do with me.

It's when I've walked out the gate in front of Clara's house and crossed the road in the direction of my own street that I notice the black car. There's no shortage of nice, dark cars in the area, but this armored monster of a vehicle stands out all the same.

The driver is staring straight ahead of him, perhaps talking on the phone; he sees me for sure but shows no sign of it. I saw him when he drove Clara home earlier, but also when he stepped in to protect her from the crazy lady during the ceremony on the Palace Square. He did it discreetly and elegantly, led Clara back to the prime minister and the crazy lady out and away, without making a commotion about any of it. That was *la classe*, as the French say. He's a pro.

Actually, I should be pleased that this is the man who will be driving Clara around, but something or other about the guy already irritates me to no end. It doesn't improve things that he's sitting inside there and looking straight ahead, talking on his hands-free phone. I am apparently invisible to him, although I'm sure that he sees me and is probably also fully aware of who I am.

Being under surveillance and overlooked at the same time is a lousy combination, unpleasant twice over.

For a second, I consider knocking on the car window and asking him what he's doing here but dismiss the idea. I have no interest in antagonizing the Police Security Service or whoever it is he represents. Instead, as I pass, I walk close to the car, so close that I almost brush up against the shiny polished enamel.

All of a sudden, he is standing beside me, having exited the car in a nanosecond. I jump, stop.

"Axel?" he says.

Exactly. He knows my name.

Then he leans against the car and puts his hands in his pockets, as if to demonstrate that he is not going to attack me. Something about this animal, alpha-male energy of his makes me feel like fighting him. That would not be wise.

"You've been at the cabinet minister's?" he says.

"I've been at Clara's, yes," I say.

It's possible that she's the cabinet minister to him. That's not who she is to me.

"Been babysitting," I add, although I don't strictly speaking owe him an explanation for anything at all.

"Yeah," he says. "She's going to need it in the time ahead."

"I know," I say, a bit reluctantly.

"They're also going to need a lot of security, more than she understands."

"Is that why you're here now?" I ask. "To stand guard?"

"No, I'm just checking things out," he says with a cryptic smile.

"I see," I say, shivering. Autumn has tightened its grip, and I sat on the front steps at Henrik's house for a bit too long. "Yes, I saw you at the ceremony today."

He nods, for a moment looks a little tired, a touch of something human.

"There will be other such episodes. She will be a magnet for people like that. We'll have to get her used to the idea gradually . . ."

"Is this when you ask me to convince her to do something?" I ask, sighing. "That's out of the question."

"Not at all," he says. "I'm just saying you should get used to the idea of it being a new era. It's not a given that it will be as simple as being a friend of the family here in the future."

With those words, he gets back into the car.

For my own part, I am left standing there, feeling strangely foolish. What was that, exactly? An attempt to get to know me? Was he checking me out? Or warning me?

Whatever the case, as I walk home through the cold, clear evening, an odd queasiness settles in the pit of my stomach.

CHAPTER 8

CLARA

I am up by five o'clock, do my breathing exercises, skim the newspapers quickly, make coffee and oatmeal. Then I take out clothes for the boys, make their lunches, and prepare their breakfast. I must teach them to do this for themselves soon, but not today.

At quarter past six, I wake them.

"Mommy," Nikolai grunts from far beneath the duvet. "Are you waking us up *now*?"

It took ten minutes of nagging to get them up and on their feet.

Finally, they are sitting at the table and eating. Both of them glower at me sullenly.

"Okay, boys," I say. "Mommy has a new job. Do you remember?"

Neither of them says anything. They're not going to let me off easy.

"I'll be picked up by my own driver, isn't that neat?"

"Sure," Nikolai says, but without much enthusiasm in his voice.

"I have to leave for work a half hour before you usually leave for school. But I set the alarm on your cell phones so it will ring when it's time for you to go. I can also call you from work, okay? Remember your book bags. Your lunch boxes are packed and ready there. All right?"

Both of them nod seriously.

"Is this really allowed, Mommy?" Nikolai says.

"Yes," I say. "You're old enough now that leaving for school on your own is normal."

"But Dad . . . ," Andreas says, and then stops himself.

"I know," I say, trying to smile. It turns into a grimace. "Dad liked to be here in the mornings and accompany you to school."

Nikolai's lower lip starts to tremble. Dammit. This in particular always gives me pangs of guilt. My sons, who miss their father so much.

"Now we just have to try and manage the best we can," I say. "It will be fine as long as we take care of each other. Did you have a nice time with Axel yesterday?"

"Yes, we played *FIFA* and I won," Andreas says.

"That's not true, I won," Nikolai says. "You're lying!"

There we go. Now they are behaving more like themselves.

With every passing year, they have become more and more obsessed with soccer in general, Premier League in particular, and above all Liverpool. Oddly enough, it's as if this interest has waned this past autumn, though I don't understand why. Lately, they've at least started playing something called *Soccer Manager* on their phones. They each manage their own team, discuss injuries, fitness curves, red cards, and who is and isn't going to start. Now they've also been playing *FIFA* with Axel. Maybe things will settle down with time.

I pour myself another cup of coffee, pack up my things. Shortly after, I see that Stian's car is outside. It's only 6:45, but I may as well leave.

"Bye now, boys. Have a hot dog or something when you get home and do your homework. I'll be home as soon as I can, and we'll have a nice evening, okay?"

They just look at me. For a second or two, I want only to stay here with them.

"Come on," I say instead. "Come have a look at the car."

They run to the door. I give each of them a hug before I trot down the walk.

"Bye, Mommy," they shout, almost in unison.

45

The boys and I have actually grown closer during these past months, closer than we've been for many years. I have managed to do many of the things Henrik usually took care of. Bought them new running shoes. Laced up their soccer cleats. Baked cakes for the team bake sale, albeit from a cake mix. Helped them with their math homework. Stroked their hair and kissed them good night and managed to have real conversations with them many times. I have hugged them more and yelled at them less. Have felt that I managed it. I even bought them those damn hamsters.

Now, with this new job, it will be harder, but one way or another, I must manage it as well.

"Good morning," Stian says, opening the door for me when I reach the car.

"Good morning," I say.

I fasten my seat belt. The boys look like dark shadows against the light from the hallway as they stand in the doorway, waving. They look so small. I wave back.

"Are they all alone now?" Stian says. He waves, too.

"Yes," I say. "But they are independent for their age. Do you have children?"

He nods.

"Twins, like you. Two five-year-old girls and one two-year-old boy."

"Oh, that must be quite a handful," I say.

"Yes, especially for my wife," he says. "I'm at work so much."

"What does she do?" I ask.

"She's in law enforcement, too," he says. "But right now, she's working for the armed forces so she can work days . . ."

He glances at me in the mirror, holds my gaze, as if to make sure I've heard what he said. I have.

She's in law enforcement, *too*.

Now I get it. Mona and PSS, the Police Security Service, and everyone else is pretending to go along with my wishes, letting me get away with only a car service, no bodyguards. On the surface. But my driver is not from the car service. Of course not. He's from PSS, a covert body-guard who's here to protect me, not to drive me around. I lean against the window and stare out.

At the office, Vigdis has placed all the newspapers on my desk. I am featured on the front page of several of them; the photos show me holding my bouquets and smiling, with wet hair and a clingy blouse, dark rings under my eyes.

The white lilies from Munch are on the windowsill, giving off the stink of a funeral. I must move them, no, throw them out.

Several of the editorials are also about my appointment and more positive than I had expected. "Clara Lofthus is an exciting choice," they write. "The time has come to bring some younger, fresh energy into this position. Lofthus has had a solid law career. The past half year, she has made her mark as a state secretary with vision and great integrity, known for having procured new firefighting helicopters last summer. She knows the ins and outs of the Ministry of Justice after having spent many years there and is highly respected by the staff of permanent officials."

Goodness. I am a bit unsure about whether there is any basis for the last claim in particular. Of course, I understand what the media is up to. They are building me up to the best of their abilities, adoring me and worshipping me. I'm relatively young. I'm a woman. I'm from Western Norway. I'm a breath of fresh air. The other side of this coin is that they are doing this so my fall from grace will be even more dramatic when, in a month, six months, a year, or two years, they pull me down off the pedestal.

I put aside the newspapers when Mona and the director of com-munications enter my office. It's nine o'clock, and I am going to lead my first morning meeting.

"Hello, have you seen the rest of the gang?" I ask.

Mona shakes her head. I get to my feet, walk out, and stick my head through the door to the largest of the state secretary offices, where I find both the state secretaries and the political adviser. They are standing hunched over a cell phone, grinning and laughing.

"Hello," I say.

They look at me like high school students when the teacher enters the classroom.

"It's past nine," I say. "The secretary general is waiting in my office."

"Okay, we're coming," the adviser says in a listless tone.

He is the lowest-ranking member of the political leadership, in fact the lowest-ranking member of the entire system. I am now on top, on paper also above the secretary general, who is the permanent administrative director of the ministry. Since the adviser and I know one another and have worked together, he apparently believes that he can still do whatever he wants here.

"Now," I say, irritated. "Bring the other two along with you."

Five minutes later, they are finally seated in my office, all three of them.

"Fine," I say. "First I want to apologize to the secretary general and communications director, who have been waiting for you for ten minutes."

Mona nods, her mouth curving in a little smile.

"You've also wasted ten minutes of my time, and that time is important. This is disrespectful. From now on, I want you here on time, or you can find yourself something else to do. I have no need for people who can't be bothered to show up for the first morning meeting. Understood?"

They stare down at the table and nod. Usually, the state secretaries are relatively professional, while the advisers are lightweights recruited from the youth parties. Here everyone seems to be a lightweight, as if they were three political advisers.

It is only after the meeting is over that I remember that I forgot to call the boys and check to see if they arrived at school. I send a message to both of them: Did you arrive on time?

Nikolai replies, **Yes, Mommy,** with a thumbs-up.

Then I walk out to speak to Vigdis.

"What does my day look like?"

"Your next meeting is at ten o'clock. Another at eleven. A cabinet meeting with lunch at twelve. After that, it's one meeting after the next all week, or, the whole month, actually. See," she says, pointing at the calendar.

"Good Lord," I say.

My calendar is full. My days will be filled with talking to people, me, the one who doesn't like people, who is most content when I can sit in peace and work on something requiring concentration.

"Oh, and Mona wants a word with you," Vigdis says. "Can you drop by her office?"

I nod. Once again, I am supposed to go to her. Fine by me.

"Clara, come in," Mona says when I knock on her door.

I peek discreetly at her shirt front; today it's a starfish.

"Munch called me," she says with a little smile. "He's read your interview in *VG*. It's been posted online. The man is furious."

I remember it now. The *VG* journalist yesterday, after Munch left.

"I was just being honest," I reply. "Munch did close to nothing for the most vulnerable, those he was supposed to be serving as a cabinet minister, and he shelved my bill."

"And now you're going to put things right," Mona says. "'Lofthus says she's determined to make up for the negligence of her predecessor. "It's a new day," she concludes decisively.'"

She raises her eyebrows as she looks up from the tablet.

"And?" I say. "It's the truth."

"Whether or not it's the truth is irrelevant," Mona says drily. "Was it *smart*?"

I shrug.

"He wondered why I'd let you attack him. Also, he points out that you would still be a civil servant were it not for him. Now he's going to make sure that both you and I regret this bitterly . . ."

She pauses, looking at me over the rims of her glasses.

"Yes, he's a stooge, but it would no doubt make sense for you to show some party loyalty. Otherwise, you won't be around for long."

I don't respond. I am fed up with Munch, fed up with Mona's commands. I want to get to work on the job itself.

"He's exaggerating, of course," she says. "Your appointment is apparently popular within the party, not least among young women who are sick of Munch and his cronies. Something else . . ."

She pauses deliberately, straightens her brooch.

"You will hear this soon enough from others, but as you know, PSS monitors threats against the cabinet minister and the ministry at all times. It turns out that the level of threat has risen in the few short hours since you took over. In part, this is logical. A new cabinet minister receives a lot of attention. And you are receiving an *unusual* amount of attention because you are a woman, blonde, beautiful, provocative in a thousand different ways . . . It shouldn't be that way, but that's how it is. Regardless, PSS is going to propose immediate measures."

"Such as what?" I ask.

She shrugs.

"You will receive more details from them, but I'm guessing a camera. A safe room in your home. A security detail."

"*That* is out of the question," I say, and picture bodyguards on the stairs, camera lenses everywhere.

"I'm afraid it's not up to you," she says. "Either way, you need to have a conversation with PSS, and even I won't be allowed to be a part of that."

On my way back to my office, I receive a text. Hope everything's fine with you and the boys. Thinking of you. Dad.

Dad. I've barely thought about him. I told him about the appointment the evening before, that was it. Tonight I have to find the time to call him.

CHAPTER 9

LEIF

Everything fine here. Call you later. C., she wrote. I close my eyes and sigh.

Shortly afterward, I hear a car driving into the yard. Nothing wrong with my hearing. It's not every day someone stops by here.

I stand up, my body immediately vigilant. I've been like this since I came back from Lebanon all those years ago. Anything unexpected and my body goes on the alert. When I left as a young man, the only dangers I really knew were bad weather and udder infections. I returned as an old man who knew far too much about the misery in the world.

It was so mixed, the whole Lebanon thing. I was happy to be home again. At the same time, I yearned to return, go back to the place where everything was a matter of life and death, where there was never any doubt about what you had to do, and we were all working together on something big and important.

Here at home, everything just seemed strange and wrong to me at first. It scared me, and people scared me. In the evenings, I often sat by the window, staring out. My shotgun hung on the wall of the storeroom. For a while, I even kept it under my bed.

It was as if nothing would ever be easy or good again, and then all that stuff with Agnes and Magne and Lars happened.

It's taken me many years to recover. This is my safe haven. Nobody can sneak up on me here. Actually, I don't want to see anyone but Clara and the boys here, and I know they aren't the ones paying me a visit now.

I go out into the hallway, open the door, and walk down the stone steps.

The car is small and fancy, white, with a newspaper logo on the side. It's been less than a day since I last saw the car and its owner.

"I think you've come to the wrong place," I say.

"Hi," Kjellaug's son says. "Aren't you Leif Lofthus?"

I nod, walk toward him, mostly to prevent him from intruding any farther into my territory.

"I'd like to talk to you a bit," he says, and takes two more steps toward me.

"About what?" I say.

"About the car they hauled out of the fjord yesterday, how you feel about it."

"I'm *not* interested," I say.

"Fine," he says. "Then I'll call your daughter. She's the one I'm most interested in anyway. There are also other family members I can talk to."

"Like who?" I ask.

"Your wife, for example," he says.

"I don't have a wife," I say.

"Oh?" he says. "Are you sure? What about Agnes?"

I squirm. Agnes and I are actually still married, on paper. I should have straightened that out a long time ago, with an eye to the inheritance and other such formalities. I tried, in fact, but since she was sick, it turned out to be so difficult that I finally just gave up.

"Talking to her is complicated," I say. "She's in the Kleivhøgda psychiatric hospital, has been for thirty years."

"How strange," he says.

"What do you mean by that?"

"I just saw Agnes at the store," he says with a nasty little smile. "Is it possible your info isn't quite up to date, Leif? Your wife has been discharged from Kleivhøgda."

I freeze. Can this be true? Have they let her out after all these years? Can she have recovered enough for that to be possible?

"Where's she living, then?" I ask after a moment.

"In Buzz's boathouse."

A hundred yards away from his own house, Buzz has a boathouse, which he has converted into a kind of cottage.

In the summertime, he rents it out to tourists, mostly Germans, but sometimes, new single mothers have stayed there temporarily.

"It surprises me that you didn't know. But it's nice to be the one to give you the news."

"I think it's time for you to leave now."

He stands there looking at me for a few seconds, as if to give me time to reconsider, before getting into that idiotic little car of his, backing up against the barn, and driving down the hill and out of sight.

I haven't told Clara about the recovery of the wrecked car, haven't even spoken to her since her appointment; she has certainly more than enough on her plate right now. She never reads the local paper, not online either, she's said.

I spoke to Buzz yesterday, but he didn't say a thing. Maybe he didn't dare? Now that I think about it, it seemed like he was dying to tell me something, but I thought it had something to do with the wrecked car they pulled out of the fjord. Then I left in a big rush.

Yes, I can call Clara and warn her, but will that help? What if Halvor Haugo doesn't call her, and I worry her unnecessarily?

It's bloody unbelievable. Agnes. Damn Agnes, out in the world for the first time in all these years. A loose cannon on deck, a savage and dangerous stray dog running wild in the village.

Last spring, the ever-zealous nurse Bodil had informed me that Agnes was talking again, after many years of silence. Clara had even gone to visit her there and reported that there didn't appear to be anything to worry about.

The leaves that have fallen from the maple tree in the middle of the yard still crunch beneath my feet. Not for long. One more heavy rainfall and these small works of art will become a kind of slick, sad film that I must be careful not to slip on as I walk. Then autumn will be over, and winter will come.

I sit down under the maple tree, thinking, look out across the fjord, the way I've looked out across the fjord pretty much every day of my life, with the exception of the half year I spent in Lebanon. When I get to my feet again, I have made a decision. I must go down to the village, must find out whether this is really true.

I park the car a short distance away. The gravel lane leading down to the house on the water's edge is steep, an abrupt turnoff from the highway. Buzz lives in one of the houses himself. The other is his boathouse, which has been fitted out like a kind of dollhouse, where you can spit from the kitchen window directly into the waves.

It would have made more sense if Agnes had gone east, to Oslo, or to the tiny, white town by the fjord she comes from. She doesn't know anyone here, but then she doesn't know anyone in other places either. Besides, it's cheaper to rent here. It's actually unbelievable that she is capable of living on her own here, *if* she is actually here.

For thirty years, Agnes has been dependent on others. How could they discharge her now? Is it safe? I should call and ask but hesitate to do so; I have been so rude to those people.

On the left side of the lane leading down to Buzz's house and the brown-stained boathouse he rents out is a yellow birch, its foliage aflame. It's not exactly my beloved maple, but it's a tree at least. I sit down with my back against the trunk.

The boathouse is only fifty-five yards away. I can walk down there, raise my hand, knock on the door. When she opens up, I can talk to her, for the first time in all these years.

Before I get around to doing any of this, the door opens. The woman who, on paper, is still my wife steps out. Under her arm, she is carrying a pink plastic basket. With light steps, she walks over to the rotary drying rack set up between the houses and spinning slowly in the wind, and starts hanging out clothes.

I saw Agnes for the first time as she was stepping off the bus. That was in 1975. Birdsong, the blue sky, the shimmering air, the warm soil, her long hair sweeping across my face at night. She looks almost more like the way she was back then than she did the last time I saw her.

Now she bends over, picks up a garment, hangs it over the line, and fastens it with clothespins. How light and agile her movements are. Her long hair hangs down between her shoulder blades. She is wearing blue jeans and a white jersey, so transparent that even from here I can see her white bra underneath.

I should get up and walk down to her. Then I could talk to her without having to knock on the door, go inside, all that, but I just can't bring myself to do it. It's all I can do to keep breathing, as I sit here staring at her, the woman I married, with whom I had children, she who has hurt me more than anyone else.

Long after she's gone inside, I stay seated. Everything I was going to talk to her about, ask her about, convince her of, drains out of me, disappears into the mold from which the sad birch absorbs nourishment.

I have at least established that it's true, what Kjellaug Haugo's son claimed, regardless of how inconceivable it was.

Agnes is no longer in the psychiatric hospital.

Just as I am about to get to my feet, I hear quick footsteps on the gravel. I turn my head slightly and see a man pass by on the road down to the house, just a few yards away from me. He is staring at his phone as he walks, doesn't see me, takes a right and heads for the boathouse, stops, knocks on the door.

I sit still, don't dare breathe, don't dare more.

So he beat me to it, damn journalist bastard.

For a long time, the door doesn't open. I hope that he will have to leave empty handed, but finally the door opens. Agnes stands in the doorway, smiling. She says something, he goes inside, and she closes the door. I get up.

It's as if the apathy that overpowered me a few minutes ago has been blown away. So too the surprising nostalgia. All that remains now is rage.

CHAPTER 10

SABIYA

Victoria is the closest I have to a friend in here, though that's not saying much. Actually, she is the only one I even talk to, and until now, it's been on a pretty superficial level.

Most of the women in here are trashy as hell, including those I know from back in the day, who've been disappointed when they understand that their joy over seeing me again is not reciprocated.

I guess I've gotten a reputation for being stuck up. Had I been in a better mood, I would perhaps have laughed at that description.

Victoria is different. She looks clean cut. Long, dark hair in a ponytail. A wedding ring. No makeup, skin that has been well cared for. A face expressive of a sharp, strong character; she looks French or Italian. She talks like my colleagues at the hospital, apparently studied for the priesthood, but has worked with development aid or something like that in recent years.

The big mystery is, of course, what she's doing here. She hasn't said anything about it, and I haven't asked. For all I know, she's as innocent as I am; I don't really care. Either way, it's liberating to talk with a right-minded human being. I can't bring myself to talk to the other women. They have an intense and artificial sisterhood, exchanging intimate secrets one minute and fighting tooth and nail the next, because somebody's socks fell onto somebody else's bed.

"Stuck up, right," Victoria says. She and I are standing out in the yard, leaning against the fence. "How's it going?"

"Badly," I say. "My lawyer says my best option is to confess so I can avoid jail time."

"So you're innocent, too," Victoria laughs. "Odd, isn't it, how *all* the inmates are victims of a miscarriage of justice."

"I can tell you the details," I say. "But you're going to think I'm nuts . . ."

"I've actually been around the block a few times," she says with a laugh.

"Fine," I say, drawing a breath. "Henrik . . . we went to medical school together, were in the same class. We had a really good connection, hung out all the time, but never anything more. Afterward, we both married and didn't see each other for a long time. A few years ago, I was accepted as a resident in pediatrics at Ullevål Hospital. It was no small feat, and I was very pleased. On my very first day, I ran into Henrik in the hallway; I had no idea he was working there."

I pause for a moment, as my chest tightens. Victoria is wise enough not to comment. I haven't told anyone this story before, except for Roger, who worked with Henrik and me. He'd become a sort of friend that spring, before everything went to hell in a handbasket.

To my surprise, I can feel myself blushing as I continue.

"Anyway, I noticed how I got all agitated and strange whenever he was around, much more than when we were at school, oddly enough. It was like there was a kind of magnetic field between us. Yes, I know it's a cliché, but that's how it felt."

Victoria smiles, warmly, indulgently.

"I was actually the one who kissed him, finally. We were in the kitchenette in the ward, and suddenly, I just did it. It was like I couldn't bear to hold back any longer . . . At first, I felt that things were sort of under control, but eventually, we did things we shouldn't have done. It was as if I just got carried along on a warm current. My life was my kids and my job and my husband, all the little things that should and had to be done every single day. Henrik was something that just happened now and then, small oases of light along the way . . ."

I stop, noticing how implausible it sounds, but Victoria nods.

"I thought that we couldn't continue in this way, that it was a dangerous game, but I wasn't able to stop either. No matter how much I tried to break it off, I was drawn to him, like a junkie to heroin. Before every meeting, I thought that this would have to be the last time. Simultaneously, I just wanted more, I had grown so fond of him. Do you know what I mean?"

She nods again, and we walk for a bit. Then I really have to struggle to hold back the tears.

"Well, then spring came, and these awful things happened. A four-year-old boy was brought in unconscious. He had been beaten to a pulp, was brain dead. The same evening, his father, who everyone knew was responsible, was shot in the prayer room at the hospital."

"Goodness," Victoria says, glancing at me, her eyes wide.

"We were all interrogated and felt we were suspects. It was completely crazy. Lots of questions about key card entry and exit times and things they couldn't make sense of. Then another woman was murdered, at Lysebu, where Henrik and I and some other staff were attending a seminar. And then there was a third murder, a woman who was killed in her bathtub. Sorry, I know this sounds crazy . . ."

"No, no," she says, and laughs a bit. "Or, well, yes, but keep going."

"When the third murder was committed, Henrik was being held in police custody under suspicion for the first two. So he had an alibi. I, on the other hand, did not have an alibi for any of them."

"But why were you even suspects?" she asked, her brow wrinkling. "I don't understand."

"Because we were in the vicinity when the first two murders were committed, and it turned out that all the victims were shot with a pistol I kept in a drawer in my office. I told Henrik that I'd acquired a firearm because I was afraid of my husband, but that was just bullshit. Actually, I just wanted to be able to defend myself, I've seen so much shit . . ."

"*That* part I understand," she says with a crooked smile.

"I showed Henrik the pistol, don't ask me why. Maybe I just wanted to show him how tough I was or cast my husband in a bad light. But after the first murder, it turned out that the pistol was missing. Only Henrik and I knew it was there, but it wasn't Henrik who took it, I'm sure of that. He could never shoot anyone. Maybe I could have, but it wasn't me. Still, somebody found and used my pistol. What's really sick is that the police found strands of my hair in the bathtub where the third victim was found, but I've never been there, never met her. Do you see?"

She furrows her brow, shaking her head slowly.

"Not really, except that someone must have intentionally gone to the trouble to nail you for this."

"Exactly," I say.

"What about Henrik?" she asks. "What does he say? Do you have any contact with him?"

I swallow. She doesn't know, of course.

"What is it, Sabiya?" she says gently.

"Henrik . . ." My voice cracks, damn it all. "Henrik is dead," I say, after a few seconds.

"What?" Victoria says. Now her eyes are huge and round, her mouth open, the crease between her eyebrows even more pronounced. I swallow. I have repressed this as best I can, to prevent myself from drowning as well.

"He drowned last summer, in a lake in the mountains in Western Norway, while he was swimming with his wife, Clara. He was caught by the undertow and dragged over a waterfall. They never found his body."

"How awful," Victoria says. "Did she die, too?"

I shake my head.

"Nope," I say. "She must have found out about the two of us and devised a way to frame me."

"But why?" Victoria says.

"I think she wanted those people to die, and I can sort of understand that. It turned out that what all the victims had in common was that they beat up their children. Henrik knew it, he had actually made a list of such cases, thinking in that way he could save the world. He must have shown the list to Clara, or she must have found it. Apparently, she has a manic obsession with child abuse. Do you know what the worst part is?"

Victoria shakes her head.

Am I really going to say it? I don't really have anything to lose, and right now I have nobody else to confide in.

"I believe Clara must have had something to do with Henrik's death."

"You mean . . . ?"

"That it wasn't an accident," I say.

"But . . . why?" Victoria says, looking shocked.

"He'd been unfaithful," I say, swallowing. "Maybe she was also afraid he would find out that she was behind all these murders? She must have lured him into some kind of trap out there in the water. The problem is that nobody believes me, and I can't prove anything."

"Shit . . ."

"Yeah, that's all I can think about, how much I hate her. And you still haven't heard the worst part. Yesterday, the woman we're talking about was appointed our new minister of justice."

"What?" she burst out in disbelief. "Are you kidding me?"

I shake my head.

"On top of everything, I have the world's most hopeless lawyer. He doesn't listen, has decided that I'm guilty. So I don't have a chance."

"Good God," Victoria says. She seems genuinely shocked. "You need a good lawyer. Mine's a real pit bull, and also head over heels in love with me. Would do anything for me and will get you out of here, I promise."

CHAPTER 11

AXEL

My youngest daughter is sitting at the kitchen table and watching a cartoon on her tablet, tuckered out after kindergarten, while I chop onions and carrots that I plan to sneak into the pasta sauce.

The two eldest are in the living room. The deal is that they are supposed to be doing their homework. Most likely they are playing on their tablets. I should probably care, but I don't. I have enough weighing on my mind, or on my heart.

The fact that Clara actually needs me, combined with how often I get to see her now, however brief our encounters, has intensified all my old, suppressed feelings.

Yesterday, I was there all evening. I threw together a pizza with chèvre, red onions, and spinach, one of my specialties. We drank a good Chilean red wine with the meal, talked about her new job, about the kids, about everything and nothing.

She was wearing a white cotton V-neck T-shirt and a pair of light-blue Lee jeans. The clothes were baggy. Clara has always been thin, but this autumn, she has become downright skinny, skinny and pale.

It's as if the images of her have been etched into my brain. Long, slender fingers with short nails, transparent polish, grasping the large round red wineglass. Her blonde hair falling into her face. Lifting her arms to capture her hair in a rubber band, a glimpse of hair in her armpits. Caro would rather die than be seen like this. Clara doesn't care, is above such things.

I want to help her, make her life easier, make her smile, do whatever I can for her, actually.

Now the doorbell is ringing. Once. Twice. It could be a door-to-door salesman. Children collecting empties or selling toilet paper. Most likely it's friends of the children.

It's none of these things. Outside stands a huge guy, dressed in a kind of shiny pilot's jacket, a dirty T-shirt, jeans, all of it in different shades of grayish black. Around his neck is a headset, in his hand a cell phone.

"Halvor Haugo, *The Fjord Post*," he says, holding out his hand. "Do you have a moment to chat?"

"About what?" I say, accepting his hand in mine hesitantly. "Wait a sec."

I run back into the kitchen and turn down the burners on the stove before walking back to him.

"Can I come in?" he asks when I return.

I sigh. "It's not a good time, I'm in the middle of making dinner."

"It's about Henrik Fougner," he says. "And Clara Lofthus. The minister of justice. Is it correct that they are friends of yours?"

Fuck, I think, and almost say it out loud.

"Henrik *was* a good friend. He's dead, as you perhaps know."

I shouldn't have to stand here saying these things. Still, even though I *know* that it's true, I jump every time I am forced to talk about Henrik's death, or think the thought of it to its completion. A part of me is still waiting for news that it's a lie, that he is alive after all.

"Yes, my condolences," the guy says, running a hand through his hair. "I work for the newspaper that's covering the scene of the accident. We would like to—"

"As I said, I'm in the middle of making dinner," I interrupt.

"I just need a few minutes of your time," he says.

I give up, waving him inside. I have never been good at saying no to people.

"You really can't stay long," I say. "I'm all alone with three hungry children, and I *don't* want to be quoted. No need to take off your shoes . . ."

He takes them off anyway. He hangs his jacket on one of the hooks, on top of one of the kids' jackets. It's too full there, so it falls down, and he has to hang it up again.

He smells of aftershave that's a bit too potent. Strong perfumes for men always remind me of Henrik's imitations of Roger, the nurse he worked with who always doused himself in sweet scents. Henrik asked him to tone it down, but Roger was apparently unreceptive to input. Now I can hear Henrik laughing.

In the beginning, I heard his voice in my head around the clock. Even when I was sleeping, he appeared. Now I hear him less frequently, but it still hurts every time it happens.

"What exactly are you looking for?" I ask as I pour pasta sauce over the vegetables.

"First, I would like to know what Henrik was like," he says. He has taken a seat at the kitchen table.

"Henrik was fantastic," I say.

"You don't say," he says in an irritating tone of voice, as if he doesn't quite believe me. "He must have had some bad qualities, too. Or didn't he?"

"No," I say, taking out a pot and filling it with water. "You know, I don't think this is such a good idea. Seriously. The man is dead."

The guy makes a kind of face. There's a steely gleam in his eyes.

"Okay, let's move on to Clara," he says. "She is minister of justice and comes from the region I cover, so I hope you can understand why she's of interest to us. We noticed that you attended the ceremony on the Palace Square when she was appointed. You know her well, then?"

I nod, curtly. Who are *we*? The people from his newspaper?

"What can you tell me about Clara?"

"Great lady," I say.

"How was the relationship between her and Henrik toward the end?"

"What kind of question is that?" I say, a burning sensation in my chest. "And what relevance does this have, really? They had a good relationship, I think."

"Clara is alone with the children now?" he says. "How's that going?"

"It's going fine, given the circumstances, I think. Why don't you ask her?"

"Cabinet ministers aren't easy to get hold of."

"So then you've come to see me instead?" I say. As I stare into the pot, waiting for the water to boil, I suddenly feel a desperate need to get him out of here. "As stated, I am *not* interested in giving an interview. Now I have to finish making dinner and you have to go. Sorry."

Ever since he sat down, I've felt a kind of fear that he would never get up and leave, that I would have to physically throw him out. He is, after all, a large man. To my relief, he actually gets to his feet, albeit sluggishly.

Thank God I haven't said a thing, nothing that can be used against me, nothing for Clara to get angry about.

"As stated, I haven't given an interview, I don't want to be quoted in any—"

"I heard you," he says in a haughty tone of voice.

"Do you have a card or something?" I ask, suddenly unsure about whether he is even a journalist. "So I can contact you if something comes up?"

"Yup," he says, takes out his wallet, and fishes out a dog-eared business card. "You see much of Clara?" he says, pushing his wallet back into his pocket.

I shrug. "We're friends and almost neighbors. So we see one another, yes."

"She maybe needs a lot of help right now? Do you help out?"

"I have no further comment," I say, while I try to lead the journalist bastard toward the hallway.

"I'm a little surprised that people like you aren't more concerned," he says when we get to the hallway.

"What do you mean?" I ask.

"Well, nobody seems to be worried about the kids, and that's strange, considering what's happened."

He raises his eyebrows, passive-aggressively now. I have to get him out of here.

"The children are alone with a mother who doesn't have time for them. The father dies or is squeezed out. The mother has more than enough on her plate. It's classic, but since you have three children of your own here, you probably wouldn't understand."

"Bye now," I say, as I open the door, place a hand on his back, and push him gently toward the steps. As soon as he's out the door, I slam it shut behind him.

CHAPTER 12

LEIF

This time I also park a short distance away, cross the road, and walk down the small hill to the boathouse with steady, determined steps.

No stopping to rest beneath any trees today. No stopping at all. If I hesitate now, I will never manage to go through with this.

I resurrect some of my secret mantras, those I used to repeat to myself in Lebanon. I can do this, I say to myself. Don't stop, just keep going. Keep calm and carry on, as the English say.

Even so, when I reach the front stoop, I stand there for a few seconds, close my eyes and open them again. The sound of lapping waves is just a yard away. Beside the door, there's a small black-and-white doorbell. I ring it but can't hear any sound of movement inside. I knock, once, twice, before taking hold of the handle, opening the door, and poking my head inside.

"Hello?" I call. "Hello?"

Then I see her. She is standing completely still at the other end of the tiny hallway, in the doorway leading to the interior. I draw a breath and take hold of the door frame to steady myself.

Once upon a time, we were a couple, got married, moved in together, had two children. The last time we stood face to face was on the front porch at home on the farm, right after Lars's funeral, a dark, rainy evening when the wind was blowing something fierce. She came to the door, as wet as a drowned rat, wanted to talk about the children.

I became furious. All the smoldering rage I had attempted to stifle just burst into flames. In the end, I threw her out. I haven't seen her since.

Now she's standing in front of me, silently. So it's true, what they've said, that she doesn't speak. She does smile, though, and the smile scares the bejesus out of me. She tilts her head, as if to signal that I should follow her into the living room. We enter a square little room, over-crowded with impersonal furniture, mostly of pine. Probably furnished by Buzz; everything looks slapdash.

Agnes sits down on the love seat and motions for me to sit down on the couch.

Then we sit there, facing one another.

I see to my relief that it's not true, the young girl impression I got from a distance the other day. Yes, she is slender and neatly dressed, her long hair is still blonde, her skin is unusually smooth, she absolutely looks younger than her sixty-five years. But her two-colored eyes are dull, her hair, too. There is something faded about her, a weary, bitter expression around her mouth. She doesn't look as resoundingly healthy and lively as she did the other day. Although she is sitting six feet away from me, I can detect a sweetish, floral odor emanating from her body, of medicine, perfume.

I clear my throat, wanting to take charge of the situation as I planned, but she beats me to the punch.

"What do you want?" she says, and a cold shiver runs down my back.

So she does speak.

Yes, what do I want, actually? I want to know what she knows and what she wants from us, and I want her to leave us alone. Preferably, I would like her to disappear from my life for good.

"What on earth led them to discharge you?" I ask.

"I got better," she says. "I even started remembering things. For many years, my memory was gone, due to the electric shock treatments, but now I remember everything."

She says it with a kind of triumphant smile.

68

"Then you must remember what happened to Lars, too?" I say.

"I remember that you made everyone believe that I was sick," she says. "And that I belonged in that place."

Her voice is not the thin, desperate voice she had on the porch all those years ago. This voice is rough, grating, as if she's had throat cancer. Is this because of all those years of silence? Electric shock treatments?

"Good God," I say. "You *were* sick, Agnes. Or off your rocker, whatever you want to call it. I am reasonably certain that you still are. What you're doing here, God only knows."

"You didn't come to see me," she says. "But now you've come . . ."

What she says is all well and good, but the creepy, grating voice, the two-colored gaze and, above all, what it's transmitting—it's all skewed, distorted, strange. I don't want to be around her, want only to stand up and run away.

"I came because of Clara," I say.

"Yes," she says. "Of course. Why else?"

Ah. Jealousy, the foul, old, dirty jealousy of her own child. Mustn't let her provoke me. Stay calm. I clear my throat.

"Clara is now a single mother and has a demanding new job—"

"I watch the news," she interrupts. "I know she's been made a cabinet minister."

"Yes, so she's having a tough time," I say. "You must leave her in peace."

Now she just sits there in silence, looking at me. Then her face breaks into her most dazzling smile. Shit. I can feel my desperation itching under my skin. Five minutes in the same room with her is more than enough. I lean forward; she does the same. We perch on our respective ugly couches, upholstered with a floral-print fabric, and are simultaneously the bull and the bullfighter circling one another in a stadium.

"Listen, Agnes," I say, trying to invest more authority in my voice than I actually feel. "You're out now. There's little I can do about that. But I will not allow you to make any more trouble for us."

She studies me with her two-colored eyes.

Looking at her feels almost unreal after all the years I've tried to believe that she was dead.

"What is it you're threatening to do?" she says, squinting at me. "Throw me into the fjord? Or a waterfall?"

I don't answer. The word *waterfall* hangs in the air. She said it. Shit. It's she who is threatening me, not the other way around.

"Coffee?" she asks, sweet as pie.

I shake my head. "I want you to leave us alone," I say, slowly, emphasizing every word.

She shrugs, says nothing. I get the urge to pull her up off the love seat she is sitting on and shake her. I picture myself picking up one of the pokers over by the fireplace, smashing her head, finishing her off, once and for all. I can either simply leave her there, lying on the floor, and let the chips fall where they may or pick her up, carry her out onto the veranda, and dump her into the water.

Yes, I would be in trouble, but she would be gone, and I would be spared having to hear that grating voice of hers again, spared having to be afraid of what she might do or blab about. Ever since I learned that she was out, it's all I've been able to think about.

"You have no idea, do you?" she says. "How these years have been for me?"

That part is true. I didn't get involved, didn't see it as my responsibility, wanted as little as possible to do with her and the psychiatric hospital. For me, she's been just as dead as in the story Clara told Henrik and the boys. But Agnes isn't dead. Agnes is alive and looks as if she could live another fifty years, having been on the back burner for all this time.

"While you went on living as you'd always done, with Clara, while Lars was dead and Magne was dead, I was locked up in Kleivhøgda. You have no idea, no idea what it's like to be drugged senseless or put in restraints, to lose all your freedom."

She stops, makes a little choking sound, as if trying to strangle herself. Then I see that she is turning something over and over in her hands, her gaze fixed on me at all times. It is a letter opener of the more exotic variety, with a miniature elephant on one end, so out of place in this cramped little wooden house on the pebble beach. She runs her finger along the blade, as if testing how sharp it is. Is she planning to defend herself with it? Or attack?

Suddenly, I feel listless, faint. If I had accepted a cup of coffee, I would have believed she'd put something in it, but I haven't had anything to drink; it's just the effect she has on me.

"Agnes," I say. "Pay attention to what I have to say now."

She looks me straight in the eyes. There's no fear there, only contempt.

Then I surprise myself. I don't say a word of what I had planned to say. All of a sudden, I clap my hands. It is instinctive. The impact loud, sharp noises have on her is one of many things I repressed, but it is now in the process of reawakening.

Balloons that burst, things that crash onto the floor. It didn't take much. It *doesn't* take much, because it works like a charm now as well.

She flinches, cowers in her seat, fidgets with the elephant, then puts it down, hooks her index fingers together, and tugs at them until the knuckles turn white.

I managed it. I have actually succeeded in knocking her off balance.

"Stay away from Clara," I say, and get to my feet. "Otherwise, I will have you sent back to Kleivhøgda. No, actually, I'll make you wish you could go back."

CHAPTER 13

CLARA

I enter the boys' bedroom, determined to ignore the hamsters spinning their wheels, reminding me far too much of myself.

It is when my sons are asleep that I feel closest to them. When I see their calm faces, hear their steady breathing, when they are far away and have no idea that I am there. When all the pride, obstinacy, and rebelliousness is washed away and they are just children, clean and clear like water in a mountain stream.

Andreas in his bed, Nikolai on the floor.

In a little while, Nikolai will wake up, go to the bathroom to pee, and then come back and get into bed with his brother. There they will lie, nestled together. They still need to be together, even more now that their father is gone. It is mostly Nikolai who needs Andreas, I think, but it's not easy to know for sure.

Their relationship is like an intricate, checkered artwork in black and white, which I will never fully fathom.

Love and hate, demands for freedom and autonomy, while at the same time being so attached to each other and with so much to talk about, at the breakfast table, in front of the television, in their bedrooms. They argue and fight, yes, but also have a bond that I have never fooled myself that I can become a part of, which even makes me envious at times, even though I also don't care. Woe unto he who dares raise a hand against either of them. He hasn't made himself one enemy, but two.

We and Nikolai, Andreas used to say when he was younger. We and Andreas, Nikolai said. They talked like that for many years. They've stopped doing it now, but the sentiment prevails.

During the day, I don't think they resemble one another, although everyone claims they do. Now it's as if the moonlight has tossed fairy dust upon them. In the dark, they have the same profile; I could almost mix them up.

Two scruffy lions with porcelain skin.

Their bodies, which I can only see a small part of but know so well. I often see them naked still, when they shower or change clothes, but soon they will not want me to see them without clothes on, and the years of childhood will be over. They will grow taller than me, turn into lanky, pimply oafs wearing earbuds, who scarcely grunt at me as they walk past.

Soon. For now, they are still children. They still need me.

I lie down on the edge of the bed, my face toward Andreas's. He is silent, doesn't make a sound, but I can smell the warm, child scent of his body. The smell of milk, wet diapers, and zinc balm from the first years is gone, but they still smell clean, soft, a smell that is oddly touching. Carefully, I place my forehead against his, one arm over him and his duvet. We lie like that for a while, until I kiss him on the forehead and get up.

I will spend more time with them. Soon. I just have to clear the first hurdles of this cabinet minister thing. After only a few days in the minister's chair, I am already feeling more and more like an octopus, each of my many arms being pulled and tugged by others. Before, I always used to scoff at all the talk of time pressure, thought it was a ridiculous, pathetic, faddish expression constructed by a spoiled middle class. Now I am being punished by the mother of all time pressures.

There is such an infinite number of things I can accomplish as minister of justice, but I must act quickly. At the same time, in one way or another, I must manage to take care of these children who are lying there, looking like tiny sculptures, small alabaster angels.

The image of the little and somewhat garish sculptures of children on the dusty square outside the Ullevål Hospital, just a stone's throw away from the prayer room where Mukhtar Ahmad died, flashes through my mind. I shot him from the doorway of the prayer room. I remember the mother-and-daughter sculpture on the wall of the swimming pool at Lysebu, where Melika Omid Carter swam her final laps, before I shot her in the sauna.

Both were killed by Sabiya's pistol, that was the brilliant part.

They deserved to die, Ahmad, Omid Carter, and Susanne Stenersen in her bathtub. The world is a better place without child abusers. Henrik, on the other hand, was a good father, nobody could deny that. But these pangs of conscience that have started surfacing are a luxury I can't afford. Thoughts like these serve no purpose, make nothing better.

I stroke Andreas's hair and kiss him, then repeat the procedure with his brother on the floor. Sometimes it makes them murmur, move in their sleep, like sleeping cats reaching one paw above their heads. Other times, like now, they don't react at all.

It's going to be fine. I have no natural talent as a parent, the way Henrik did, but neither am I my mother.

I will figure this out, I will manage it.

I feel like smoking a joint but should get to work. I walk into my office, which used to be Henrik's, and his father's before him, and which I now occupy. The cases I am working on as a cabinet minister deserve a more dignified location than the kitchen, which is full of backpacks and lunch boxes and unwashed pots and frying pans, and a jumble of shoes is virtually spilling over the threshold from the front hallway and onto the floor.

I removed Henrik's papers, emptied his drawers, aired out the room, and took down some Liverpool banners. I have the same system here as I do at work. One stack of papers for each department lies neatly on the black leather surface of the antique desk. I can therefore see right away if something is out of place.

On the desktop, amid all my stacks of documents, lies a sheet of paper that wasn't lying there when I turned off the lights here last night. I walk over and pick it up carefully.

It's a classified government document about the threat of a pandemic, which I received on my first day as cabinet minister, a document so classified that nobody is allowed to bring it home or send it electronically. I did so anyway but placed the document in the desk drawer I have reserved for papers that shouldn't be here.

Many people may have seen it. My state secretaries, my executive officials, the heads of my department, the advisers, and the department heads and executive officers of the Ministry of Defense and Ministry of Health and at the prime minister's office.

Mona has seen it. Cathrine Monrad. Munch, before he stepped down.

Many people could have had access to this document. But who has been in here, in my home, and placed it on my desk?

I run down the stairs. After Henrik died, I phased out my daily evening joint, cutting back to a few times a week. When I became a cabinet minister, I decided to limit it to just Friday or Saturday. Once a week, and then preferably only *one* joint. Now I say to hell with it, go out to sit on the veranda, dressed in a wool sweater and an old parka, and smoke.

It was Henrik who introduced me to joint smoking when we first started dating. For him, it was a party thing. No demons were haunting Henrik; he didn't have Lars, Magne, or my mother.

While I, on the other hand, need the joint, have probably become addicted to it, to escaping from myself for a little while.

My phone buzzes. I reach for it and see I've received a message from Cathrine Monrad, the police commissioner. I have asked her to keep me apprised of any new developments in the Sabiya Rana case. Now she informs me that the investigation has determined that the forensic evidence of the case is insufficient. Laboratory tests of the hairs found at the last crime scene have proven that they must have been planted.

Sabiya will therefore be released from custody tomorrow. This is, of course, strictly confidential. I thank her and put the phone down again.

I would have preferred for Sabiya to rot in prison for the rest of her life, though a trial would have quickly become awkward, especially now that I'm a cabinet minister. The fact that she was Henrik's lover would almost certainly come out. And the evidence was also too flimsy, she wouldn't be convicted anyway. This way, I will perhaps be spared having the press dig into the case. But on the other hand, Sabiya is out in the world. She is a ticking time bomb, vengeful and uncontrollable, free to talk to everyone and anyone.

I feel the paranoia rising inside me. Things have been going well lately. I've had a sense of calm, and the children appear to be managing. I have made a decision about what I will and will *not* do in the time ahead.

Now it's unraveling. I was attacked and had to be rescued by Stian. Somebody's been in here going through papers that I shouldn't have brought home with me. Sabiya will be out of jail. Maybe I should have agreed to home security cameras after all? If it was freedom I wanted, I shouldn't have become a minister, but instead moved back home to the village.

A metallic taste fills my mouth as I am swallowed by a gray mist of anxiety that resembles the smoke rings I am sending into the sky.

CHAPTER 14

SABIYA

Just two days after the new lawyer got involved, it happens—what I've been longing for but didn't really dare hope for.

I am told to pack up my things. It doesn't take me long. Then I am flushed back out into the world. Taking the subway into the city is surreal. All these people, everything that looks the same as before, that is the same as before.

I will finally see my children again. While I was inside, I had to try and think about them as little as possible, that was the only way to survive. Now that they are within reach, it's impossible to think of anything else; now it's as if I can't stand to be away from them for one more second. I almost run the final stretch of sidewalk leading to our house. I am happy and excited, yes, but I am also afraid, more than I was able to admit to Victoria when we said goodbye.

During the time I was in custody, I saw the children on one single occasion and then only for ten minutes. Their father stood in the background, his eyes on me at all times, as if I were dangerous. His arms crossed, not a smile, not a word. Whenever I was allowed to make a phone call, it was impossible to reach them, and they never called me either.

My husband has many good qualities, or he used to, before all of this. If the two of us can find a way to live together, I can see the children every day. It seems a bit unrealistic, but if I can just see the children, hold them against my body, I will be able to manage just about anything.

The first letdown is that the house is dark and locked. Nobody is home yet. I take out my keys and insert the front door key in the lock— or *try* to insert it. It doesn't work, the lock must have been changed.

I sit down to wait, hoping that none of the neighbors will come walking by and see me on the front steps, locked out of my own house.

When Victoria boasted that her lawyer was in love with her, I had envisioned a man. As it turned out, a well-dressed, elegant woman, her hair as long as Victoria was tall, showed up.

She introduced herself as Marion Høivoll and had me tell her everything I told Victoria and then some. While I was talking, she sat in deep concentration, with her elbows on her knees, leaning forward, her eyes on mine, listening.

Wait, she said, placing her fingertips against her temples, as if she'd developed a migraine or something. She sat like that for a minute, perhaps two, while I didn't dare move or say anything.

I think I know how she's done it and how we can prove it, she said. It has to do with the strands of hair, they must have been planted.

I was so happy when she left, full of new hope. That was just a few days ago, and already it feels remote as I sit here waiting on the steps.

When my family arrives, I'm so cold that I'm shaking. Three children tumble out of the Tesla, the car I splurged on for us during my first year working at Ullevål Hospital, even though I really couldn't afford it.

"Hi, sweetie," I say, opening my arms to my eldest son, and I can feel the tears welling up.

My children. Finally.

The boy just glances at me with sad eyes. My youngest, my daughter, starts running toward me but is stopped by her father.

"Stop," he says. "Kids, go inside. I'll be right there."

The children scurry into the house. My husband and I stand facing each other a couple of yards apart.

"Please," I say. "I must see them. I have the right to see them."

"You listen to me," he says impatiently. "There's nothing for you here."

A loud ringing fills my ears. This is worse than I feared. Inside are my children, already within reach, but lost to me. I try to speak calmly all the same, to conceal my panic.

"They're my children, too," I say. "And we own the house together."

"That's something you'll have to take up with your lawyer," he says. "But you can kiss goodbye any hope of gaining custody."

"Please," I say. "Listen to me—"

"Leave now," he interrupts. "Or I'll call the police."

Then he goes inside, slamming the door behind him. In the living room window, between venetian blinds that I bought, I can see my youngest pressing her face up against the pane for a few seconds until she is yanked away.

I gave birth to her two weeks after my due date. Even though she was the third child, they had to induce labor. She was breastfed longer than the others, allowed to sleep with us longer than the others. Before I was arrested, she used to lie on top of me on the couch in the evenings while we watched TV. She wanted to be close to me constantly. Her favorite thing is to dress up in my clothes, braid my hair, bake cupcakes, all the things that are so intimate and at the same time so incredibly distant.

The door is locked. I pound on it, but it doesn't help, and I am probably just frightening the children. Good God. Now that I am no longer locked in, but locked out, it actually feels worse.

Everything I've hoped and dreamed and longed for in jail now seems wholly unattainable.

What should I do? Must I swallow my pride and ask my parents for help? Or my brothers, although for sure they are also angry with me? Right now, the thought of facing their wrath is not exactly appealing.

Perhaps I can go to one of the city's secret hideouts, the air-raid shelter, the disused factories and breweries, places where I spent a lot of time during my adolescence. Many years have passed since then, but presumably some of those places are still intact. Didn't I hide a pistol somewhere? Where can it have been? In the old sausage factory?

In truth, I should just spend all my energy finding out how I can recover something of my former life, at least the chance to see my children again.

And yet I can't stop thinking about Clara Lofthus sitting there in her big house. She killed Henrik, robbed me of my life, and is now Norway's minister of justice. Life is really not fair.

CHAPTER 15

——

Clara

This is my first dinner at the palace after a month as cabinet minister, but I've been here once before, just after I was appointed state secretary. When I received the cream-colored, monogrammed, and embossed invitation to a dinner at the Royal Palace, I knew what to expect. I was familiar with the requirement to report to the main gate between 7:20 and 7:40, knew about the noisy symbiosis of voices and the orchestra playing *musique de table*, about the pompous program bearing the gold royal crown insignia and the menu in French.

Dinner will be *Tartare de langoustines*, then *Flétan*, subsequently *Filet de bœuf*, and finally *Gâteau Forêt-noire*.

Everything is described in detail, though I don't get much out of it. French is not my strong suit.

The *programme musical* informs me that the entrance music for the arrival of the procession will be the military march "Kingdom of Norway," no surprises there, followed by the national anthems of Iceland and Norway, respectively.

Later, a mezzo-soprano and a pianist will perform Georges Bizet's *"L'amour est un oiseau rebelle (habanera)"* from *Carmen*, then Sigfús Einarsson's *"Draumalandið"* to be concluded by the familiar "Valdres March" for the exit procession.

I am also familiar with the feeling of rustling silk against my legs, the ache in the small of my back after wearing high heels for so many hours, concentrating and conversing, holding a drink in my hand, and a shawl over my shoulders.

Now I raise my glass in a toast, at the suitable height. I wasn't exactly spoon-fed all this as a child and have had to learn it little by little. I sip, swallow, smile, doing it with apparent lightness and ease, but this is also work. A message from the prime minister on my way up the stairs. A veiled dig delivered into the ear of the police commissioner once I reach the top. A quick exchange of information with the minister of defense under the chandelier.

People talk to me differently now, look at me differently, treat me differently. I don't know whether I like it, but everything *is* different, including me. I am the same, but still I am different.

I am the minister of justice. I am also a single mother.

From now on, I *must* keep myself on the straight and narrow, take no risks. Attend to my job, look after the children. That is more than enough.

Approximately one month has passed since I stood out here on the square with the stones pressing through the thin soles of my Christian Louboutin shoes. The first, most paralyzing feeling of time pressure has begun to abate.

This will all work out, somehow. The boys appear to be managing quite well. Their spirits seem to have improved of late.

Perhaps the shock of Henrik's death has started releasing its hold on them?

The last time I was here, I learned that it is not wise to leave the party before it is officially over. It takes time, but it is at long last finally over, and I can walk to the black wrought-iron gate with gold ornaments, then between the big columns outside of it. A convoy of governmental vehicles, taxis, and private cars awaits there. The guardsmen stand watch. Curious passersby are kept at a distance by security.

I am on my way over to my car, about in the middle of the line, when a small parade of demonstrators comes toward me. The group of young adults is carrying signs and banners; they are shouting something; I can't make out what.

How I despise these militant activists who think they are something, think they mean something, who aren't of any significance whatsoever.

A girl wearing braids, heavy makeup, and a ring in her nose heads straight for me.

"You damn traitor," she screams. "Damn fucking traitor."

A red cloud, a powder of some kind, is thrown at me. It looks artificial, like the kind of sprinkles you put on an ice cream cone. It drifts down on me; I can feel it on my face, my lips, in my eyes.

Damn it all. I back away, glance behind me. The car. Stian. Can he see me? I am gripped by a surprising panic. Is this how life is going to be now?

A second later, Stian is there, leading me toward the car while the guardsmen or the police, I can't see who, remove the demonstrators.

"Traitor," the girl screams as she is led away, so loudly that they must be able to hear it inside the Royal Palace.

I walk toward the car, trying to brush off some of the red powder. It looks like blood, and I get it on my hands.

"Are you okay?" Stian asks, watching me. "And does it itch?"

"No," I say, and try to breathe.

"I'm sure they were reasonably harmless," he says. "Classic much ado about nothing. But listen, this won't do. There are threats against you from many different camps. You must have proper security; you understand that, don't you?"

I don't reply, just lean back in the seat and look down at my dress. No dry cleaner will be able to fix this. Maybe I can write it off as an expense since it was a work-related incident.

I close my eyes, notice how tired I am, and at that exact moment, my skin starts itching like all hell.

When I have walked through the front door into the hallway at home, I see an envelope with my name on it and without postage lying on the floor. Someone must have stuck it under the door in the course of the evening. Åsa the perfectionist would never have left it lying around like that. I put it on the kitchen table with the rest of the mail and walk into the living room.

Åsa is dozing on the couch in front of the television. She sits up and looks around her dazedly when I gently shake her upper arm.

"Ah, there you are," she says. She glances down at her watch and then looks at me in horror. "Goodness! What in the world happened to you?"

"Nothing," I say.

"I see," she says doubtfully.

"Well, there were a few young protesters who wanted to spice up my day. They threw a cloud of red powder at me. I guess I should stay away from the Palace Square."

I stop talking and have to scratch my arms and throat, which are itching and burning something terrible now, as if I dove into a swarm of jellyfish.

"Probably just itching powder," I say with a grimace.

"Heavens . . . ," she murmurs.

"But I'll be fine. How have things been here?"

"Fine," she says. "They're good, your boys."

I hesitate. Mentioning Henrik will make her even more sad. At the same time, I know that all she wants is to hear his name.

"Henrik did a great job with them," I say.

"Yes," she says, smiling wanly.

Others would have perhaps attempted a phrase such as "So did you," but not Mother Åsa, and I like her for it.

Henrik was his father's boy, the boys were Henrik's boys, that's how it was.

Åsa has been walking around like a zombie for the past few months. I hope spending time together helps both her and the boys, that it gives her days meaning, that they can console one another.

Of course, it could be that her grief only makes the boys' sadness worse, that it isn't healthy for them to spend so much time together, but I have no choice. Dad lives many hours away. I must allow her to babysit the boys every bit as much as she likes. It has actually been Åsa and Axel whom they've seen the most of in the past weeks.

"Hey," she says, biting her lip. "Sorry, don't take this the wrong way . . ."

She pauses. I brace myself.

"But you're surrounded by so much drama. I worry about you and about the boys. Are they safe? They don't have any security, as far as I know."

I swallow, trying not to let her see how much her question irritates me.

"Åsa, it's fine," I say. "I promise. They are safe. Everything will be fine."

She nods, gives me a kind of wan smile. My skin itches.

On the way through the kitchen after having accompanied her to the front door, I see the envelope I put down on the table earlier. I stop, open it, take out the letter. There is one lone sentence on it, in an ordinary font of some kind, in huge letters on the middle of the page.

Somebody knows what you've done.

Five words. Just five words, but they do the trick.

My hands start trembling as if I have developed Parkinson's disease. My knees start shaking, too. A wave of discomfort rolls through me. What the devil is this? Who is out to get me? And who is it that knows something about what? Are they referring to the murders of last spring? To Henrik? Magne? Or something else entirely?

I sit down, breathe. Okay, the letter was addressed to me personally, but it *could* still be one of these idiots who write to me and whom I am not informed about. Such letters are usually sent to the ministry and screened there. I never see them; I just know that they exist.

Without giving the matter further consideration, I tear the letter and the envelope into small pieces and shove them down into the recycling bin. Then I go upstairs, take a long shower, and get dressed. I stop in front of the mirror above the bureau to see whether I look different or simply feel different.

I look the way I usually look. A bit skinny, middle aged, and tired, Henrik would have said, but nothing unusual.

When I turn away from the mirror and start walking toward the door, I notice something, almost like a small shadow out of the corner of my eye.

There's something about the sewing mannequin, Edith.

Usually, she just stands there, unclothed, such a given part of the furnishings that I don't really see her anymore.

Now I see her. It's as if she were standing there beaming at me in the darkness. Over her petite, narrow French shoulders hangs one of Henrik's favorite white shirts, neatly buttoned.

The sight gives me chills.

I never dressed her, and neither had Henrik. So who was it? Axel? Åsa? The cleaning lady? Most likely, it was somebody else entirely, from outside the family.

The pandemic document. Now this letter. And the shirt on the dummy. All these things are messages to me, from somebody out there who wants to show me that they can intrude on my life, do whatever they want.

One thing is certain. Over the weekend, I am going to contact PSS and agree to everything they suggest.

CHAPTER 16

—

CLARA

This is my second cabinet meeting.

The atmosphere before we start is ostensibly more jovial and relaxed than the many suits and ties and attending titles would suggest. But when the prime minister clears her throat and says it's time to begin, a gravity descends upon the room.

Everyone sits up straight and opens the folders on the table in front of them. In the folders are all the Memoranda to Cabinet that have been circulated for comment.

I was up at four this morning to read all the documents thoroughly after an anxious night.

It is usually in the morning, when the rest of the world is asleep, when my brain has just woken up and I have staggered out of the bedroom and into my office and pushed the button on the Moccamaster in there, that I am at my sharpest and function best.

After the episode on the Palace Square, the letter, the mannequin, and a sleepless, itchy, shitty night, I now feel only distracted and tired.

Item number five on the agenda is the new draft of a regulation relating to so-called child abduction cases from the Ministry of Children and Families. The prime minister says pretty much the same thing she says for each item, that we have received a memorandum about the draft and that it is good.

I raise my hand. The prime minister looks at me in surprise but nods.

"Personally, I am unfortunately not impressed by this proposal," I say.

"You're not?" the prime minister says.

Her tone of voice is not encouraging in any sense, but I have no intention of letting her psych me out.

"It's far too weak, barely an improvement on current practice," I say, and pause for dramatic effect. "On a couple of points, it's actually worse than what we have now. It is presented as progress, but it's not. I can't understand why the minister of children and families isn't willing to do more."

I see that the secretary to the government looks at me in shock, that the prime minister's face darkens, that the other ministers smile maliciously, but there's no turning back now.

"I think this issue would be better suited in my hands, at the Ministry of Justice, a ministry with heft. There, it will receive the attention it deserves. I would be happy to explain in further detail . . ."

"Thank you, Clara. But we have to move on," the prime minister says without looking at me. "I would otherwise remind you that the Ministry of Justice had no comments when the document was circulated."

For a couple of seconds, the room is completely silent. The only sound is the minister of local government's heavy, irritating breathing. I stare down at my notebook and say nothing more. The prime minister clears her throat and continues through the agenda.

Afterward, I sit behind closed doors in my office with my head in my hands. My blood is seething and boiling under my skin.

The cabinet meeting made me feel weak and humiliated. Now I am furious.

I was probably the only person in that room who really wanted to accomplish something, and I had to sit there and be ridiculed.

I said yes to becoming a state secretary and subsequently a cabinet minister to accomplish something, to make sure that what happened to Lars would not happen to other children. That is why I'm here, and now I am obliged to navigate this quagmire of useless people. The prime minister and her yes-men will be forced to eat their words. I'll show them how to do something that actually makes a difference, unlike the pathetic measures the minister of children and families proposed.

I call Vigdis, unable to find the strength to get up and go out to her.

"I want to see the secretary general in my office immediately," I say, and hang up.

"You wanted to speak to me?" Mona asks when she comes into my office ten minutes later.

"Close the door," I say, skipping the usual pleasantries. "And have a seat."

She nods and sits down in one of the conference table chairs, angling it toward my desk. I have purposely not gone over to take a seat at the table beside her.

I am a cabinet minister. The secretary general has been called into my office, and I remain seated behind the minister's desk. That's how it must be now.

"I was at a cabinet meeting today," I say. "It didn't go very well."

"No?" she says expectantly.

For all I know, she may have already received a report about my gaffe. Secretaries general are always informed of such things, sooner or later.

"The minister of children and families' new bill came up. It is completely without content. I gave my opinion, that it was an empty egg, that the matter would be better off here in my hands."

She makes a face, starts to say something. I raise one hand.

"I mean it," I continue. "But I shouldn't have said it there and then and not in that way."

"No," she says smugly.

"So now I'm wondering why you didn't brief me properly before the cabinet meeting?"

"What do you mean?" she says, surprised.

"You know that I'm new, you know I'm not familiar with all the codes, that the amended children's bill was on the agenda today, and that we didn't make any comments when it was circulated. Besides, you know that I'm passionate about this issue."

"Yes," she says.

"So you should have put two and two together and warned me," I say. "This is not to happen again, understood?"

A few seconds of silence.

Mona's face is white and strained. I can see that she wants to object, but finally, she nods.

"Fine," she says, and gets to her feet.

"Wait," I say. "Sit down. I have a job for you. The bill that Munch stopped is to be prepared for circulation to the ministries for comment. ASAP."

"Listen," Mona says, leaning forward. "That's difficult for a number of—"

"It was not a request, it was an order," I interrupt. "*Now* you can leave."

She gets up and leaves without saying another word.

An hour later, Vigdis puts three pieces of crispbread with cheese and a cup of tea in front of me, even though I didn't ask her to. When I took over as minister, I thought I wouldn't use her for such things. Munch had, and I thought it was embarrassing. I would manage to prepare my own lunch.

In reality, there's no time for anything, and more and more often, I must ask Vigdis to take care of something. Today she has done so without being asked.

Vigdis is so much more than a subordinate. There is nobody who knows more about what happens in the manifold corridors and offices of the ministry than the minister's secretary. Beyond this, there are few, if any, who have the same detailed knowledge of the cabinet minister's affairs.

"Thank you," I say. "But aren't you going home soon? It's late."

"Yes, I'll be leaving now if that's all right," Vigdis says.

"Fine," I say, and take a bite of the first piece of crispbread without looking up from my papers. "Thank you for your help today."

The security guard comes in and says hello, and then checks in again a while later, without batting an eye. He has probably seen cabinet ministers working late into the evening here before and will see it again.

All members of government have jobs that a single person cannot manage on their own, regardless of how much they delegate or how skilled they are at using the staff of permanent officials. Some ministerial positions imply even greater responsibility and are more demanding than others. The position I have is among the most demanding. I am still thinking about the day's gaffe in the cabinet meeting, ashamed about having miscalculated, lost control, made a fool of myself, about being an amateur. But at least I set Mona straight.

This is how it must be moving forward. It's the only way I'll manage to get anything done here.

During all my years as an executive officer—yes, even as a state secretary—there was always something or other that made me feel superior, elevated above the others, yes, better than them. I have received more respect than I deserved.

Now, however, I am in over my head. The other cabinet ministers, the police commissioner, Mona, my own political leadership, nobody has respect for me. I must change that now, by working even harder. So I can't just log off and go home. I must write emails and comment on memoranda and drafts, do everything that it is impossible to find time for in the course of an ordinary workday.

Thank you, Åsa, I write to my mother-in-law, who has canceled a theater date with a girlfriend so she can stay with the boys a bit longer.

I will do what I can to prevent this from happening too often, I add, and throw in a heart, something I otherwise never do.

I'll sleep in Nikolai's room, if that's okay? is her reply.

Of course, I respond.

It's good that she's spending the night; then I won't have to rush home.

I have just sent out an email full of lengthy and intricate instructions to one of the technical divisions, feeling so tired that my vision is blurry, when somebody clears their throat in the doorway. I hadn't heard any footsteps, and I jump. Then I look straight into Stian's steady blue gaze.

"You?" I say, and burst into something resembling laughter. "I thought it must be the security guard again. What are you doing here?"

He leans nonchalantly against the door frame, points at his watch, and gives me a stern look, with a light shake of his head.

"Find your coat," he says. "We're going home."

"I understand that *you* want to go home, but *I'm* not finished here . . ."

"It's not me," he says. "I'm on duty all night. It's you."

"What?" I say, feeling dazed. *It's you.* What does he mean by that?

"Time's up," he says. "You can't sit here any longer. It's not good for you to sit here burning the midnight oil, it's not good for the children or your mother-in-law—"

"She's actually spending the night," I say.

"—and not good for tomorrow. So pack up your things, let's go."

Something about his voice causes me to obey. I stand up, close my laptop, and am about to take it out of the docking station.

"You won't need that until tomorrow morning," he says.

I shake my head but do actually leave the computer where it is.

"Your wish is my command," I say, closing the door to my office.

It feels like he guides me with a feathery-light touch of his fingers against my back as we walk toward the elevator.

I can't help it. I like it.

CHAPTER 17

CLARA

The next day, I am, in fact, picked up outside the government building R5, as agreed, by four o'clock in the afternoon, far earlier than I usually go home.

In addition to the promise I made to myself and Stian the night before, I am tired of all the idiots on whom I have wasted the day, and I have used up all favors from my mother-in-law for a while.

"You know the lady who came after you on the Palace Square? During the ceremony?" Stian says, glancing at me in the rearview mirror. "It turns out she's a pro-life fanatic who blames you for the current abortion legislation because you happen to be minister of justice right now. And no, it's not logical, but that's how it is. Now we think that we have her under control for a while. Either way, no need to worry about her specifically."

"Good," I say. "Thanks."

I turn toward the window and look out. The colorful palette of the autumn foliage is still beautiful. This weekend, I will finally have the chance to go for a run or two like I used to.

I have been running for thirty years. It started with runs up and down the mountain by the waterfall, to the summer farm and back after Lars died. The runs were punishment and consolation at the same time. Had I been another kind of person, I would have perhaps started smoking hash behind the bleachers on the soccer field, taken the bus to the next village and gotten drunk, reeled around in the forest with a bottle in my hand, allowed someone to lay me on my back in the woods and pound away on me. Or I would have started a systematic destruction of my body by stuffing it with sugar and trans fats, allowing my body to expand until all my feelings and edges disappeared.

I did none of these things. I breathed. Ran. Breathed. Ran. I've been doing this for years, ever since then, until now.

During these weeks as cabinet minister, there simply hasn't been time. Everything is just work. A glimpse of the boys now and then. A glass or two of wine with Axel, who has lately been bombarding me with messages and invitations to go out and eat, offers to come over and prepare dinner or for me to come over and eat at his place. You'd think life was all about food. One evening, I let him make a pizza for me. It was nice, but I don't often have time for that kind of thing. Sorry, too busy right now, I wrote to him yesterday. It's true, but maybe I can invite him over this weekend. The boys would like that.

Most of all, I look forward to seeing the children, making tacos, and reading to them and not looking at my phone again until after they're in bed, no matter what PSS has to say about always keeping one eye glued to the phone.

A run or two, otherwise I will dedicate the entire weekend to the boys.

On Monday, I will seriously get back to work on the job I barely made a dent in yesterday evening, after putting Mona to work on my bill. This time, in this chair, I plan to use well. Achieve real change, make up for the incompetent Munch. My probation period, the first month, is over. Now it all starts for real.

"Have a nice weekend, Clara," Stian says when he opens the car door for me.

"You, too," I say, smiling at him.

On my way through the gate, I glance at my watch: 4:30 p.m. The boys are probably sitting on the couch, drinking chocolate milk, absorbed with something on their tablets.

"Hello?" I say as I open the door.

It is dark and silent in the hallway. No shoes or knapsacks in sight.

"Hello," I say again, and peek into the living room. Silent and empty. I walk up the stairs, look in their rooms. Games, library books that should have been returned a long time ago, dirty clothes that should be in the washing machine, dirty dishes that should be in the dishwasher, tangled duvets, stuffed animals they should have grown out of. No children.

I walk downstairs again, go into the kitchen, pour myself a glass of water. Maybe they stopped at the park to kick the soccer ball around with Olav, maybe they went home with him, without letting me know? I can call Axel and check.

They are children. It's Friday. No homework. No scheduled activities. I should let it go. Not scold them, not get irritated.

It is when I turn around, away from the sink, while swallowing the final gulp of water from the glass, that I see it. A letter. On the kitchen table.

For a second or two, I think it's a note from the boys. But nowadays, children don't write notes; they send messages on their phones. Now I also remember the other letter that was lying here when I came home from the dinner at the palace a few days ago, the one I chose not to worry about, to ignore, repress, say to hell with. I pick up the letter, start reading, and my world explodes.

My hand quivers and trembles, the trembling spreads into the sheet of paper, and it drops to the floor. I pick it up, read it again.

This can't be true. This is not happening.

There are some who know everything you do. You will be punished.

More information will come later. In this period, do not do anything. Most importantly, do not tell someone something.

If you want to see your sons again, you have to be quiet.

If you do not, they will be killed.

Strange wording, probably written using Google Translate, but I get the message. A message that fulfills its presumed intention, to scare the living shit out of me. Literally. I dash to the bathroom and relieve my twisting bowels. There's a prickling sensation in my hands, in my head, everywhere, like I'm going to faint. Then I start hyperventilating, I pull up my trousers, start walking in circles, stumble, and fall.

Sounds come out of me, sounds I don't recognize.

My children. My beautiful, brave boys.

PART 2

THE CHILDREN

CHAPTER 18

ANDREAS

It seems like Nikolai has dozed off; anyway, he's completely silent. We maybe shouldn't sleep now, really, but it's wonderful that he did, so at least he's quiet. I'm actually a bit envious.

I just keep seeing these films inside my head, again and again, even now. The first film shows Daddy coming home from the cottage. We throw ourselves at him, hug him, sit down on the floor in the hallway. He teases and plays with us, tickling us, throwing us up into the air, like when we were younger.

Then the doorbell rings, and we jump up, the way we always do, because it's almost always somebody for us, who wants to play with us or get us to go outside with them to do something. That's not what it is now, though. Now there are three policemen on our front steps. They are wearing uniforms and boots and hats. One of them opens his mouth and asks for Daddy. I have always wanted to see real policemen, but now I just *know* that something is really wrong.

Although there are actually sounds for this film, although the policemen talk and Daddy talks and Mommy talks in her work voice, it's completely silent. It's like watching TV with the volume off or ducking your head under water in the pool, so you can no longer hear the noises around you.

That's how it is, until Nikolai starts bawling. His bawling cuts through me like a knife. We cling to Daddy, and he says we must go to

Mommy, but I don't want to let go of him, I just hang on tight, while Nikolai screams and screams and doesn't stop, how typical of him.

That part of the film ends there.

Both the policemen and Daddy said that he was just going to help them out with a few questions, but I understood that he was under arrest. There was something about how there were three of them, in uniform, and their faces were serious, something about the way they talked and Daddy's face, which turned completely white, something about Mommy, who spoke all sharp and stiff and strange.

She tried to stop them, but it didn't work. They left, they took Daddy with them, and we were left alone with Mommy. I was so scared that we would never see him again. I remember almost nothing from those days, just my heart beating and beating and beating. The whole time I thought that it was going to stop, because Daddy was gone and everything was so awful, but it didn't. My heart kept going. Everything kept going. We went to school like nothing happened, too. Mommy went to work like nothing happened, and Daddy sat in jail under arrest for two murders. Inside me, everything turned to ice and became totally unreal.

Grandpa came, Mommy's father. I almost couldn't remember the last time he'd been to visit at our house. One time, he came for our birthday, but not every year. Mommy always said he was happiest at home, and also he had to stay at the farm to take care of the animals and all that, and we saw him quite often in Western Norway. Still, I thought it was too bad he never got to meet our friends or see our soccer games. So it was nice that he came, but nothing could be really fine, not so long as Daddy was gone.

Every day, I asked Mommy if he would be coming home soon. Every day, she answered that she didn't know, but that she was working on it, we just had to be patient. Grandpa stroked our hair and watched TV with us and read to us and looked at us like he was worried when he thought we didn't see.

The whole time, I heard the same questions inside my head. What happened? Did Dad really do something wrong? And will he ever come home again?

Then I thought that if only Dad came home, everything would be fine, but really, it was only the beginning.

CHAPTER 19

CLARA

For a while, I lose it completely, just lurch around, a creature of fluid desperation. I weep, kick, punch the wall, take a shower, end up vomiting in the bathtub, have to pick up the vomit with my fingers and throw it in the toilet so the drain won't be clogged the next time one of the boys wants to take a bath.

Nikolai loves taking long baths. Andreas prefers showers.

Naked and wet, I sit down on the toilet, something wants to come out, but it's only my bowels inside there, they seem to be twisting and curling in a savage death dance. I lie down on the bathroom floor, press a towel against my face, in my mouth, as if to suffocate myself, to take control over everything inside me that wants to come out. Then I sit up and rock back and forth, with my hands around my knees.

I have no idea what to do.

Finally, I manage to climb to my feet, dry myself off, and get dressed. I walk into the kitchen, take out the largest, sharpest knife, sit down on the floor, place the blade against the inside of my wrist, apply pressure, close my eyes, and pull the knife toward me.

A burst of pain, more overwhelming than I could have imagined.

Then the soothing, white dizziness, which drowns out everything else for a few seconds while I place my lips against the gaping wound and swallow my own blood.

My boys. They used to sleep in the carriage outside the door here, only the tips of their noses and their heads visible under the duvets and blankets. I would check on them constantly. Was the carriage still there? Were they awake? Was anything covering up their faces? Were they breathing?

Later, at zoos and playrooms, where parents sat with their eyes glued to their phones, I walked around and tried to keep an eye on my two children at all times. Those kinds of places had to be a paradise for pedophile bastards.

Then in one way or another, the children became more Henrik's domain. I became more interested in other things. They got older, became more independent. Or I thought they were older and independent, because I wanted them to be, because I couldn't bear for them to need me. I had enough on my plate, I was so self-absorbed.

But actually, they were still so little, so young.

Recently, even after becoming minister, I haven't even considered the possibility that something could happen to the boys, even though I'm alone with them now and have put us in a position where we are suddenly in the public eye, a public target. I could have posted someone outside here, someone to protect them, but I said no, because I was so stubborn, wanted to be so free.

Dumb, that's what I was. Dumb and selfish.

With trembling hands, I find Andreas's phone number, want to hear their voices saying that everything's fine, that they are in the park with Olav. It must be the person or persons responsible for the pandemic document, Henrik's shirt, and the first letter, who has taken things a step further.

My call goes straight to voice mail. I try Nikolai's number, and there, too, I'm sent to his voice mail. Their cell phones must be off. I am about to call Axel, get him to come, along with my father-in-law. Then it hits me. I can't call Axel. I can't call Dad or my father-in-law. I have to handle this alone.

I run up to their rooms, where everything lies in a blissful chaos—duvets, pillows, clothing, stuffed animals, all the books they've been given and don't read, toys, socks, trousers—it's barely possible to see the floor anywhere. Since Henrik died, I've just closed the door to their rooms when the cleaning lady comes, turning a blind eye to the mess, thinking I would get to it eventually.

Now I move things around, lifting, rearranging, trying to do it systematically.

There are no cell phones here, just their clutter, everything that reminds me of them. Now it's as if a restlessness has infected my skin. I scratch my hands and chest desperately, the way I did after I was bombarded with the red itching powder a few days before.

CHAPTER 20

ANDREAS

I must wake Nikolai soon, even though it's nice that he's asleep, instead of fussing and crying.

After spending a few days in jail, Dad came back. It was summer, and everything was green. I stood at the window in my room and saw Grandfather's car stop outside, watched Dad get out.

There he was. I almost couldn't believe it. I was so happy, was about to run downstairs and hug him tightly. Then something strange happened. I had been so angry the whole time, at Mommy, at the police, and at the world, but now it was as if all my anger suddenly became a cannon that was aimed at Dad because he had been away. I had been so worried, and now I was suddenly just *so* angry.

Instead of running downstairs to give him a hug, I sat down on the floor to play and tried as hard as I could not to cry. Nikolai was, I think, feeling the same way, because he sat there with his LEGO pirate ship and didn't move either, even though he'd been standing beside me at the window and had seen the exact same thing.

A few minutes later, Dad came upstairs, and then he came into our room, opened the door, and I saw how happy he was. For a little while, he just stood there, beaming, but when neither of us got up, it was as if the light went out. I should have stopped then, but it was already too late. So while Nikolai accepted a hug and let Dad talk to him a little,

I just sat there being angry. And when he came over to me, I pushed him away.

Afterward, when I heard him walk down the stairs, already I regretted it. I regretted it while I heard him arguing with Mommy, regretted it during the barbecue we had in the garden, regretted it every single day since, even though we had a nice time. I will probably regret it every day of my life. Don't, you smell bad, I had said, pushing him away.

Now I shake Nikolai's shoulder gently.

"Nikolai, wake up," I say.

CHAPTER 21

CLARA

After an hour, during which I have frantically tried to scribble ideas down on paper, make a mind map and lists of suspects and clues, the way I imagine a detective would do, I crumple up the pages and throw them out.

Then I run back into the bathroom, tear off my clothes, and pull on my sports bra and leggings and an old T-shirt. In the hallway, I tie the laces of my favorite running shoes, put earbuds in my ears and my phone in my bra, saying to hell with it to the minister's phone. That's not where these people will contact me if they make contact.

Then I run out the door. After emptying my stomach, after all the trembling, after cutting myself, I don't really have much energy left. When your two children are abducted, a mother also probably shouldn't be going out for a run, I understand that, but I have to do *something*. In one way or another, I must make my brain clearer, cleaner. And this is the only way I know how, except for taking out the knife and cutting myself again, and I can't do that, I must not do that. I have wanted to do it so many times and managed to resist. I can't start with that now; if I do, I'll end up cutting and cutting until there's nothing left.

I run to the edge of the forest, scale the steep hill where I usually warm up by walking at a sprint. My muscles cramp immediately, but I power through, defying the burning in my muscles and lungs.

When I reach the place where I usually stop and catch my breath, I keep going with increased determination. Where I usually hold back a bit, I sprint, ignoring the pain in my lungs, thighs, shins, everything that's locking, everything that's burning. I didn't bring a headlamp, so there's darkness all around me. I can't see where I'm running, but I can feel the ground, and I don't care anyway, just keep pushing myself. It's like running in a dark tunnel. The pain thunders in my ears. Every now and then, I trip over roots, stones, on the verge of falling.

Andreas. Nikolai. Their names in each throb of my pulse, like small explosions, like the crackling of their sparklers on New Year's Eve. I can't lose them the way I lost Lars; I won't survive it.

The pain I drive myself to has released a lightness. I am as light as the wind, as light as the child I once was, as light as cotton grass and baby-bird down, as light as the weight of nothing, I *am* a nothing: I fly away and everything around me disappears. All that remains is the feeling of flying, the one I've been chasing since I was a little girl.

My boys, who are so different but so attached to one another, like day to night and night to day. I just hope with all my heart that they are together, can console one another until I find them.

Andreas was born first, Andreas who pushed his way through the birth canal spontaneously and head down, saw daylight a half hour before his brother had to be pulled out bottom first. He led the way, has always led the way, is sharper than Nikolai, sharper than everyone his age. I have intentionally never told him so, and I regret this now. So many things I should have said, so many things I should have done.

Andreas will one day inherit the farm at home. He should have been named after Dad, but Dad vetoed this, he doesn't like his name. Instead, Andreas was named after his grandfather on his father's side.

I run fast and hard all the way home. Once inside the door, I fall onto the floor and lie there for a long time. Everything in front of my eyes is red and flickering.

After what feels like several hours, though I have no idea how much time has actually passed, I clamber up from the floor and sit down again with a pen and a piece of paper. I must think clearly and rationally now. Who has a motive? Who wants to hurt me? That's where I have to start. I scribble down a few names. Work names. Munch, for example. I hear his voice in my ear, soft, bitter, the way he said bitch. Vengeful. Yes. The question is whether he is crazy enough to kidnap two children.

Full of doubts, I nonetheless write down the names of the relatives of the child abusers I have done away with this year, even though I don't really think any of them could have figured out I am to blame.

After a while, I rest my head in my hands and moan, registering how tired I am. I have to eat something. There's nothing in the refrigerator. I go to the freezer to look for a frozen pizza. Nothing there either except for a bag of shrimp. It will have to do.

I pace restlessly around the living room, trying to organize my thoughts, every bit as queasy as when I try to write emails in the back seat of the minister car. It doesn't help. I am unable to think a single coherent thought.

Finally, I walk up the stairs, into the bedroom, and lie down under the duvet, curling up into a ball. I have to try and disappear for a bit. Maybe sleep for a couple of minutes, wake up with sharper, clearer thoughts.

The only time I am ever in bed is when I turn in for the night after a long day. I never lie in bed during the daytime. Never. It reminds me too much of my mother. Even when the boys were little and slept in the baby carriage outside, I tried to spend the time doing something constructive, no matter how groggy I was.

The silence in the house reminds me of the one at home after Lars moved out with Agnes to live with Magne, and later after his death. Silent and empty. The kitchen clock with its sluggish hands. Ticktock, ticktock. Finally, Dad had to take it down. I still can't stand that kind of wall clock.

It all comes back to me now.

I used to carry Lars with me, pointing at everything and telling him what we saw. Flower. Lars. Cow. Lars. Barn. Tractor. Barn bridge. Grass. Dad. Mommy. Tree. Wheelbarrow. Cat.

Dad had taught me all the words; then I taught them to Lars. I led him around by the hand when he started walking. I taught him to ride a bike. I watched television with him, told him stories. I changed his sheets when he wet the bed and let him sleep with me whenever he wanted.

I never told Dad how it was while he was away, didn't want to make him even sadder than he already was after Lebanon.

Then suddenly, Mommy was going to move out and take Lars with her. At first, I didn't believe it. He was mine. I was the one who took care of him while Dad was away. I looked after him; she didn't care about him. I said she wasn't allowed to take him. Then she just laughed, shook her head, said that I could come along with them. I didn't want to do that, I couldn't. I had to stay at the farm with Dad. I howled, I screamed, I tried to hold him back. It didn't work. This is what I am unable to forget, that she took him and laughed at me.

He left and I stayed behind.

After he died, we never talked about Lars. Neither of us could bear to, but that didn't mean that I didn't think about him. Sometimes, I could go ten minutes, a half hour, maybe an hour without thinking of him, but never a whole day. Besides, I could hear him, especially at his graveside. He said the same words over and over again.

Avenge me, he said.

So much was destroyed back then. Even so, I created my own life. A job. A house. A family. When my sons were born, I believed that my thoughts about Lars would fade. Instead, everything about them reminded me of my brother. Their puffy diaper butts, their wobbly gaits across the living room floor, the lightning-quick steps here and there, holding out their arms like airplane wings.

The years went by so fast. My sons grew, became thinner, taller, legs like small drumsticks on soccer fields all over the city. At first, they could barely kick the ball or run in the right direction. We laughed at them, Henrik and I, but it was as if I'd just blinked, closed my eyes for a second or two, and when I opened them, the boys had not just learned to kick the ball and run in the right direction, but also how to dribble and score goals.

I wasn't home as much as I should have been. But even so, the worst part was that I was only here in body when I finally did show up. My mind was everywhere else. I didn't have time to be a mother; my head was full of my job. It was like a Rubik's cube; I thought that if I just twisted and turned the sentences, sections, and paragraphs enough, the pieces would slide into place, an opening would appear.

Eventually, I threw away the cube. I had to do something more hands-on, intervene personally. I pictured all the children I saved from beatings and kicks and burn marks by doing what I did to their parents, felt that I was now making a difference, but my mind was still everywhere else.

Maybe I tried to protect myself by not being too close to the boys, in case I lost them the way I lost Lars. Now it seemed it was all a waste of time, none of it does me any good now. How could this possibly be more painful?

Henrik always talked about how he wanted to make books for Andreas and Nikolai, where he would write down what they said, when they took their first steps, when they lost their first teeth. He talked about it and talked about it but never did it. Sometimes, I teased him about it. It would never occur to me to spend time on something like that.

Now he's gone, and the boys are gone, too. Now there is no family left. And I have no idea when they took their first steps, said their first words, lost their first teeth.

We run and run, toiling away, have so much to do, so much that's urgent, waiting. We think that we have so much time, that we will have the chance to do the things that are really meaningful sometime down the road.

Then one day, we wake up and understand that's not how it is. That it's already too late to do what we really wanted to do, what's really meaningful.

Now I am lying in bed, completely still, the way my mother used to. The duvet is pulled almost over my head, my legs tucked underneath my body. You would think there would be comfort in curling up this way, that that's why people do it, but it only seems to make everything worse. The feeling of a smoldering fire, or caustic acid, which I've had in my diaphragm since I got home and found the letter, only intensifies.

I'm on fire. The bed is on fire. The house is on fire. The world is on fire. Who set the fire? And why? I say it out loud: "Who? Why?"

I try to make contact with Lars, long for the feeling of the wind blowing through my body, the wind that always comes before it happens.

I used to be able to talk to him sometimes. I could really hear him talking to me, from heaven or wherever he might be. It was so nice, but it's been quiet for a while now, ever since the last time. I haven't managed it since the business with Henrik.

"Lars," I whisper. "Can you hear me? Where are the boys? Who has them?"

He doesn't answer. Doesn't want to. It's pointless.

The answer to the second question lies in the third, I am sure of that. Somebody has done this to me, to me personally, to hurt and diminish me, avenge themselves on me, or maybe both.

Who has the greatest cause to hurt me?

Again, I review my list. Most likely, I have countless invisible enemies due to my position as minister, but who else could it be? Somebody I know?

112

Munch, the families of those I have killed, and Sabiya.

Sabiya. That makes sense. A child for a child. Two children for three children. My children for hers.

That is the moment when I sit up in bed, the moment that I see them. On my nightstand. Two identical cell phones, Andreas's with an LFC sticker on it and Nikolai's without, so they don't get mixed up. I try turning them on, but the batteries of both are dead and need to be charged. Someone has intentionally left the cell phones here, in a place where they know I will find them. That presumably means that whatever information is to be found on the telephones will not help me.

It's 9:00 p.m., the time I usually call Dad, but the thought of talking to him now and pretending nothing is wrong, of lying and saying everything is fine—no, I just can't do it. Neither can I tell the truth.

I have chosen to believe whoever it is that has taken my children. Maybe I shouldn't. Maybe I should just call the police right away. It's guaranteed that they would do everything to find the minister of justice's children. But the only demand I have received so far is not to tell anyone or the boys will die. I don't dare take the chance of calling their bluff. I have to figure this out myself, the way I have always dealt with the major issues in life.

On my way downstairs to see if I can bring myself to eat some of the shrimp, I write a quick message to Dad, saying I have a headache and can't call him today. I press send.

CHAPTER 22

LEIF

Get well soon, I write back to Clara, but I don't like it.

All these years, she has called me every night, no matter what. We will often talk for just a few minutes, but all the same, hearing her voice makes me feel less alone. I understand that she is checking up on me, in a way, and I like that she does it.

Even during the months that have passed since Henrik died, she has called every evening. Something new has materialized between us during this period, maybe a little uneasiness on my part due to something I suspect but can't talk about. Maybe she's wondering what I think about his death, I don't know, she has never said as much.

Henrik was a kind of stabilizing element. I felt a sense of security on behalf of Clara and the boys when he was in the house. Yes, he was a spoiled papa's boy who no doubt had his own skeletons in the closet, the way those kinds of men always do. Still, he was there, was a good father for my grandchildren.

Some mornings when I wake up, the thought of Henrik is burning in my chest until I manage to get out of bed and drown it in coffee and chores. Over the course of the day, I feel better, but in the evening, the thoughts are there again, no matter how much wood I put in the stove, how much I read about the war, or how much I ply my Dutch courage.

Sometimes, it's like I see him outside in the darkness, standing with his face pressed up against the window. Then I hear him walking into the hallway, kicking off his boots, entering the living room door. He is so dark in these visions, Henrik, who in real life was always easygoing and light. Would I be happy if he were standing here in front of me, dripping wet, straight from the waterfall, emaciated and nasty, like a ghoul, with the same hateful gaze that Agnes had when she talked about Kleivhøgda? Or would I just be frightened?

Then there's this new job of Clara's. It's as if it has added fuel to my Henrik thoughts, of which I had almost succeeded in ridding myself. Has something happened there maybe, something she doesn't want me to know about? Has Agnes called her? Or has she learned that her mother is out and wants to spare me the anguish of finding out about it? She has no idea that I know.

Dammit. All these thoughts going round and round.

I walk into the biggest room facing west, facing the river, one of the rooms I almost never enter. Neatly made beds with crocheted bedspreads, elegant night tables, rag rugs on the floor made by my mother, old black-and-white photographs on the walls. The room has not been touched since my mother was alive. There is a fine layer of dust on almost everything; otherwise the room is as it has always been.

Now I walk through the room and open the door to the tiny attic inside, which serves as a storeroom. All kinds of things have been stowed in here. Garbage bags filled with old clothes, crates of all kinds of junk I will never have the strength to go through, boxes of Christmas decorations. Clutter, clutter, clutter.

Far in the back of the narrow little room, far away from the window with flies on the sill and a faded old curtain, is a box labeled *1988*. I climb over an old rocking chair, stumble and curse, but finally reach the box, take it under my arm, and walk out again.

There are seven bedrooms in the house. I use only one. When Clara and the boys are here, we use three. All this space, for nothing. Clara or Lars should be living here with their family now. I should have built myself a little retirement cottage on the property. But that's not how things worked out. Lars is dead and Clara is living her life in Oslo.

Now I take the box with me into the living room, put it on the table, open it, and start taking things out. Medical records, the death certificate, police report, notes, pictures.

I know that Clara thinks I never did anything. That's not true. I collected all of this in secret, contacted a lawyer, had plans of pressing charges, going to the newspaper, anything to avenge the death of my son. I was going to take Magne and Agnes down. Agnes because she neglected the children and the animals and everything while I was obliged to go to Lebanon in order to save us from financial ruin, because she threw herself straight into the arms of the biggest psychopath in the village when I came home again, because she took our son with her, allowed him to be abused to death. Magne for everything he did, everything he took from me.

The car accident in Storagjelet when Clara was twelve years old changed everything. Suddenly, Magne was dead and Agnes was in a home. There was nobody left on whom to wreak vengeance. I could not get my son back. On top of that, I risked making everything worse for Clara.

In the end, I put it all away. None of this has been out of the box in thirty years. Now I empty the box, spread the contents across the table, take out a legal pad and a pen, and start making notes.

CHAPTER 23

Clara

When I open my eyes, at first I've forgotten about it. One second, two, three, my life is fine.

Then I remember. The boys are gone.

The clock on my phone reads 3:02. I have slept for two hours, and I won't be able to sleep anymore. Lying here is like being boiled in a kind of corrosive acid bath. So I get out of bed, walk out into the hallway, go toward the boys' room, and hold my breath as I open the door.

I must have had a nightmare. They are lying there, warm mounds under their duvets, rumpled hair, small bodies, beating hearts. They have slept in this house for so many nights. They're not lying there now. This isn't a nightmare, this is reality. I walk over to the bed, climb into it, inhale the scent of the bodies that are not here, start to cry. I lie there like that for a long time.

Almost half a day has passed already since I came home, even longer since someone took them away from here. They could have been transported far away by now, could be on the other side of Europe, or even farther away.

While I haven't gotten anywhere. I have no plan.

I glance at the time, the smartwatch on my wrist shows 3:35. Then I realize something. The boys also have watches like this. Maybe they are still on their wrists? The watches were nowhere in sight when I was searching for their cell phones. That I didn't think of this before now, after many hours have passed, just shows how befuddled I've been.

I write a couple of short messages and send them. Where are you? Did you receive this message? Please let me know if you can see my messages.

It must be possible to track the watches, but I can't do that by myself.

I lie on the bed for a while, thinking, until I am unable to lie there anymore, with the hamsters spinning their wheels around and around. I get up and go downstairs.

It's sink or swim. I must try to do it in a way so my enemies, whoever they might be, don't find out. But I *must* have help. I'm not capable of doing this alone.

I consider asking the police commissioner to track the watches. Monrad definitely owes me a favor, but she could become suspicious and investigate why I am asking, and then all hell will break loose.

No, I must ask somebody else, and now I know whom. Just telling one person about it isn't the same as alerting the entire police force. Whoever it is that has my children need never know about this. I take out my phone, spend a long time composing a message, writing, deleting, starting over.

Can you call me when you wake up?

CHAPTER 24

ANDREAS

It's so cold in here. Nikolai has snuggled up against me. I have actually put my arm around him, even though it feels a little dumb, so we can stay warm.

The film that's playing in my head now is the one from when we went on summer vacation, not long after Dad came home.

We had just gotten into the car, after Dad had crammed the last, almost-left-behind things into the trunk and fastened our bikes on the roof, and we were finally rolling out the driveway, toward Western Norway, and I remember thinking that now everything was going to be great.

Grandmother and Grandfather came over to say goodbye. They stood at the gate, waving. It was as if they shrank a bit more every year as we grew larger; soon we would maybe meet each other in the middle.

The way they were standing there, it almost looked like it was their house. It used to be their house, before we moved in. In our Oslo family, the children took over the parents' home when they grew up. That's how it was in Western Norway, too, except we *hadn't* taken over the farm. I felt a bit sorry for Grandpa, who was so old and lived there alone and had to do everything himself, but I didn't want to move to Western Norway. Daddy absolutely didn't want to move. In fact, I don't think Mommy wanted to either. Well, I knew she was fond of Grandpa and the farm, but I thought she was even more fond of her job, that's how it seemed anyway.

Dad insisted on playing music by the Norwegian singing duo Knutsen and Ludvigsen, because his parents used to play Knutsen and Ludvigsen when they went on trips when he was a little boy and because we had also really liked this music when we were younger. Nikolai and I tried protesting, and Mommy sighed something awful, but Knutsen and Ludvigsen it was until we had to stop for the first bathroom break, and then it was Radio Rock for the rest of the trip.

First, we stayed at the farm for a few days. I liked being there, even though the television was little and old and the internet was slow and it smelled like dust and half-rotten apples everywhere. Grandpa made meatballs and beef stew and grilled mountain trout. We made him brownies and swam in the river and played in the barn. In the evenings, the adults sat around the picnic table in the garden and drank plum wine. Everything was fine, almost as if Dad had never been arrested. He had explained to us that the police had made a mistake and that they were sorry about it. Now he had decided not to think about it anymore.

The best day of summer vacation was always the day we moved up to the summer farm. It was kind of like traveling to Narnia when we walked along the river to the spot where the waterfall came down before we started following the path up the mountain, through the dense green forest where there were ferns taller than Nikolai and me, and birds and waterfalls everywhere.

Another thing that was good was that Mommy always changed when she got to the farm, and even more when she got to the summer farm. She got happier and started doing lots of things.

At home, it was Daddy who mowed the lawn and painted fences and stuff, if anyone did. Actually, it didn't seem that either of them liked doing that kind of thing. When Mommy finally got to the summer farm, though, she, like, turned into a milkmaid or farmhand, as Daddy used to say. She rushed around and fixed things and cut the grass with a scythe and hammered away on the roof. I thought Mommy was cool when she was like that, and I think Daddy did, too. He lay in the grass and read a book and seemed completely relaxed.

Sometimes, I could tell that he was far away, as if he weren't really there, and then I got a little scared. Maybe he was afraid he would be sent to jail again? But most of the time, everything was fine.

That summer, I tried really hard to make both Mommy and Daddy happy, especially Daddy. I try to remember that when I start thinking about the day he came home, that I was nice to him for the rest of the summer, after all, and that I've tried to be nice to Nikolai because I know that Daddy would have been pleased about that.

Now Nikolai's teeth are chattering. I am really freezing, too. How long will we have to sit here waiting like this?

CHAPTER 25

CLARA

By 6:37, he calls. He is already awake. He has young children, or maybe he is going out for a run before breakfast, the way I imagine guys like him usually do, the way I used to before. I have no idea, I don't care.

"Yes?" I say when I answer the phone. I picked it up when it rang and ran out into the garden in case the house has been bugged. I sent the message from my minister phone, and that is the one he calls me on now.

"Clara," he says, his voice hoarse. "Everything okay?"

How much can I say? As little as possible, even though I'm out-doors, even though the phone should be secure.

"Yes, no, well," I say. "Any chance you could come by?"

If I hadn't before understood the extent of his professionalism, I understand it now. He doesn't hesitate, doesn't ask, doesn't sigh.

"I'll be there in fifteen minutes," he says.

"Fine," I say. Then we hang up.

When he parks down the street, I am sitting and waiting on a bench outside. To be on the safe side, I have left all my phones inside.

He gets out of a car I've never seen before, an SUV, which must be his own private vehicle. He crosses the street with long strides and walks up the hill toward me.

Something about him is so different, probably because he isn't wearing a blue shirt or dark tie or suit pants, just a pair of blue jeans and a light-blue hooded sweatshirt with a big purple *J* and *L* on it and a black leather jacket over that.

Until now, I have only seen him as an extension of the car, the uniform, the situation. He is all of that, but he is also a man, a father, a human being, and a person I desperately need right now.

Now as Stian comes trotting toward me, I see how he freezes when he catches sight of my face.

"Clara," he says, his voice warm, and he lays one hand on my neck, lightly, carefully and naturally. "What's going on?"

"When you drove me home yesterday," I begin, "I was looking forward to spending time with my children, but . . ."

"Yes? What happened, Clara?"

"Something . . . happened. The boys weren't here."

"They weren't?" he says, and I see something guarded infiltrate his gaze. "Where were they, then?"

"I don't know," I say.

For a moment, everything stops again, but now he doesn't urge me to continue. There's no warm hand on my neck.

"They haven't come home since then either," I say, struggling to get the words out. "There was a letter on the table."

He sinks down onto the bench beside me, but I look at the ground, unable to meet his eyes. I summon my strength.

"Someone has taken them, and I'm not allowed to tell another living soul . . ."

For a second or two, I catch a glimpse of surprise and shock in his eyes. Then it's gone and his calm is apparently restored.

"Not allowed by whom? By the person behind this?" he asks.

I nod. "But I can't manage this alone. So I'm telling you, but you have to promise not to tell anyone else. They will kill the boys if I say anything . . ."

"Was there a ransom note?" he asks.

I shake my head. "It just said that I would receive further instructions later. For the time being, the only demand is that I keep my mouth shut."

"Hmm," he says, and the grave expression on his face scares me.

Although I am more afraid than I've been since Lars called me that day thirty years ago, I have, in a sense, grown accustomed to the idea of this, the way one is somehow able to get used to everything inconceivable.

I have started absorbing it now, through my pores, into my flesh, into my blood. It has circulated through my body several times now. I've started to think it, feel it, breathe it, the way a person absorbs alcohol or cannabis or other active chemical ingredients and, for a time, makes them a part of oneself, something that eventually feels more real than the person one actually is or was.

"It has to be someone who hates me," I say.

Now Stian actually puts his arm around me, pulls me into the crook of his arm, not like a bodyguard, driver, or policeman, but like a big brother. Given how calm, sober minded, reserved, and ever professional he is, his behavior is oddly physical. What is strange is that it doesn't bother me. I like it.

"Clara, we'll find them, trust me."

And then I actually cry into his jacket for a little while, before straightening up, drying my tears with my mittened hands, and taking a deep breath.

"Forgive me," I say. "You mustn't tell anyone, promise me?"

He raises his eyebrows. "Oh, Clara," he says, shaking his head. "That's not possible, you know that, don't you? I have to involve the agency, my superiors."

"Don't make me regret telling you," I say. "They will *kill* my children if I tell anyone."

I stop. I can hear the panic, the desperation in my voice, and feel embarrassed.

"Clara," he says calmly, the way an adult speaks to a hysterical child. "If I do what you want, I will lose my job and be guilty of offenses punishable by Norwegian law."

"I know," I say in despair. "I know, I know, but . . ."

"What do you need?"

"Their smartwatches," I say. "Their telephones are here, but their watches aren't. Maybe they can be tracked?"

He nods. "Can you go inside and get the cell phones? And the letter you found? Wear gloves, put it in a clean plastic bag, and bring it out to me."

I run inside, come out again with the letter in one bag and the cell phones in another, and give it all to him. Could this mean that he will help me after all? That I didn't beg in vain?

Stian examines the letter through the plastic, his brow furrowing.

"Looks like something that was generated using some kind of translation program," he says. "I'll have to check to see if there's anything unusual about the paper, the ink, fingerprints."

"Thanks," I say. "Thank you so much."

"But, Clara," he says gently. "I am a civil servant, a policeman. I want to help you; I'm a parent myself, but I can't. I *have* to report this."

My heart sinks into my stomach. I am unable to utter a single word. My entire body is bristling and prickling and sizzling with panic. For the first time, I have asked someone for help, and this is how it turns out.

"Sorry," he says, sounding like he genuinely means it.

My brain is working on a kind of unconscious plan. I can't give up, not yet. There must be a way to get through to him. I can't lie, he would see right through that. I have to tell the truth.

"This is the first time I have *ever* asked someone for help," I say. "It's not in my nature."

"No," he says with a hint of a smile. "I can imagine."

"There's something I never talk about," I say, swallowing. "I had a brother . . . When he was seven years old, something happened."

It is already difficult, but I do it anyway, taking a deep breath.

"Yes?" he asks, looking at me attentively.

"My mother moved out suddenly. She found a new boyfriend, Magne; he was a teacher and a local politician . . ."

I stop. Magne, with his piercing eyes, powerful jaw, the nasty mole beside his nose. Sometimes that mole would sprout a black hair, which he used to pluck out with a pair of tweezers, and he talked about having the mole removed.

I clear my throat.

"Magne was, by all appearances, a great guy," I say. "Actually, he was the biggest bastard you can imagine. Even so, my mother left us. I refused to go with her, but she took my little brother, Lars. At first, he stayed with my father and me on the weekends, but then he stopped coming or came very seldom. And he . . ."

I have to stop for a moment. Luckily, Stian doesn't say anything.

"He became quiet and strange and completely different from the Lars we knew. I remember once, my father sat on the couch and cried after Lars had gone to bed. He had seen Lars in the bathtub, seen that he had bruises and other scars all over his body. After that episode, my father really tried, he went to talk to a woman at social services, but when he came home, he was completely demoralized. None of the people who were supposed to help him wanted to listen to him. Everything got worse and worse, and Lars became quieter and quieter. Then he stopped coming to stay at our house. He didn't want to, my mother said, but we didn't believe it. My father said the whole time that he was going to do something about it, but somehow it never happened. I think he actually had no idea what else he could do . . ."

Again, I stop, my mouth is so dry, I have to swallow.

"Then one day, Lars called. I was home alone and could hear immediately that something was wrong. I had to come right away, he said. He was frightened, because he thought they were going to hit him, give him a real thrashing. I got scared, too, jumped onto my bicycle, and rode it as fast as I could up the hills to Magne's farm. I rode the bike really fast, but even so, I got there too late. He was lying there on the floor of Magne's house, already blue, and not moving at all. It felt as if I was dead, too, you know? It sounds like something people only say, but it's true, that's how it was. Afterward, I saw everything I did from a place outside of myself . . ."

"Oh, Clara," Stian says.

"Nobody punished them, nobody cared, nobody wanted to listen, nobody wanted to see. That's often how it is. I have spent my entire career trying to do something about that, specifically that."

"Are they alive?" he asks. "Your mother? And your stepfather?"

"My mother is alive," I say.

It is the first time I have spoken those words. Henrik thought my mother was dead. The boys believe it. My in-laws. Axel. Everyone here.

"Magne died in an accident not long afterward. I was with him . . ."

And then I tell him about Magne and the accident, and I don't lie. I just give him the truth I gave the policeman on that day thirty years ago, the one about how Magne had been drinking and driving too fast and drove off the road and just sat there inside the car as if he were paralyzed until I just had to swim away.

"Maybe I could have saved him, if I made an effort," I say finally. "But I let him die and I didn't care. Do you understand?"

I have never told anyone so much about this before.

Stian nods. Then he takes my hand, which is still stiff and odd after what I did with the knife yesterday. I almost snatch it back but stop myself just in time. On top of the bandage, I have both the sleeve of a knitted sweater and wristlets; it's impossible to see what I've done.

"You were a little girl and scared to death, Clara," Stian says. "He put you in that situation. Nobody could expect you to save him, no matter what your feelings for him were. Do you understand?"

I nod. "But don't you see? This makes it even worse that I failed to take care of my boys," I say. "Like I messed up again. And I can't take any more tragedies. Neither can my father. Still, I let this happen, by saying yes to becoming a minister, by leaving them alone, refusing security. And now I've told you more than I've ever told anyone."

"Thank you, Clara," he says, his voice hoarse. "I really appreciate your trust in me."

He is silent for a few seconds, a tiny flame of hope, until he starts talking again.

"Believe me, I wish I could help you without involving others, the way you want. I just can't. It would be completely irresponsible."

"Okay," I say, swallowing. Panic prickles through my body.

We sit in silence for a while.

"Can you think of anything out of the ordinary that has happened lately, someone who might have something against you?" he says.

"There is one thing, actually," I say. "You know those murders my husband was in jail for before the summer?"

He nods. Of course, he has been drilled on this.

"One of his colleagues, Sabiya Rana . . . they had an affair. After he died, she was in jail under suspicion for the same murders. I think she's guilty. The police commissioner does, too. Even so, she was recently released, due to insufficient evidence. And that woman hates me."

"Shouldn't it be you who hates her?"

Now it's the policeman talking, the one trained to do more than chauffeur cabinet ministers around, open doors, smile.

"Yes," I say. "But she was pathologically in love with my husband. I think she blames me both for the fact that he wouldn't leave me and for his death. She is obsessed with getting everything that is mine. Henrik. The boys. I know it sounds sick, but it's true."

"Do you know where Rana is now?"

"Unfortunately not," I say. "No idea. Can you give me one day? Please?"

He shakes his head. "I have to go now. I'll be in touch. Or we will."

Every fiber of my being screams *no*.

No to being alone here for hours and hours. No to having to sit tight without knowing what has happened. No to staying here without being able to do anything useful, while waiting for a battalion of special agents to arrive.

I have always loved being alone, but now I feel an overwhelming sense of anxiety at the prospect of being left behind here with only myself for company.

I have gambled and lost, bared my soul, to no end.

He is going to involve the agency. The people who have my boys are going to kill them, and it will be my fault. All my fault.

CHAPTER 26

ANDREAS

We're inside now. It's not as cold here, but it's still dark. Besides, we're locked up again, except now, there's no droning noise or shaking. It is completely silent here.

I miss the outdoors, the water and the trees and all that.

When we went to bed at night, Daddy always used to say that we should think about the nicest thing we know, picture it in our minds. Usually, I pictured the next time we would be at Anfield Stadium together, Dad and Nikolai and I, and maybe Axel and Olav.

One thing Mommy and Daddy and the two of us liked to do was to go hiking in the mountains, like the guys' trip we took last summer. Mommy wanted to stay behind to chop down a few birch saplings on the summer farm, and nobody complained. Because even though it was nice when the four of us were together, it was always more relaxed when it was just us guys, as Daddy used to say.

We went on this hike on one of the first days at the summer farm; they were always the best days, before everyone got tired of hot dogs, card games, sleeping bags, and living on top of each other.

Daddy suggested we walk up to some small lakes located an hour farther up the mountain on foot. It was mostly to make Grandpa happy, I think, since he always talked about all the fish he had caught up there when he was a little boy, and always tried to get us to go fishing.

We had tried the river down on the farm and a lot of other places and never got more than a nibble, but this time, each of us actually caught a fish. The fish were small, but that didn't matter. We were so happy when we left. Dad took a picture and sent it to Grandpa. When it was time to leave the lake, we even saw a brown hare hopping away.

I liked that this was *our* place, that we never met anyone else there. Sometimes someone would walk past, but not often, maybe just once every summer. I think wanting to be alone was something I inherited from Mommy. Sometimes it seemed like she didn't like people at all. Daddy, on the other hand, jumped on anyone who walked by and offered them hot dogs and coffee while Mommy stood there scowling at him, irritated because he talked to them and asked them all kinds of questions while he patted their dogs and explained about the trail ahead.

Mommy and Daddy were so different that it was impossible to understand what had made them get married and have children together, but maybe all grownups are like that? My grandparents on my father's side have almost nothing in common. Uncle Axel and Caro didn't seem like they were much alike in any way at all either before they got divorced.

As we were walking down from the mountain that day, Daddy asked if we wanted to check out the scree. I wasn't all that interested. From a distance, it just looked like a big pile of rocks, but Dad seemed so interested in it that I said yes.

That scree was the coolest thing we'd ever seen. It had huge, long crevices and big hollows you could climb into, neon-green grass on the ground, and small brooks and stones as big as a house and tiny ponds. It was like we were on a different, awesome planet.

Dad pulled out a map that Grandpa had made for him, along with an explanation of where all the best fishing spots were. Once, I guess, someone had tried to make a kind of quarry here, and the people had built a little stone hut inside the scree, Grandpa had said. When he was a little boy, hunters and others would spend the night in the hut.

We looked at the map, and suddenly there was the stone hut, right in front of us. It was so small that Dad couldn't stand up all the way inside. Nikolai and I could, but only just. The walls were made of stone, as were the roof and the bench inside. Everything was stone, except the door, which was wood.

Imagine, this hut has withstood all kinds of weather for a hundred years, Dad said.

Can we sleep over here? I asked.

Maybe, Dad said. Or you two can sleep inside, and I can sleep in a tent in the cave over there or something. Because there isn't enough room for all three of us inside this hut.

Yuck, I don't want to sleep here, Nikolai said. It's cramped and gross.

Yeah, the summer farmhouse is a luxury hotel compared to this, Dad said. When Mommy wasn't around, he always said "summer farmhouse" like she wanted. When she was with us, on the other hand, he always called it a "cottage," even though he knew it irritated her. I always thought that was weird.

For some reason or other, I remember every single word Dad said on that vacation and everything we said. Or maybe I just *think* I remember everything because I want to so badly, because I'm afraid of forgetting.

He's still sort of alive in me. That's something people say, but it's actually true. I feel like he's living inside me and will be for as long as I can remember him. But if one day I forget his words, or his voice, or how he smelled, how he hugged us and how it felt to hold his hand, then he will be gone. That can't happen.

That day on the mountain has, in a way, stuck to me, like the day he came home from jail, even though one of those days was nice and the other was awful.

I was so sure that Dad and I were going to sleep in the scree many times and go fishing together even more. Now it will never happen, none of it.

"I'm hungry," Nikolai says.

"Yeah," I say. "I know. We'll probably get something to eat soon."

CHAPTER 27

CLARA

It isn't until twenty-four hours later, a full day during which I barely sleep, don't eat, don't manage to call Dad and lie, just wander around in a kind of feverish state, go out running twice, smoke, have diarrhea, try to create a mind map, try to work, am unable to accomplish anything, sit there holding the knife in my hand several times, consider cutting myself again but manage to refrain, that Stian finally comes back.

In the meantime, I have been expecting a police team to arrive on my doorstep. Maybe it would be just as well? Now I am just sitting here, without doing anything, without knowing what Stian is doing, *if* he is doing anything.

"Everything is more difficult when it's the weekend and none of the higher-ups are at work anywhere," he says when he shows up. "I don't know anything more about the watches yet, but I have been able to get hold of some surveillance footage."

"You have?" I whisper, barely daring to breathe.

He has apparently done this without yet involving the agency.

There is no doubt in my mind that he is going to notify them. He is the type to do what he says he's going to do, stick to the decisions he has made. Still, he has actually given me the day I requested.

"This is footage from a camera at the convenience store across the street from the school, where you can see a bit of the schoolyard. There's something of interest. Take a look."

He finds an image on his cell phone, holds it out to me. I automatically back up a bit, the way people my age do when they need reading glasses and haven't yet realized it.

My boys. There they are, in the identical green winter jackets with fur collars that they got from their grandmother. It has never occurred to her that maybe they don't want to dress alike. One is wearing a purple hat and the other an orange one. Both of them are wearing scarves and mittens.

They have gotten so good at dressing themselves, even when I'm not there to help out. How small and childlike they look in their winter clothes, even as tall as they are.

A kind of vagrant is standing with his back to the camera, short and slight of build, talking to them. On the back of his dark-blue fleece jacket are the words *Vålerenga Soccer Club* in big letters. Can it be a teenager? Not likely. A teenager in this part of town would rather die than be seen wearing that outfit, I am sure of it.

"What in the world," I mumble. "Who is that?"

"Nobody you recognize, then?" Stian asks.

I shake my head.

"Fine," he says. "We were unlucky with the angle there. I'll check out a few more things and pick you up early tomorrow morning, okay?"

"Yes," I say, swallowing.

It is only then I realize that, unless Stian has already reported me and everything that has happened, tomorrow, I must go to work, be a cabinet minister.

I must play my part, behave as if nothing is wrong, as if my children aren't still missing after three days, as if the world hasn't fallen apart all around me.

CHAPTER 28

Andreas

It's better being in the little cellar where we are now than lying in the dark baggage compartment. Here, it's not as cold and it's less cramped, so we can move around. But we can't go anywhere.

The whole time I keep hoping that Dad will, like, walk through the door. I know it's stupid, but I can't help it.

Because he has just disappeared, because nobody has found him, I keep imagining that one day he will suddenly be standing in the doorway of our house and everything will be like it was before. Maybe it will turn out that he just needed a break and found an empty house to live in for a few months.

Most days, I know this won't happen.

The funeral was horrible. Mommy stood there wearing a black dress and, all of a sudden, wanted to hold our hands. I couldn't cry, felt like I had been lying in a bathtub for too long, so the water was cold. I would have given away half my life to spend just one more day with Dad.

Since he was never found, not in the lake or in the waterfall or in the deep pool at the bottom of the falls, we held the funeral without his body. There was a coffin there, but it was empty. On the altar were things that were supposed to remind people of him, a picture of him and us, his Liverpool jersey, his favorite sneakers, his coffee cup, things like that.

I held on tight to the key ring in my pocket. It was a special Liverpool key ring from when we won the European Cup Final in 1984, after a penalty shoot-out against Rome at the Stadio Olimpico. LFC became the first English club to win a treble.

The key ring was Dad's favorite thing; he always said we would inherit it the day he was gone. Now we argued about who should have it. Grandpa suggested that we could take turns having it six months at a time. In the end, Nikolai and I had gone along with that. Now I mostly keep it in my pocket all the time, even though I was terrified I might lose it.

There were so many people there, at the funeral, the parents of the kids in our class and our neighbors and people who worked with Daddy and people who worked with Mommy. Her minister, the one she didn't like, was there too, and a crowd of media people were standing outside.

I hadn't ever really been in a church before. We hadn't been baptized. Neither Mommy nor Daddy believed in God, and seriously, I almost freaked out when I saw Jesus on the cross and heard the crazy things the pastor said about Jesus's blood and body and saw the flowers and all the faceless men wearing black suits and white shirts. It was almost impossible to breathe in there.

It was like I was standing far away, watching myself and everything; that's actually how it was every day since Dad disappeared.

After the funeral, we noticed that Mommy actually tried to do some of the things that Daddy couldn't do for us anymore. When school started again, she woke us up extra early every day and had lit candles and made hot cocoa for us when we came downstairs. If Nikolai doesn't want to wake up, he can be a real slowpoke. Sometimes she would lie down beside him, with her forehead against his, stroking his head and talking to him softly until he woke up and stretched.

It was nice, really, but I also thought it was awful to see how happy he always looked when he woke up. For a little while, he was a happy kitten, until he remembered that Dad was gone, and his face would crumple.

I dreaded starting school again after summer vacation, didn't really want to go. Mommy and Grandmother and Grandfather and everyone said that it would be fine and just like before. I knew that wasn't true, and in fact, everything was even worse than I'd feared.

The teacher had tears in her eyes and treated us differently than she did before, talked to us in a soft voice, didn't nag us about anything, tousled our hair in that stupid way. The other parents were startled when they came to pick up their children and saw us, as if we were ghosts. Nikolai *was* actually kind of ghostlike, walking around crying and sitting on the teacher's lap at recess. I tried to talk to him about it, said he had to stop, that it was embarrassing, but then he just started crying again.

The other children were different, too, as if they'd been told to be careful with us or something. They gave away things we used to fight over. Nobody teased or shoved us. Nobody interrupted us or made fun of our packed lunch. Nobody called me Nikolai or Nikolai Andreas for fun.

It should have been nice, but it just felt fake, like soccer players who fake injuries, like instant mashed potatoes instead of the real thing, like candy spray—does anyone really like that?

One day, I said to Olav, our friend, that he had to tell the others that it would be better if they just acted normally. When everyone behaved differently, it made everything a thousand times worse, I said. I don't know if he understood it, but he nodded, and since then things have been a bit better.

After Dad died, Nikolai started climbing into my bed every single night. Usually, he slept there, too. It was pretty crowded, but I let him stay.

Nikolai is different from me, softer, always has been. I think maybe he is more like Dad and I am more like Mommy.

Mommy borrowed books to read out loud to us and fussed about how we should read to her. She talked about how we would go to the theater and the movies and the Christmas market and build a snowman and go skiing when winter came, even bake gingersnaps, but I *knew* that she wouldn't be baking anything; it was just something she said.

We also knew how busy her job is. It's like she lived somewhere inside it, even before she became a minister.

CHAPTER 29

CLARA

It feels so bizarre to stand in front of the mirror and put on my cabinet minister face, applying the black eyeliner along my lids and brushing mascara onto my lashes with a trembling hand so the thin black line ends up crooked and choppy and the brush leaves behind small black dots on the space between my eyes and eyebrows.

Afterward, I apply powder on my face using a small brush. Usually, it sort of melts into the skin, becomes a part of me. Now everything lies on the outside. My skin has become so dry over the course of the weekend. I have gone without bathing or fixing myself up or smoothing on face cream, but it must be more than that. Something must have happened inside me, something that provoked an outbreak of small, dry scales on my skin.

I take out a lipstick, draw it across my washed-out lips. They are also dry. I still have blue rings under my eyes, my face is swollen and my skin flaky. It makes no difference. I have been wearing more makeup since my appointment, as if to don a cabinet minister persona, along with the suits and the blouses, but I have never been vain. Now I care even less. The lipstick at the very least makes me look like I'm alive.

I drink a cup of coffee while waiting for Stian but can't bring myself to eat anything. The coffee alone makes me sick; everything turns my stomach.

Stian jumps out of the car, strides through the gate and up the walk toward me. I pick up my handbag and coat and go to meet him.

"Behave normally," he whispers, placing my handbag in the car. "Don't talk about the issue. Leave your handbag on the seat when you get out; then we'll talk briefly, and after that you can retrieve your bag. Okay?"

I nod, feeling even more dizzy and unwell.

I have begun to realize the amount of intel PSS must have about everything I do, even though I have refused to accept a camera and other forms of surveillance. They just don't have enough intel to know what happened to my boys; I have refused to give them that.

In the car, I am incapable of reading emails or updating myself on the news. I just lean my head against the car window, watching the city shimmer past in the early morning darkness.

Usually, I like the autumn, the cool air and yellow leaves and dark evenings. Now all of this just increases my anxiety, reminds me of the great darkness in which I am fumbling around.

Once, when I was a teenager, I rode my bike into a tunnel on a desolate road in the neighborhood. The tunnel was just a few hundred yards long, but it was unlit, and I didn't have a headlight on my bike. It wasn't possible to see what was in front of me, behind me, above, below, to the right or the left. I had to get off my bicycle, make my way forward with tiny steps, all the while holding my arms out in front of me to make sure I didn't crash into the stone wall. All sensation of space, time, direction disappeared. Everything was just pitch dark.

That's the feeling I have now, too, that I am fumbling around in absolute darkness, without direction.

"Well," Stian says from outside the car. "Any news on your end?"

"Unfortunately not," I say. "I stayed home, like you told me to . . ."

"Clara, this can't go on any longer," he says, his face full of regret. "Today, I have to let them know. It's well overdue. I've tried, but the footage doesn't get us anywhere. I can't get anything out of the letter. It's irresponsible of me that I still haven't brought in help."

I don't say anything, am unable to speak, just feel paralyzed.

"Are you going to the Parliament building later?" he asks as I reach into the car to retrieve my handbag.

"Yes," I say. "But I can walk over there."

It takes just five minutes to walk from the ministry over to the Parliament building, and a little fresh air will do me good.

"Now?" Stian says, shaking his head. "No, you can't. You shouldn't walk down Akersgata Street alone anyway, given the level of threat directed at you, and now it's especially out of the question. I'll drive you over and wait for you."

"Whatever," I say, holding up my hands in mock surrender.

Long before I became a minister, I felt that I must be the one to take charge, assume responsibility, lead the way. At work, at home, everywhere. I had no respect for Henrik, and definitely not for Munch. Mona? Hardly. My driver, on the other hand, emanates such authority that protesting feels futile.

Besides, it isn't important to me whether I walk over there later. There's not a single policy or anything else for that matter that is important now that my children are missing and their lives are on the line.

I walk through the revolving door, toward the security turnstile, slide my card through, enter the scan, and exit on the other side. Almost ten years have passed since the day that led to an extreme tightening of security in all government buildings, the day that changed all the procedures for cabinet ministers and other VIPs.

In the elevator, I meet my own reflection in the mirror.

A cabinet minister who is not a cabinet minister, who is unable to do her job.

A mother who is not a mother, who is unable to take care of her children, who has made their lives even more difficult than they were before.

I am a robot, a robot who must walk through the doors, smile at Vigdis, say yes to the question of whether I've had a nice weekend, hang up my coat and put down my bag and start the computer and open emails, look at them one by one, go through the folders that are lying on the desk in front of me.

Two and a half days have passed since I last sat here. Did it really happen? *Are* the boys missing? Or is it all in my head? Everything feels unreal, as if I have finally smoked too many joints and lost my sense of reality. In one way or another, I manage to go to the morning meeting, sit there, and talk about insignificant things, while I am burning up from the inside out.

Afterward, I walk into my office, close the door, and do a phone-number search online. It comes up empty.

I sit for a while with my head in my heads until I get an idea and try a search for another number. This time, I get results. I call. A husky voice answers. It sounds like he just woke up.

"Hello, Roger," I say. "This is Clara, Henrik Fougner's wife."

"Oh, hello," he says. "Congratulations on your new job, if we can call it a job."

"Of course," I say. "Did I wake you?"

"No," he says. "Or, yes, I had the night shift, but . . ."

He sounds a bit aloof. We ran into him in the city once, stopped to chat, and then he was incredibly upbeat and chipper. A kind of straight-laced guy, an inveterate homosexual, apparently a skilled nurse.

"Thank you for coming to the funeral," I say with as much warmth as I can muster.

"The least I could do," he says.

"Listen, I was wondering about something," I say, drawing a breath. "I would very much like to have a chat with Sabiya about something. I understand she's been released from police custody. Henrik told me that the two of you are good friends . . . You wouldn't happen to know where she is?"

He sighs, heavily and dramatically. "You and Sabiya, I don't know," he says. "I wasn't born yesterday. Don't the two of you have a complicated relationship?"

"Yes," I say.

"So why do you want to see her?"

"It has to do with Henrik," I say. "And with the boys. They need to see her. That's all I can say. You'll just have to trust me. I need a little help, not as the minister of justice, but as a mother and a human being. Maybe there's something I can do for Sabiya . . ."

Silence on the line for a few seconds. Then he answers and his tone is completely different.

"She actually stayed here for a few days after her release, cast aside by her husband and children, and by her own parents and brother. Can you believe it? It's awful. Now, I'm not used to having people living here, but I did my best to be hospitable in every sense of the word. I emphasized that she was welcome to stay as long as she wanted. I don't have much room, but where there's a will there's a way and all that . . ." Then he laughs, a smug little chuckle.

"She's not there anymore, then?" I ask.

"Exactly," he says. "That's exactly how it is. I tried to get her to stay, but she was so restless, like a caged animal, I had no choice but to let her leave. I have no idea where she went. Sabiya has a checkered past, and she has her demons. Maybe she's with old friends or at a homeless shelter? No, I have no idea. I have to try and track her down soon."

"Fine," I say. It was time to cut to the chase. "Do you have her telephone number by any chance? I can't find anything online."

Yet another silence, followed by a dramatic sigh, before he replies.

"Yeah, she has an unlisted number, but she bought a burner phone while she was staying here," he says. "That's the only phone she uses now, I think. Wait a second, I just have to look for it on my phone."

A few seconds later, he is back on the line and reads off a number. I write it down, thank him, hang up, and try calling the number using an encrypted app. No answer. Dammit. I type in a message.

Sabiya. Clara Lofthus here. I would like to meet you to discuss something. ASAP. Can you?

If she doesn't reply, maybe I can ask Stian to trace the number. Is that possible? I'm not sure why Sabiya would bother to meet with me if she is the one who has my boys, but I have to try, I have nothing more to lose. I get to my feet, drape my coat over my arm, leave the office, and stop in front of Vigdis.

"I'm going over to the Parliament building," I say.

"Can I come with you?" the tiresome adviser asks. He is loitering nearby, reading the newspapers.

I shake my head. "No need for that now," I say.

"Okay," he says, looking offended and turning on his heel.

I already feel exhausted by this day, by the lack of progress, from pretending, while at the same time the fear is knocking and bleeding with every heartbeat.

Fear is an illusion. I have to remember that. Fear is an illusion.

Upon arriving at the Parliament building, no sooner do I enter the central hall than Erik Heier comes walking toward me with that calculated, slouching, fifty-five-year-old, boyish presence of his. Dammit. A conversation with him is the last thing I need, but there is no escaping him now.

Heier is one of the more experienced TV journalists and has had a kind of fixation with me ever since we met at my first dinner at the palace, while I was still a state secretary. He invited me out and did a glossy, in-depth TV interview of me after Henrik died.

At the time, I believed I had him under control, but now he's constantly on my heels, overly attentive and irritating.

"Lofthus," he says. "You've built your career on a bill for the protection of children?"

"It's an issue I am committed to, yes," I say. I've already started counting to ten in my head.

"Right," he says, dragging it out. "I received an advance copy of the upcoming report from the Office of the Auditor General. It documents a greater incidence of violence against children than previously and a greater delay in response time. So I'd like an answer as to what you've done to stop this development, which affects the weakest and most vulnerable among us."

I try to think. Usually, I manage to come up with something intelligent to say. Not now. My brain is like molasses. Pointing out that I was just appointed minister of justice a month ago seems overly defensive.

Then something happens. A message pops up on my smartwatch.

Come alone, don't tell anyone. At 24 Fredensborgveien Street. When?

"Sorry," I murmur to Heier. "I just have to . . ."

I turn around and walk toward the lavatory. Once inside, I walk into one of the stalls, take my cell phone out of my bag, and tap in a quick reply. I have to respond before she changes her mind, must try to gain a bit of an advantage by responding quickly.

Everything has moved slowly the past three days. It's high time something happened so I can do something other than just wait. Stian has also said that he will report it today. Time is running out, in every sense.

Be there in a half hour, I write.

CHAPTER 30

ANDREAS

Nikolai sniffles again. Just when I thought I'd gotten him to stop. It makes me crazy.

Just because he's so soft and cries so easily, everyone thinks that Nikolai is always so nice. He's not. He takes my things, lies about me, and hits me when no grownups are watching. All they see is that I hit him back. I try to tell Mommy, Uncle Axel, Grandmother, Grandfather, that he's almost always the one who starts it, but nobody wants to listen.

Nikolai is like Grandpa's multicolored lambs, whose wool is gray and black and white. Still, it's as if people only see the white parts of him and think he's completely white, while I'm just black.

That's how it is with twins, Dad always said. People need a way to tell us apart, on the inside as well as the outside. That's why they say Nikolai is like this and Andreas is like that, he explained.

Dad was actually the only one who didn't carry on like that. He never referred to us as the twins. Grandmother, his mother, on the other hand, says things like "I'm with the twins" or "I'm babysitting the twins" all the time. It irritates me, as if we're just twins and not people. "The twins" sounds like aliens or something.

Since Dad died, we've barely had the energy to argue or fight. It feels like we have to stick together. I guess that means it's really a crisis.

One thing Nikolai is actually really good at is snooping. He's always been a busybody, going through Mommy and Daddy's drawers and phones and jacket pockets ever since he was in kindergarten.

He was the one who said we had to go into Daddy's office at home and see what was in there before Mommy threw out all kinds of things. If there's anything we want, we should move fast, he said. I almost didn't understand that he was able to think of that then. I was so tired after everything that happened and after the drive back to Oslo that I felt like I had a cold *and* a tummy bug.

That same evening, while Mommy was unpacking, we took a box from our room into Daddy's office. We opened the drawers of his desk and took out all kinds of things. Not flyers or work papers, but pictures, tickets he had saved from soccer games, handwritten letters.

Dad liked to write letters. He had a computer, of course, but even so, he often wrote letters using a pen and paper. A long time ago, he apparently promised his French grandmother that he would write proper letters to people who were important to him, so once in a while, Nikolai and I received letters in the mail.

We hid the box in our room, inside the messy closet. Mommy never went anywhere near that closet. Neither of us could bear to look at the things in the box now, so we hid it until one day when Nikolai called me.

He was sitting on the floor surrounded by all kinds of things.

Look, he said, and pointed at something he had in his lap, a letter in Dad's handwriting, which was almost impossible to read.

I sat down beside him, and we started reading through it together.

Dearest Sabiya . . .

CHAPTER 31

Clara

Sabiya and I. This was meant to happen, the whole time. That the two of us would meet. Two warrior women, face to face. I have to meet her, find out what she knows, what she wants, whether she has my boys.

At this moment, I have nothing to go on but a gut feeling, that I know she probably hates me more than anyone else and that she was released from prison right before the boys disappeared.

Outside, Stian is standing beside the car, waiting. He will stop me if I involve him. Maybe he has already reported it, used the time I've been inside to get it done.

Now I'm the old Clara again, the one who does things alone, fixes things by herself, who doesn't sit around passively waiting for help. The question is how I'm going to get out of here without his noticing. There are underground tunnels here, as there are between the government buildings and under Ullevål Hospital. This city is full of secret tunnels and passageways, like the ones mice create under the peat in the mountains, a subterranean system that has always fascinated me.

I was taken on a tour down here recently. Now I am trying to think back, remember where we went down to see the tunnels. My memory is unclear and vague, but I *think* I have to walk through the central hall, down a long carpeted corridor, around a corner, down another corridor, down a flight of stairs, and through a door.

The question is whether I will be able to open the door once I get there.

Either way, the first thing I have to do is walk through the central hall. I put on my coat, throw my bag over my shoulder, pick up my telephone, press it against my cheek, walk out the lavatory door, nod at an MP from another party on the way in, and walk purposefully out into the central hall without looking to the left or right, all while pretending I'm talking on the phone.

Through the corridor, down another corridor, down the stairs.

I glance at my watch. About ten minutes have passed already: 11:35. At 11:55, a half hour will have passed.

I need some kind of alibi for stepping out and call the secretary of the Standing Committee on Justice, whom I've met a few times lately.

"Clara Lofthus here," I say. "I'm here in the Parliament building and need to make a few calls of a sensitive nature without being disturbed. You don't happen to have an office I could borrow?"

"Sure," she says, clearly relieved that I am asking for something she can provide. It still astounds me that people are willing to do virtually anything for me just because of my title. "You can use mine, 2501. It's open right now. How much time do you need?"

"I don't know," I say. "An hour? Hour and a half?"

"No problem, I'll stay away for the next hour and a half and make sure nobody else bothers you either."

"Thank you so much," I say, and hang up.

I walk down the stairs and come to a white steel door. There is a key card reader beside the revolving doors leading out into the corridors. Of course. Of course, there's a reader here. Dammit. My only hope is that I will be able to open that door. How likely is it that I can just open and close key card–secured doors leading to more-or-less secret escape routes? Here, of all places? In theory, the chances are pretty small. But I believe I've heard that my key card is supposed to function on all the doors in Parliament, in case I should find myself alone in an emergency evacuation situation. It's worth a try.

I take out the key card, draw a breath, close my eyes, open them again, and slide the card through. A never-ending second. Then a beeping sound. The door buzzes open. It's unbelievable, but it actually works. I rush to pull the door toward me and walk through it, then break into a run along the passageway, a white, anonymous corridor.

Before long, I reach the end of the passageway. Another steel door. Another flight of stairs.

After running up the stairs, I exit the building around the corner from the café Halvorsens Conditori. I don't need the GPS to find the address on Fredensborgveien Street. I quickly pull out my phones and turn them off. Now it shouldn't be possible to track my movements.

I trot down the streets Prinsens Gate and Øvre Slottsgate. Stian is sitting in the car without a clue. He has delayed reporting it, helping me even though he has actually refused to do so, gone against his own principles and all the rules. I should let him know, involve him, but I can't. I must do this alone, and I must do it quickly.

Will Sabiya be alone, too? I don't know.

I have no illusions about her. She was supposedly a juvenile delinquent in her youth, and she's tricky, sly, mendacious. I have no idea what awaits me, but this is my best chance, the closest I've been. I just have to do it, see it through, keep telling myself I can do it, like the slogan the boys used to chant back when they were in kindergarten: Do it, do it, see it through.

CHAPTER 32

ANDREAS

The letter had no ending. Dad must have forgotten to finish it, or changed his mind; he could be a little scatterbrained. Still, he'd kept it. We read it together, out loud. Now and then, we glanced at one another.

Sabiya worked with Dad. He'd told us that she had three children, two who were our age and one a little younger, and that she lived on the other side of the city. We understood that Dad liked her. Sabiya was his best friend at work, and his voice always got strange when he talked about her. Yeah, sometimes his eyes even got shiny, like when he was going to tell people about something Nikolai or I had done or said.

We'd met Sabiya several times, mostly when we were with Daddy in his office. I liked her. She was nice and easy to talk to, always smiling. The way she and Dad looked at each other almost gave me a jabbing feeling in my stomach, as if they had some kind of big secret.

'I can't do this anymore,' Nikolai sounded out.

'I can't take anymore,' I sounded out.

'Life is like a desert,' Nikolai read.

'Where I find water only when I'm with you . . .' What does he mean by that?

'I love you . . .'

'And I've always loved you . . .' Geez.

'I've been trying to hang in there, but I won't manage another ten years of this.'

This? Nikolai said, and looked at me. This?

He means Mommy, I said.

Toward the end of the letter, he wrote that Clara was becoming more and more cold and manipulative and that he didn't think she was wholly right in her head.

Good grief, Nikolai said angrily. He *is* writing about Mommy.

Yeah, I said. But it's sort of true, too . . .

'I dream . . . that one day we and . . . all our children will live under the same roof,' Nikolai read.

Afterward, we sat there staring at the letter. It was as if Dad had come back to us through it, to talk to us, even though we knew it had been written a long time before he died.

Should we call her? Nikolai asked. Ask if she wants to meet us?

Why? I said. Besides, she's in jail.

Oh, Nikolai said, and slumped. That's right . . .

Shortly after Dad died, we had seen on the internet that somebody else had been taken into custody under suspicion of the same murders for which he had been arrested. The article said the new detainee was a female colleague of a former suspect. We understood that it had to be Sabiya. We were even more sure when we checked her Instagram account. She usually posted all kinds of things, but now there was no activity.

But could she really have killed someone? I couldn't believe that any more than I could believe that Dad supposedly did it. The pieces didn't fit.

CHAPTER 33

CLARA

This reminds me of the puzzle that Andreas always works on with incredible patience, lying on his stomach. Although he will often struggle with it for hour after hour, feeling his way, testing one piece first in one place and then another, the pieces in my puzzle fall into place before me, lickety-split.

I think I know, I think I understand, but do I, really? My ability to make cool assessments, which has always served me well, has apparently evaporated in the past few days.

By the old Krist cemetery, covered by orange leaves, I have to stop for a few seconds. I glance at the monument and the old cross at the entrance, commemorating the plague of the seventeenth century.

Memento mori. Memento mori.

Suddenly, it hits me that turning off my phones is not enough. PSS will still be able to track them. I should have left them behind in the Parliament building, but it's too late now, and I have no idea where I could have stashed them either.

I quickly empty the contents of my makeup pouch into my bag, put both of the turned-off phones into the pouch, place the pouch down in the mulch, and cover it with some leaves, burying my cell phones. There. They should be safe here for a little while.

I look around me. Nobody in sight. I get to my feet, brush off the knees of my trousers, and start trotting in the direction of the address on Fredensborgveien Street.

Less than ten minutes after I exited the catacomb by Halvorsens Conditori, I arrive at the address Sabiya gave me: 24 Fredensborgveien Street, just two hundred yards from the ministry.

I didn't recognize the address when she sent it, but I know the place well. This block has been the site of both a school of advertising and the Ministry of Government Administration. Mona used to work here, in the State Directorate of Personnel. Once, she told me just to call it the personnel theater.

Sabiya is nowhere to be seen. She didn't actually say anything about exactly where in this area we should meet, inside or out, only the address. I also don't have any phone on which to reach her, since both of mine are lying beneath the plague monument. For all I know, my absence from the Parliament building may have already been discovered. Maybe they have sounded the alarm while I stand here waiting for Henrik's girlfriend.

One minute. Two. Three. Four. Have I been set up? If ten minutes pass without anyone showing up, I must just leave again, I can't just stand here waiting.

Mona also told me that the sausage factory owned by Norwegian author Axel Jensen's grandfather Axel Jensen Sr. was located here back in the day. The sausage factory had taken over the huge premises of the Fortuna brewery or something like that. The younger Axel has apparently described the place in several books.

Five minutes. Six minutes.

The most special place she worked, Mona said. Now there's a kind of construction site here. Just the big, white, stone building remains standing where the "personnel theater" once was, between the cranes and trucks, temporary walls and gates, like a final reminder of the sausage factory. Despite all the mess, it's dead and deserted here today. The construction work must be on hold.

Seven minutes. My nerves are seriously on edge.

Then I hear a kind of screaming whine from the wall of one of the buildings. I look in the direction of the sound and see that there is a stairway there, almost hidden behind a tree and some bushes. The stairs lead up to a partially hidden, dark door. That must be where the sound came from.

Standing in the doorway is Sabiya. The once-so-immaculately-groomed Sabiya, with her deep skin tone and beautiful wavy hair and pearl earrings, feminine and soft, now mostly resembles a scabby alley cat. She is so thin, and her skin is sallow, gray, in spite of her natural brown tone. Her hair is greasy, hanging limply, and she has a rash on her face.

Henrik wouldn't have given her a second look now.

"Clara," she says from where she is standing on the stairs.

I glance around me. Nobody in sight.

"Where are my sons?" I ask.

She looks at me for a long time, scrutinizing me with a strange smile I have difficulty reading. It's as if the pearl-earring lady has just been a disguise, which has now been shed, discarded.

What remains is the gangster chick she once was, and actually has always been, just older, more hideous.

"Come with me," she says finally, waving me inside through the doorway.

I shiver beneath my thin, rust-red autumn coat. Sabiya has a big jacket knotted around her waist. Everything she is wearing looks like something she has found in the back room of the Salvation Army.

The concrete door slams shut behind us. For a second or two, it is dark, until Sabiya turns on a headlamp.

"Down there," she says, pointing to a darkened stairway.

I am alone and impossible to track, but I can't turn back now; it's too late for regrets. Far off in the distance, I can hear a dog barking. Even in the faint light from Sabiya's headlamp, it is a spectacular sight that greets me as I walk down the stairs. Above ground, everything appeared reliable, ordinary, and modern. Down here is another world entirely, an underworld and another century.

A parallel world, two minutes away from the Government Quarter.

Thick layers of dust on the floor. Spiderwebs on the ceiling. A mouse scurries across the floor in front of me. We are in a long, narrow hallway. Then we enter an enormous room, with many big vats, maybe used for salting meat.

Sabiya is so tiny; if she is to attack me, it should be an easy match, even though I am not in the best shape of my life. If she has an ally in here, though, I'll have my work cut out for me.

No sounds from the city out there, up there, can be heard down here. I can just discern thick concrete walls and ancient vats and barrels in the dim light from Sabiya's headlamp. Still, I get the same feeling as in the tunnel at home that time, the feeling of being at the center of absolute darkness.

CHAPTER 34

ANDREAS

When Sabiya was arrested, we started looking through Mommy's newspaper every day to see if there was anything new about the case.

One day, we saw that there was a short article about a woman who had been released. It had to be her.

We have to give her the letter, Nikolai said. Imagine how happy she will be!

Why should we make her happy? I said. Besides, it will probably make her sadder. It will just cause trouble. Mommy is cross enough as it is.

We didn't think Mommy seemed to like her new job, even though she was the one who told us that this was an offer she could not refuse. She was driven home in a really nice car, but her face was always cross when she came in the door. I thought that if she disliked it so much, she shouldn't have become a minister, but I didn't say so. There was no point trying to argue with Mommy.

One day, Nikolai said that now he was going to contact Sabiya, no matter what I thought. He *wanted* to meet her, he said.

I gave up then. I also wanted something to happen, and it felt like Sabiya had a little of Dad inside her, since she was maybe the one who knew him the best and had been the most fond of him, besides us.

We couldn't find her telephone number online, but she still had her Instagram profile, so we sent her a message there. It didn't seem like she was active on Instagram, so we didn't think we'd get an answer, but she replied almost immediately.

Of course, she wrote. When? And where?

The next day, we met her.

CHAPTER 35

CLARA

We reach a corner, where a kind of improvised, dusty bar has been set up. On the bar are some huge, white, lit candles. In front of the bar are two red velvet armchairs, with a round teak table between them, everything covered with a thick layer of dust.

"Have a seat," Sabiya says imperiously, nodding toward one of the chairs. "This is where I've been staying the past few days. This is my living room now, my life."

"Where are the boys, Sabiya?"

"I don't know," she says. "I don't even know where my own children are."

She leans toward me, coming so close that I pull away. The back of the chair is cold and raw against my body.

"You killed Henrik," she says. "Then you took my life away."

I cringe when she says this about Henrik, so bluntly. What happened to him is something I have intentionally not mentioned to Stian. Did I really kill Henrik? I got him to go for a swim with me, yes, and I am a better swimmer than he was, but is that really the same as killing him?

In a flash, I can see his face, his final look of desperation, before he was whirled toward the falls. And then the feeling afterward, the one I haven't had before, after any of the other times, the feeling of having made a terrible mistake. I try to shake it off, I need to concentrate.

"Where are the boys, Sabiya?" I ask again.

"So they're gone?" she says, shaking her head. "Is that why you're here? Well, I really have no idea."

As she is speaking, she unties the jacket around her waist, puts it on, and my heart skips a beat or two.

It's a fleece jacket with a Vålerenga Soccer Club logo on the back, the jacket I saw just yesterday on the surveillance footage from the school.

"It was you," I say. "You *have* met my boys. I know it, I recognize your jacket."

Then she nods, smiling an odd little half smile.

"They contacted me, wanted to meet me. Nice boys, probably in need of a real mother. Could be they would also prefer me, given the choice."

I try to stay calm, not let her provoke me, remember why I am here. Then it happens.

Suddenly, she's aiming a pistol at me. I look up, our eyes meet, and I understand that she means business.

This is why she agreed to meet me, my contacting her was a gift.

Maybe she has my children, maybe not. After having seen her eyes, I know without any doubt that she wants to kill me.

CHAPTER 36

ANDREAS

The fleece jacket was all wrong for her, but you could say that about everything she was wearing, the sweatpants and the hoodie. We barely recognized her.

We met in our schoolyard. First, she hugged both of us. Then she started to cry, and then Nikolai did, too. He threw his arms around her waist, and I was so embarrassed that I didn't know what to do, but she just sniffled and laughed, and I understood she was happy that he did it.

Are you sick? Nikolai asked. You look a little pale.

She *was*, in fact, very pale and had blue rings under her eyes, as if she'd had the flu for a week or something.

Sabiya just shook her head and wiped away the tears beneath her eyes.

Sad, then? I asked.

Then she smiled and stroked my cheek with a soft, warm hand, which made my legs tremble. Then she nodded.

Because of Daddy?

She nodded again. Yes, and because I've been in jail for no reason and now I can't go back to work, and I can't see my children either.

Oh no, Nikolai said. We have something for you, by the way. It's a letter from Daddy.

He held out the letter to her. It was in a plastic folder so it wouldn't be ruined.

Oh my God, she said, and looked even paler.

It's from last spring, I said. From before he died.

She accepted the letter with such care, like it was worth a million dollars, started reading, and then stopped.

I'll read it later, she said. When I'm alone. How are you?

She dried her eyes with her hand.

Sorry, Nikolai said, and now he was all soft, I could tell.

No, no, Sabiya said. You mustn't say that. It made me happy, both that you wanted to see me and that you gave me the letter. Thank you.

We talked for a while. She tried to ask us about school and how things were at home and stuff, but I noticed she was really struggling. She was, like, sad through and through, the way clothes and shoes get soaking wet when you've been out in the rain for too long.

For some reason or other, maybe just to have something to talk about or to seem interesting, Nikolai said that maybe we should meet with a journalist from Western Norway. Just before Sabiya came, we had received a text message from a guy who wanted to talk to us about Mommy.

What? Sabiya said. Are you sure that's a good idea?

No, I said. We're *not* going to meet him, and now we have to go home.

I said that to give her an out so she wouldn't have to stay with us any longer. She didn't exactly look like she was feeling very well.

Oh, she said. It was so nice seeing you both. It helped, a little. We can meet again tomorrow if you want?

It was strange that she suggested we should meet up again so soon, but maybe it was because she couldn't see her own children? Maybe she wanted to pretend that we were her children so she would feel a little less sad?

Tomorrow we have soccer, I said.

But the day after tomorrow we can, Nikolai said.

163

Oh, okay, then I'll see you the day after tomorrow, she said, and hugged us again.

It was nice seeing her, but actually, I think we already understood that she couldn't help us or make us happy again, the way we had maybe hoped. So then we started talking about how it might be cool to meet that journalist, even though Sabiya was skeptical and for sure Mommy would hate it if she knew anything about it.

It wasn't long ago, just a few days, but it already feels like ages. Now we've been moved to another place. Here, we're allowed to move around a bit, but both the house and everything else here is really creepy.

CHAPTER 37

CLARA

"You admit that you met the boys but claim that you have no idea why they disappeared right after that?" I say.

"Yes, and it's true. They were going to meet a journalist, I think. I went to meet them again two days later, but they never showed up."

She draws herself up to her full height, the pistol still aimed at me, her arms shaking. The pistol reminds me a little of her Glock, but the police have that, so it can't be the same firearm. Anyway, it doesn't make any difference right now.

"Good Lord, Sabiya, stop and think," I say. "I'm the minister of justice."

"A lot of good that's doing you," she says coldly. "I don't see any bodyguards."

"Why do you want to kill me?" I say. "What do you get out of it?"

She stares at me. Eyes like still, black pools.

Despite how unkempt and disgusting she looks, I also suddenly understand better what Henrik must have seen in her, now that the curls and pearls and all the polish is gone. She is standing there and is a teeny-tiny, keenly sparkling black gem of hate, anger, grit, and courage.

"You know why, Clara. Because I can't bear the thought of you walking around, alive and breathing. Henrik is gone. My children are gone. Everything is gone, and you are the minister of justice. You will never be held accountable in any other way, just the way you planned it when you murdered those child abusers."

I flinch. Nobody has ever said to me what she is saying now.

Whether or not her gun is loaded, I don't know. I don't want to find out, and I know I have to act now or never, without hesitation, on instinct alone. She is a kind of juvenile gangster in familiar territory, and she has a gun. It's me or her, only one of us will survive.

I stand up and, with a single broad movement, knock the pistol out of her hand. It lands a few feet away. Then I become nothing. I no longer think, forget myself, forget the time and place, and my hands find her throat. I just act, releasing what lies ready and waiting inside me, squeeze, squeeze, squeeze until there's no air or color or breath left in her, till she stops fighting back, till she slumps down against the wall, till I do the same, and end up lying on top of her.

There's a sickening little thud as her head hits the floor. I bend down and check. No pulse. She is dead.

I stand still for a while until I am able to collect myself. Then I bend over, remove Sabiya's headlamp, and fasten it to my own head.

There can't be many people, if any, who come down here, but she shouldn't be left lying on the floor in the middle of the room anyway. I have to move her.

In one of the adjacent rooms, I find a huge salt vat, more than big enough to hold a human being. I walk back, grasp her wrists, and drag her behind me into the room where the vat is. Her head hangs down limply. I take hold of her under her arms. She can't weigh more than 110 pounds, but it's still not easy to lift her several feet off the floor and over the rim of the vat. I have to use my knee like a kind of lever. One try. Two. Three. Her body is still warm in my arms, but it is already dead weight.

I finally manage to heave her up over the rim, so she is lying on the white salt. In the dim light, it looks like she is lying in snow, her dark hair is like a fan around her head.

Sabiya no longer exists, is no more.

She will never again stand up, move, breathe, speak, or laugh.

There is something unreal about it. Just a few minutes ago, she was walking around in front of me, just as alive as I am now. Her heart was beating, her lungs breathing, her brain producing thoughts. Now only her extinguished eyes remain. The blood in her veins is still warm, but it will soon coagulate, her skin will turn yellow. It's all over.

So many lives. Magne in the car, the three of last spring, Henrik out in the water, now Sabiya in the salt vat. Six human beings. Until last spring, there was only one: Magne. And if anyone deserved to die, it was him.

The three child abusers deserved it, too. I did their children and the world a favor by eliminating them. It was different with Henrik and, now, Sabiya. There are children who will miss them. But Sabiya stood there and pointed that pistol at me. I had no choice. I had to do something, and now I have to get out of here. I close her eyes. It is the first time I've done this on a dead body, and it is surprisingly easy.

I look around me. On the floor is a big sack labeled *Sodium Nitrate*. It's heavy, but I manage to heave it up onto the rim of the vat. Then I pour salt over Sabiya until she is only a few bulges under all the white, like when two feet of snow have fallen upon black crags and rocks and stones.

When we salted meat at home on the farm, we had to add stone weights to keep the meat from floating up to the surface. Again, I look around the room. And there, in a corner, lie some weights. I lay them on top of Sabiya. There, now she'll stay down.

After I've blown out the candles, I walk back in the direction of the stairs leading to the entrance, rush up the steps, and grab the door handle. It's locked. I shake it, but it doesn't help. I'm locked in, trapped down here in these enormous, dark cellar rooms, and there are an amazing number of them.

Still, even though I know it's wishful thinking, I keep expecting to see the boys sitting huddled together in a corner, staring at me with huge eyes, or that I will find mattresses they've slept on or some sleeping bags, but there's nothing like that here. There is essentially nothing to indicate that they have ever been here. And if I can't get out of here now, there's nothing else that matters. Then I will never find out where they are, never see them again.

I can't get out the way we came in, must find another exit.

Another stairway, other than the one Sabiya and I used, apparently doesn't exist. At the other end of the cellar, I finally find an old, dusty, and dirty ghost of an elevator. The door is open; I walk in, press the button for the second floor, close the door. The elevator starts moving with a heavy sigh. Then it stops again, and I am trapped in an ancient cage between two floors.

I try yanking at the door but can't get it open. I press the same button again. No response. There must have been a tiny residue of power left in the generator, a final spasm of life, which is now gone.

What shall I do? It appears that I will die a slow death inside this more-than-one-hundred-year-old cage. Then I sit down, resting my head on my knees.

"Lars, help me," I whisper. "What do I do?"

CHAPTER 38

ANDREAS

I have no idea what time it is, I'm not even sure what day it is. But I think it's Monday. That means we have soccer practice. Practice is twice a week, on Mondays and Thursdays. We were there on Thursday, not today.

Will anyone miss us? Do they know we're gone? Are they looking for us?

This is the first practice we've missed this fall. We haven't missed a single one, even though a lot of sad things have happened. I'm actually a little proud of that.

Nikolai tries to talk to me, but I can't be bothered to answer. Yes, I'm used to being with him all day long, but this is different. Usually there are other people to talk to and we're not on top of each other all the time. At school we mostly play separately, hang out with different kids, even though we both spend a lot of time with Olav.

I've tried to talk to Daddy. Several people have said that I can, but it doesn't work, he never answers. That's too bad, because there are so many things I want to ask him, tell him, so much I miss. Especially everything having to do with soccer.

Daddy knew, for example, how high up the shin guards should be. Mommy always puts them on too far down. I've tried to tell her that they're supposed to be higher up on the shin, that's the point of shin guards, but she doesn't understand. First, I moved them up after she put them on, when she wasn't looking. Finally, I said I could do it myself, the socks, and the cleats and the shin guards. Great, she said, and nodded, as if she didn't understand. She kept doing it for Nikolai, but she was so clumsy that finally I taught him how to do it himself.

That's what's strange about Mommy, because she is so good at so many things. She is very calm and proper when she talks on TV, and she is good at everything she does on the farm and at the summer farm, knows how to do tons of things Dad couldn't do, like build fences, chop down trees, shear sheep, and things like that.

Completely ordinary things, on the other hand, like putting on shin guards and soccer socks or making dinner or making sure we have erasers and pencils in our pencil boxes, that everything isn't left lying on the table at home, that our lunch boxes are washed every day, that our boots aren't wet, or that the winter jackets are brought down from the attic and hung up on the hooks, with *those* things, she is hopeless.

I mean, I never thought about those things before. They just happened. Daddy took care of it, without us noticing. Daddy made things happen. With Mommy, they don't happen. That's how it is. I don't think she's careless on purpose, just that there isn't room in her head.

Daddy said once that maybe Mommy's head was like one of those fantastic telescopes that is set to see all kinds of things that are far, far away. When you look into a telescope and look at the stars and the moon and everything else you can see in there, then maybe you can't manage to see what's going on around you at the same time, he said.

He would probably say that again if he were here now, try to get us to understand that Mommy cares, even though it doesn't always seem like she does.

I've been really mad at Mommy many times this fall, mad at the whole world, but mostly mad at her. Now I just miss her, more than I thought was possible.

"Mommy," I whisper. "Mommy, come and get us."

CHAPTER 39

CLARA

Lars doesn't answer. Nobody answers. I get up, unsteadily, lean against the wall of the elevator. By some miracle, the elevator starts moving. So there must have been a little power left, one final tiny spark of life. Maybe it's enough to save me?

Slowly, slowly, the elevator starts moving upward. I close my eyes, hold my breath, don't dare move. This time, it doesn't stop.

I am so relieved when I slam the elevator door shut behind me, it is as if I am already standing outdoors in the fresh air, as if I have been saved, but I'm not out, not yet. Now I'm standing in a dark corridor, in another location in this confusing building, away from where Sabiya and I entered. The floor is flat, but I still don't know how to get out of here.

Then the light from the headlamp I took from Sabiya fades. It grows dimmer, flickers, until it goes out and everything is dark.

I was lucky when I got out of the Parliament building and lucky when the elevator started up again. I am lucky that it is Sabiya and not me who is lying in the salt vat. Now none of this matters after all; it's like the headlamp going out is a sign that all my luck has run out.

I start fumbling my way forward, crawling through the darkness. It feels like hours, while in reality it is probably more like minutes. Then I finally see a horizontal strip of light in all the darkness, which could mean there is a door there.

It *is* actually a door, with a kind of lock on the inside. The lock is rusted, so I have to press all my weight against the door, tug and wriggle it. Finally, I get the lock open, I yank on the door handle until it opens. Then I am standing, unbelievably, on a landing like the one Sabiya and I passed through before, which I can now see to my right. I must have moved in a kind of horseshoe path around the room, by way of a little trip to the cellar.

Air. Light. It feels so good.

I want to thank someone, but I don't believe in any god and, strictly speaking, have only myself to thank for getting out of there.

Sweaty and shaky, I jog back to the plague monument in the cemetery, retrieve the pouch containing my phones, and shove it down into my bag. I hadn't seen any sign of Sabiya's phone. I would have liked to have taken it. Maybe Sabiya has it in her pocket, so it's lying with her submerged in the salt? If so, it will be destroyed relatively quickly.

The October sun warms me, the leaves glitter like huge gold coins. For a second or two, I am so relieved to be alive and out of the sausage factory that I feel invincible, almost happy.

I look at my watch: 12:30.

One hour has passed since I sneaked out of the Parliament building. For all I know, PSS has been searching the entire Parliament for me. They might think I've been abducted; they may have discovered that my phones are turned off. Stian may have told them everything, because now he thinks someone has kidnapped me, too.

PSS and Stian are still the least of my problems. I was actually convinced that Sabiya had the boys, believed that I would find them with her, but she didn't have them, and now I've killed her.

The boys are still missing, and I'm back where I started. Actually, I've taken several steps backward. I thought I knew something. I know nothing. I thought I had the solution. I don't. Where are they? And who were the boys going to meet? A journalist, she said. What journalists do I know? Right before I left for Fredensborgveien Street, I spoke with

Erik Heier. He has always been far too interested in both me and my personal life. Could he have been the person they were going to meet?

I should have been back at work hours ago. I'm late for a meeting with the governor of Svalbard, who is on his annual visit to chat about the polar bear on display in our waiting room. I walk through the revolving doors, through the security turnstile, and take the elevator up. It works, it hums brightly, does everything it should.

Then I catch sight of myself in the mirror.

I'm a wreck. I am disheveled, have cobwebs in my hair, dust and dirt on my clothing. I quickly brush off the worst of it but still don't look presentable and won't until I have a shower and change my clothes.

I try sneaking past Vigdis, walk straight into my office and into the bathroom. There, I moisten a towel with a little hot water and do my best to remove the worst traces of my visit to the sausage factory.

When I enter my office again, Vigdis is standing in the doorway.

"The governor and his retinue are waiting for you in the conference room," she says.

"I'll be right there," I say, turning on both phones.

They buzz as an avalanche of missed calls, text messages, and alerts pours in.

I don't look at all of them, only those with Stian's name. Without looking at what is already on the thread, what he has written to me over the course of the past few hours, I write a message I had worked out on the way up here. Was waylaid by TV2-Heier. Had to be sneaked out the back way. Can you meet me outside of R5 right away? I must tell you something. Urgent.

The answer arrives ten seconds later. Okay. Nothing more.

Then Vigdis clears her throat in the doorway again.

"Listen," I say. "Tell the governor that I'm not well and have to postpone the meeting . . ."

She looks at me, eyes wide, clears her throat one more time.

"And can you have the communications people put together a list of all the journalists who have been in contact with us? Including those who were dropped after I became minister?"

"All of them?" she says, looking at me doubtfully.

"Yup. All of them. Each and every one. A complete list. I'm going home now, so I need everything printed out and delivered to my home by messenger today."

"Fine," she says, even though she looks like she wants to object.

Twenty minutes later, Stian and I are walking toward the bench in the garden, where we had our talk over the weekend. He is apprehensive, his face tense. When he opened the car door for me, I said that I had to go home, that I wanted to talk with him in the garden. He nodded. In the car, we didn't exchange a single word.

He is presumably not very happy that I ran away from him. I can only imagine what he will think after I've confessed.

When Sabiya talked about the children and Henrik, I felt how much I hated her. Henrik would have been here, tying the laces of soccer cleats and doing math homework and mowing the lawn, had it not been for Sabiya.

All the pain started with her, and then she was standing there, trembling, aiming the pistol at me, ready to shoot. This is true. At the same time, everything is all mixed up. I can no longer see or think straight. No matter how I look at it, I've committed another murder, even though I promised myself not to do it again. I have even killed someone with whom I could be connected, even though I hope she won't be found for a long time.

And now the one link to my children is gone. Now I no longer believe that Sabiya is behind their disappearance. And I have nowhere else to look, no clues to unravel, nothing more than the one sentence about a journalist.

Now I have to tell Stian what I've done, and what happens next will be up to him.

The other me, the one who kills, the one I never thought anyone would find out about, I am about to hand her over to a man employed by PSS. All my instincts are resisting. He will probably report me, report me to his colleagues. If I lie, he will see through me, and that will make everything worse. Still, I must talk with him, I need him. Everything I have managed on my own up to now is irrelevant.

"Have you spoken to someone?" I say. "Did you report it?"

He shakes his head.

"I was on my way to do so when you sent your message," he says.

"Good," I say, and take a deep breath. "There's something I have to tell you, but you have to promise not to interrupt until I have told you the whole story. You can comment and ask questions afterward, okay?"

He nods. Then I start telling my story.

CHAPTER 40

AXEL

The digital age intensifies every form of heartbreak. I am lying on the sofa, vegging out, incapable of doing anything but staring at the damn app. Sometimes Clara appears in the form of a green dot. For a little while, she glows at me, and then she disappears.

In the past few days, I have hidden our chat to avoid seeing that I haven't received a reply to my last message, or to any of the five or six messages before that. Since Clara is the person I chat with the most, it doesn't help. Her face, along with the green dot, pops up anyway every time she is online and "active." To avoid seeing her and the green dot every time I'm using the app, I would have to delete or block her, and I don't want to do that. I don't want to put an end to anything, actually. I want more.

I know I should delete Messenger, not put myself through this. It is a hopelessly outdated system anyway, a forum for pensioners, but people still use it. Young people, neighbors, colleagues, and that makes it difficult to give it up. I have disabled the notifications, so I have to open the app to see whether I have any new messages from Clara, but there is never anything new. Now I've started thinking that maybe there never will be.

Isn't it common courtesy to respond, even though she clearly doesn't need me as a sitter any longer? After the evening of pizza and wine, I haven't seen or heard from her. We've been friends for over a decade. I have really been there for her and the boys this year. Shouldn't that be worth something?

My feelings change all the time. Sometimes I miss sitting and talking to her so much, despite how aloof and reserved she is. Now and then, I just get angry, feel stupid, exploited, humiliated. I try to devise ways of retaliating but can't come up with anything other than strolling past her with a new girlfriend, if that ever happens. Would she care? Hardly.

Maybe she would even be relieved to get away from tired, clingy, old Axel.

This is all so incredibly destructive, so frustratingly adolescent. I should forget all about Clara, but it's impossible. It doesn't make it easier that she lives just a few hundred yards away.

Besides, I miss the boys. I've been over there several times a week for months, and now suddenly, I'm not wanted. It makes no sense. The children need me as a stabilizing element. Henrik used to say about Clara that she had impaired nurturing abilities. I thought that was a bit harsh, and she *has* gone above and beyond after Henrik's death, but since she was appointed minister, I've been concerned. Without Åsa and me, Clara and the boys would never have managed, and now she's apparently trying to fend for herself.

I get up, go out into the hallway, put on my jacket, hat, gloves, shoes.

It's probably Åsa, not Clara, who is there. I can say hello to the boys before they go to bed. If, against all odds, Clara should be home, she will maybe be happy to see me. Maybe she will remember how nice it was spending time together and that I'm a part of the family. Either way, sitting here and obsessing about it isn't going to accomplish anything.

Elated by the euphoria that often follows in the aftermath of a decision, I walk over to Clara's house. I just have to be patient and confident; then with time, things will evolve the way I want them to. My former despondency is replaced by a kind of cockiness.

A hundred yards away from the gate, on the other side of the street, I pull up short. Sitting on the bench in the garden where I have personally sat many times, I see Clara, and she is not alone. She's with that driver of hers. What was his name again? André? Stig? Stian. Stian, that's it, I remember it now. Stian with his Viking look and striking, dramatic face and intense eyes, like a kind of male Clara. Alpha bravo. Stian who instructed me to prepare myself for a new era. Is he the one who has forbidden her to have contact with me?

They are sitting close together, Clara with her hands in her lap, her head bowed. Why are they sitting like that, as if they're a couple? They can't be. If so, that went fast, but Clara is unpredictable, Henrik always said so. Besides, she's proud of her rural roots, her childhood on the farm, all of that. Maybe she likes slumming it by hanging out with her driver?

This would at least explain why she's suddenly gone silent. I have tortured myself over it, scrolled through our chat, seen how one-sided it is, winced. And all the while, she, who has complained so much about how claustrophobic this driver business is, is in a relationship with her driver, maybe even has had sex with him.

Should I go over, make my presence known, if for no other reason than to see their reaction? I am about to do just that when I notice how they are looking at one another. Something big starts to grow in my throat. It grows and grows, and I am unable to stop it.

Shit, I *can't* go over to them in this state.

I turn around, almost slip on the rotten, slippery leaves on the ground but manage to recover my balance just in time and walk home, struggling with something large and salty.

In the few minutes this takes, the big, heavy autumn sun disappears between the trees in the west, like a kind of red death.

CHAPTER 41

CLARA

The autumn-red setting sun slips farther and farther down between the trees. I train my gaze on it, unable to look into Stian's eyes right now.

I start with Heier, who ambushed me, and the message from Sabiya that popped up on my smartwatch, with the walk down into the underground passages at the Parliament building and through the streets. When I get to the part about Krist cemetery, I hesitate, but finally tell him that I put both of my cell phones in my makeup pouch and buried it under the leaves. Then I tell him about Sabiya on the almost invisible landing behind the tree, Sabiya who took me down to her secret bar, who started talking about Henrik and about my sons, that she was wearing a jacket with a Vålerenga logo, that she pulled out a pistol.

"I was frightened," I say. "It was me or her. I tried to take it away from her, but that was impossible."

I stop for a second, the words are stuck in my throat. Stian keeps his promise not to ask questions, not to comment, but I can feel his gaze on me. It's too late to turn back now, now I must just get this over with.

"She was the one who had the firearm, not me. She must have planned this, agreed to meet me in a place where I wouldn't be found for a long time. I had to defend myself, was just trying to disarm her, and then it went too far. It was an accident . . ."

His alert gaze, full of concern, is focused on me. I draw a breath.

"She's dead, Stian. Now I have no idea what to do . . ."

I raise my hands and hide my face in them. Sounds come out of me, sounds I've never heard before, which don't sound like me, aren't me. At the same time, they are some of the most truthful things ever to come out of me.

Maybe I don't have an authentic self. Maybe I'm just an empty shell that can be filled with whatever.

Stian pats me on the back. "Easy there, breathe," he says.

"It's just so horrible," I say. "I can't believe it happened."

"Self-defense, Clara," he says. "You haven't done anything wrong."

I remove my hands and dry my tears. Then all of a sudden, I see it. The scar. On his hand. I have seen a scar like that before. It comes along with a beret and a metal splinter from a grenade. He is that kind of soldier. One of them. One of us.

Where did it come from? Afghanistan? Wasn't that what I thought the very first time I saw him, that he looked like a veteran? I am about to comment on it, but change my mind.

"My father served with the UN forces in Lebanon," I say. "He was gone half a year, came home with a nervous disorder. That half year left a lifelong mark on us. My brother and I were left alone with Agnes, my mother, which was not good. That was when all the misery began."

Even now, many years later, with far more ruinous and immediate problems hanging over my head, it's almost impossible for me to talk about this.

"He told me a lot about his time there," I say. "What he went through, experienced. It had such a profound impact on him. Maybe he talked more to me than he should have, but he had nobody else to talk to. He was so afraid that something would happen to me, especially after what happened to my brother."

I hide my face in my hands again. I sit like that for a few seconds, before straightening up. Sorry, Dad, I think. Forgive me.

"He drilled it into me, how to be a good soldier," I say. "Taught me all kinds of things, also things I probably shouldn't have learned. Today it all came back to me, when Sabiya stood there pointing the pistol at me. I knew instinctively what I had to do to survive . . ."

A moment of silence.

"You can talk now," I say, finally. "I don't have anything more to say. You will want to contact your colleagues, report me."

Another moment of silence. Then he starts to talk.

"This was cut-and-dry self-defense, Clara," he says. "Sabiya met you there to kill you. Nobody can blame you for wanting to save your own life, but neither is there anyone who needs to know about this now. It won't bring Sabiya back to life."

I don't dare say anything, am unsure about whether I heard him correctly, afraid of messing things up. He seems so different from before and so different from what I feared and prepared myself for. Does this mean he's not going to report me? Do I dare believe it?

"Did Sabiya say anything about the boys that can help us?"

"Not much," I say. "But I'm sure she didn't know about the kidnapping. We must have been looking in the wrong place."

"Wow," Stian says, rubbing his fingertips against his temples.

"Actually, she did say something," I say. "They were apparently going to meet with a journalist, they told her when they met her. I've ordered the ministry's media log from my time as cabinet minister, was planning to go through it tonight, see whether I can find anything unusual. Now that's probably out of the question . . ."

"Clara," he says, raising the hand with the scar. "I will help you go through the media log; we will do this together."

I almost don't dare breathe. Stian looks at me earnestly.

"I had no idea where you were when you ran away today. You *cannot* violate those kinds of agreements, no matter how good a reason you might feel you have. Can you promise me that you won't do something like that again?" he says, his eyes meeting mine.

"I promise," I say, and feel that I truly mean it.

Then I actually take his hand, the way he took mine the last time we sat here. As the last of the sun disappears and just a thin red line remains highlighting the boundary between earth and sky, I am sure.

We're a team now, Stian and I, whether we want to be or not.

CHAPTER 42

LEIF

I have just poured myself a cup of coffee and am trying to make my way over to the chair and my book without spilling it, when something outside the window makes me jump. Coffee splashes onto the saucer, and the cup rattles so much that I have to put everything down on the floor.

Walking across the yard is Halvor Haugo, holding a notepad in one hand and taking notes with the other, while my cat, Bella, slinks around his heels. I run out into the hallway, shove my feet down into a pair of boots that are standing there, and yank open the door.

"What are you doing?" I shout.

He stops and looks at me in surprise, as if he hadn't thought about the fact that I live here. It is damned rude. Besides, it's the second time in a few weeks that I've seen him here.

This is my turf. My castle. Here I reign. Nobody comes here. That's how it's been, but apparently, that's not how it is anymore.

We stand just a few feet from one another, staring.

"You can't be here," I say. "This is private property."

"I'm writing a story about Clara and her childhood," he says. "Isn't that nice?"

He is making fun of me. He is damn well making fun of me.

"Have you been down to Geir's place and taken a closer look at the wreck?"

I shake my head, not sure whether he is actually asking me a question.

"You should," he continues. "It's a gem. Lots of incriminating details . . ."

He smiles, but the smile frightens me. It doesn't reach his eyes, which are shining with something else, anger, contempt, maybe even hatred.

"Leave," I say, my voice breaking, to my irritation. "Otherwise, I'm calling the police."

He studies me for a moment, that disturbing smile on his face. Then he shrugs and walks toward his car.

An angry, desperate old man, that's what he turns me into.

I walk away and sit down under my maple tree, place my hands on my knees, lean against the trunk, and close my eyes. It's too cold to sit here. I don't have the peace of mind to keep my eyes closed either. My good mood has disappeared, and it's impossible to imagine it coming back.

So the wrecked car has been taken to Geir's place, must have been there for more than a month now. What kind of incriminating details was he hinting about? Was that just something he said to upset me, or is there really something there that can create problems for Clara?

The thought that the wrecked car has been hauled up into the light of day is intolerable, as if that devil Magne himself has been brought back from the dead along with it.

At that workshop, there are certainly a lot of things that are flammable. Oil, gasoline, other stuff. A lit match is all it would take, and the workshop, along with the wrecked car from the fjord, would be a thing of the past. Geir Vassenden is virtually an invalid with that arthritis of his. In recent years, he has come to resemble Iggy Pop more and more. His workshop hasn't been profitable, not even in the best of times, which was a long time ago. If I burned down the whole shebang, the insurance would cover Geir's losses, and it would probably be a good thing for him. A fire wouldn't hurt anyone but could spare Clara a lot of grief.

I am on my way over to the car to drive down there when I change my mind. Better to wait at least until it's really dark.

On my way into the house, I pass Bella. I stop, try petting her, but our visitor has made her every bit as skittish and strange as me. Once inside, I walk over to the living room table covered with all the papers from the box, but the fighting spirit I was feeling when I took them all out is gone. Now it all just makes me feel sick. All these old memories about what I should have prevented.

It's high time I warn Clara about Halvor and Agnes. I don't usually call her, leave it to her to pick up the phone when it's convenient for her. Now I take out my phone and dial.

The phone rings for a long time. She doesn't pick up.

CHAPTER 43

CLARA

Dad calls. But I can't talk to him now, will call him back later instead. After making my confession to Stian, after agreeing to this fragile coalition, against all odds, a tiny flame of hope has begun to flicker in my chest. Probably it's necessary for survival, to be able to believe that this will work.

The printout of the media log did not arrive until I called about it several times. Stian went home for a bit, had to watch his children, his wife had an errand to run. I was slightly nervous that he wouldn't come back, but he did. Now we have finally set up in the living room, where we can't be seen from the outside. Stian has gone through the entire house and confirmed that whoever took the boys has not installed any surveillance devices. He is aware that PSS has no surveillance in place here yet.

The pile of printouts is surprisingly large. We have divided it between us. Now each of us is going through our half; when we finish, we will exchange piles.

Ironically, it's as if Stian has let me in after I told him what happened with Sabiya.

That's good, but at the same time, there are so many things that he mustn't find out about. He must never learn the last part of the story about Magne and me, that I filed down the window crank, that I grabbed the steering wheel, that I told him to stay in his seat, told him that it was the best way to survive. And it's even more important that he not find out about the murders of last spring, that I was behind them. The police have had to release first Henrik, then Sabiya. Now they have no clues or leads. I want it to stay that way.

Already Stian knows too much. At any moment, he could change his mind, go to his superiors, and tell them everything. My life is in his hands. That is the price I am paying for his help.

The words in front of me. Journalists. Scores of journalists. Here amid the log entries and registrations and names maybe lies the solution we are searching for.

"Let me know if you find any sign of Heier," Stian says. "But whether you find him or not, he's now our best lead."

"Also the only one, right?" I say.

He nods. We are silent for a long time. Both of us leaf through the pages and read, leaf and read. Deep concentration. Then I see something.

"Hey," I whisper, pointing. "Look at this."

One Halvor Haugo from the local paper back home has tried to reach me several times. He wants to talk to me about my childhood, about the tragic, fatal accident last summer, about my ministry position. Each time, his pitch is a bit different.

"Do you know him?" Stian asks, wrinkling his brow.

"I don't know," I say. "The name rings a bell . . ."

I have always been terrible with names and faces and people in general, unless they interest me for some reason or other.

"I found his license plate number," Stian mumbles. He is chewing on a pencil that he has stuck in the corner of his mouth.

His face is so full of concentration. It reminds me of the mountain landscape at home.

What's his story? Where has he been? What has given him that face and that scar? Maybe it was in fact the story about Dad and Lebanon that saved me, persuaded him to take my side, if only for the time being? Or was it his own experiences from war, far away from the black armored minister cars, that made him want to help me?

Now his phone vibrates, he wrinkles his brow, reads.

"What?" I ask.

"Just Janne," he says. "She's wondering when I'm coming home."

"And what will you say?" I ask.

"That I don't know," he says, showing me a photo he has found of a somewhat frazzled-around-the-edges guy about my age. "You know him?"

"Possibly," I say, squinting at the photo. "But I have some difficulties with . . ."

"Faces and such, yes," he says with a knowing little smile.

"You know that?" I say, astonished. "I didn't think anyone was aware of that."

"It's my job to know such things, to know more about you than you do yourself," he says. "But you know him, then?"

"Maybe," I say, trying to remember where I might have met this man.

Stian takes out his laptop, turns it on.

"I've transferred some films here," he says. "Sit here so you can see."

I move over beside him, so close that I can feel the warmth of his upper arm and thigh emanating into my body.

"First the tollbooths," he says. "Maybe we can find him. If he's been here and driven his own car. But there's a lot of footage, so it will take time. Let's start with the afternoon they disappeared."

I nod. I can scarcely breathe and barely dare to look.

EB 63970 is the license plate number. Stian has written it on a piece of paper that's in front of us. It is now permanently engraved on my retina.

The footage is strangely gray and blurry, looks like it's from the 1980s. I am concentrating so hard that my body aches, my eyes are burning.

"At work, we have equipment to simplify this and make it more efficient," Stian says. "Here we have to use the old manual method. We probably won't find anything, remember that."

"Yes," I say, staring at the computer screen, trying not to blink, even though my eyes are stinging. I would so like to see that number and try to make it appear by force of will.

We look and look, in deep, silent concentration that does not yield results. Then a white car drives toward us with the license plate number EB 63970.

"Look!" I say.

We both stare, Stian zooms in. There's no doubt.

"Okay," I say. "That *must* mean something?"

"He may have just been here to circle in on you, in one way or another," Stian says. "But he *is* a journalist, which is the best lead we have now. He has been after you, he has driven through Oslo during the right timeframe, on the afternoon the boys disappeared from the area. Now all that's missing is to find him on camera somewhere with the boys, like we did with Sabiya."

I have to smile. There's a light in his eyes now that wasn't there before. I can tell that he likes that something is happening, in spite of everything. He likes the chase, the excitement. I used to be like that as well, last spring. Now I can't feel anything but this jagged, white, overwhelming fear, but I like seeing that light in his eyes. He is somebody who likes to win, to accomplish things, to fight battles. Now this is his battle, too.

Is that why he's agreed to help me, even hide the Sabiya business, put his entire career and maybe even his personal life at risk? Is he one of those lone wolves, someone who craves excitement, who misses action and danger? Is he hiding something, too, or is it just that he can't resist helping me because he's a good person?

So many questions. Even so, it makes me feel safer having him here. Maybe fear *is* only an illusion, the way all feelings are illusions.

"Okay," I say. "Let's assume that Haugo has taken them and that he lives on the west coast. Wouldn't it make sense for him to take them there?"

"Yes," Stian says. "Although I would like to get the results on the smartwatch tracking first. They could forget to notify me in the event of a response, especially if it doesn't appear to be an emergency. I'm going to give them a call."

Ten minutes later, he's back.

"Those watches are no longer transmitting. Whoever's behind this probably discovered that the boys had them and got rid of them or destroyed them."

"Shit," I say, feeling the disappointment well up inside me.

The boys loved those watches so much, were so proud of them.

"But listen," Stian continues. "The last time there was a signal from the watches, they were in your hometown, and that's where Halvor Haugo is. Go pack your bags. We're heading west."

CHAPTER 44

ANDREAS

Being here sucks. We can't do anything, and we don't even have our cell phones or tablets to play on.

When I say that the thing I miss most about Dad is soccer, I'm actually not thinking about shin guards and socks and cleats or that he used to come to practice whenever he could, to stand there and watch while he talked to the other parents, not missing a thing.

I'm not thinking about how he came to all the games, cheered for us and consoled us and held our water bottles and our uniforms and stepped in as trainer if Hans Marius was sick or something, that, afterward, he would always say something smart about what had or hadn't gone well.

No, what I miss most of all are the Liverpool games. The way we would look forward to them and talk about them all week, about who was in the starting lineup and where we were in the ranking, and who we would be playing and who was injured and who wasn't. The way we sat there and watched, Daddy always resting his elbows on his knees, with a cup of coffee or sometimes even a can of beer in his hands or holding me or Nikolai in the crook of his arm, sometimes both of us. That he teased and joked and thought it was so cool that we had actually grown more obsessed with our club than he was, because he noticed how we were the ones really paying attention, that we knew more about the players than he did, that we could tell him things. That was cool.

Daddy even said that we were almost big enough maybe to take a trip to Anfield and see a game there, the way he had promised us our whole lives but always said we were still too young. Now we wouldn't be going there, not with him anyway, and now the whole thing is pointless.

We don't watch Liverpool games anymore either. We barely manage to play *Soccer Manager*. Without having actually talked about it, in one way or another, we've agreed that we can't bear Liverpool without Dad. So now we've actually lost Liverpool, too.

CHAPTER 45

CLARA

I am already sick to my stomach by the time Stian pulls out onto the highway.

He drives steadily, with unassuming skill, fast but with control, without making a big deal about anything. He is perhaps the best driver I've ever met. It's not his fault that I hate being a passenger. I always get sick, no matter how good the driver is and how nice the cars are. Now it's even worse than usual, it feels almost unbearable to sit here in this hermetically sealed armored car.

"Sorry, do you mind if we open the window? I need some fresh air," I say.

He nods almost imperceptibly, lowers the window beside me a few inches. For ten seconds. Then he closes the window again, and instead turns up the air conditioning.

"Hungry?" he asks. "Thirsty?"

I shake my head.

The boys are probably in Western Norway, maybe even in some place I know well, not in the Congo, Uzbekistan, Romania, or somewhere else far away. Finally, we are on their trail. I must be pleased about that, I *am* pleased about that. But my thoughts keep grinding away all the same. Are they outdoors? Are they cold? Are they locked up somewhere, in a dark cellar, like in a movie? Are they together? The thought of them being split up, separated for the first time in their lives, is the worst. It's bad enough that they are cut off from me.

I don't understand, looking back, how I actually made it through all the hours I was doing things other than being with them. It seemed logical and natural at the time, but now it feels so wrong.

In a way, it's as if the closer I get to a solution, an answer, the more my anxiety grows. What awaits me, really? What if they've been hurt? Abused? After investing my professional life in preventing all these things from happening to other children, are they now happening to my own because I didn't take proper care of them?

And just like that, I'm back there again. The car flies off the cliff, hits the water with a bang. My head is thrown forward and then back. The water pours in. Everything starts over. Over and over again.

The suppressed nausea pushes up into my throat.

"Stian," I say. "Can you stop for a minute? I think I have to throw up."

We spend five minutes at a bus stop, five minutes during which I stand behind the shelter, staring at the ground covered with cigarette butts, broken glass, used condoms, a diaper, all of it illuminated by a streetlight, and vomiting up the contents of my stomach.

I've eaten very little, so not much comes up, just large quantities of coffee and bile. Even so, I can't stop heaving. After a while, Stian comes over, puts his arm around me and straightens me up, gives me a bottle of water from the car and some paper napkins.

"Come on," he says, putting his arm around me, leading me away from the bus stop.

Ten minutes later, we stop at a roadside diner reeking of fried food that I have always driven straight past without a moment's hesitation.

"Good God, we don't have time for this," I say.

"Sure we do," Stian says. "We can't get anything accomplished there in the middle of the night anyway. And you probably haven't eaten today, have you?"

"No," I say.

As late as it was, I called Vigdis a little while ago. I told her I still had a stomach virus and to cancel or postpone all my meetings for the time being.

Tomorrow, I will have to call Mona and tell her something or other about a family emergency in Western Norway. I had packed in ten minutes. Twenty minutes after we made the decision to go, we were on the road.

I haven't eaten, not once in the entire long day, during which I somehow had time to spend messing around down in the sausage factory on Fredensborgveien Street.

"Exactly," he says. "That's what I thought. And what little you did have in your stomach you've just disposed of. You need some nourishment, and I need you fit for a fight. Come on."

Inside, we stand in front of a counter filled with open sandwiches made with sweaty cheese or pale ham and pieces of marzipan cake and almond meringue sponge and apple cake. None of it looks appetizing to me. We look up at the board of pale birch on which a white sign with black letters lists the hot dishes. Swiss steak with french fries and béarnaise sauce. Meatballs with mashed peas, potatoes, and cowberry sauce. Local salmon with cucumber salad. Cheeseburger with french fries. Sliced reindeer meat. Sausages with mashed potatoes.

I don't feel like eating anything at all. I just want to keep driving. I always want that, but now even more than usual.

"Yes?" the woman behind the counter asks, looking at me wearily.

"Sausages with mashed potatoes."

"That's on the children's menu," she says, releasing a world-weary sigh. Trine Lise is her name, according to the name tag on her chest.

"What?" I ask.

Stian lays one hand on my shoulder.

"Sausages with mashed potatoes is on the children's menu, just for children."

Her hair is long and greasy. The three rolls of her stomach can be seen beneath her T-shirt, where the name of the café is written in big letters. On her chest are a couple of disgusting stains.

"Honestly," I say, "what possible difference can it make how old I am as long as I pay for it? I can pay twice the price . . ."

"It's not about *that*," she says, shifting her weight from one foot to the other.

What is it that makes people allow themselves to go to seed like this? If I looked like her, I wouldn't want to live any longer.

"What *is* it about, then?" I ask.

"Those are just the rules," Trine Lise says.

I am about to argue but can't be bothered. "Okay. Salmon," I say, turning toward Stian.

"Salmon?" he says with surprise. "At eleven o'clock in the evening?"

"Yup," I say. "Can you get this? I need to use the restroom."

He nods and I leave. Inside the ladies' room, I stop in front of the sink. There is only cold water in the faucet. Cold water and an air freshener on the mirror. I splash water on my face for a long time.

Halvor Haugo. Who is he? What does he want with me?

"The meatballs here are never a disappointment at least," Stian says when we have sat down in a corner. I sit with my back to the wall. That way I cover my back and have a view of the premises, the way Dad taught me.

The salmon that is placed in front of me five minutes later is dry and almost cold and covered with a white film. The potatoes are greenish.

"This is impressive," I say after two bites.

He chuckles.

"It resembles something I could have made, and that's no compliment," I say. "Do you like to cook?"

"Yes, actually. I considered going to culinary school in high school."

Perhaps the five minutes behind the shelter at the bus stop, the water on my face, and the food in my belly has better equipped me to function, because when Stian says the words *high school*, I suddenly know who Halvor Haugo is.

Halvor Haugo is a fat tub of lard a year or two younger than me. He used to try to approach me in high school, apparently thought the two of us had something or other in common. What that might be, I never knew, other than the fact that neither of us had any friends to speak of. For my part, it was by choice, and anyway, that was a poor basis for a friendship.

When we leave the diner, I feel lighter and happier than I've felt since I came home on Friday. We are headed west, we have a lead, and I know who Halvor Haugo is.

Maybe it is the darkness surrounding us as we drive west, the jazz music from Stian's Spotify coming out of the speakers, or maybe I am overtired. Something or other helps me to say it.

"You didn't become a chef," I say, and take a bold chance. "What was it you did in Afghanistan?"

"Special operations commando," he says after a few seconds of silence. "I guess I can reveal that to the minister of justice?"

Of course. SOC. I should have known.

"I did some things there that were a little unorthodox, you could say . . ."

"Like what?" I ask. "I need the distraction."

I try to brace myself, remembering Dad's stories from Lebanon. They were always dark, always involved fatalities.

"Well," he says. "In 2010, or around then, we were on assignment in the eastern part of the country in the Kunar Province. A hairy place, you could say. We were on our way back to the forward operating base, after having finished a tough mission involving the capture of a Taliban leader, but we were short on time, and the security was sketchy, to put it mildly. Suddenly, a boy around your sons' age, maybe a year or two older, came running toward us. In Afghanistan, you can never be sure who's friend or foe, but there was something about his face; it seemed so open and sincere. Of course, we didn't understand a thing he said, but the interpreter told us that his mother was giving birth and they believed that something was wrong. Everyone understood that this could be a trap and that helping him would at any rate be in clear violation of all the regulations, but all the same, we decided to follow him to his house, which turned out to be an impoverished brown Afghan house made of clay. In the doorway, a group of gesticulating, burka-clad women waved us in. They didn't want us to see the woman who was giving birth because we were men, which led me to believe that it wasn't a trap . . ."

He paused for a moment, took a sip of coffee from the paper cup in the holder between the seats. I waited for him to continue. Had it been a trap?

"I said that they had to let us in, that both the woman and the newborn could die if they didn't receive help. The interpreter translated. Finally, they let us enter an unfurnished, dark room where the woman in labor was lying on a carpet on the floor. On their knees beside her sat two old women. The woman in labor wailed and moaned, around her lay blood-soaked rags and garments. All the SOC units have a medic with advanced medical training, often at about the level of a nurse, but childbirth was not exactly one of their areas of expertise . . . On the other hand, we were experts in the art of improvisation. I remembered that Janne's mother, who lives in Toten, is a midwife. She's a great woman, has seen just about everything, and is not easily flustered. I connected with her on Skype."

"On Skype?" I say with surprise.

What kind of tall tale is he telling me?

"Yes, of course, we had a satellite phone with us. So my mother-in-law, who has given birth to four children herself, spoke calmly and firmly in Norwegian through the screen to the Afghan woman."

Now I see that he is far away in this memory.

"The woman pushed, but it did little good. It seemed like she was screaming more than she was pushing and wasting a lot of energy on it. My mother-in-law instructed her to change positions, first onto her back, then her side, on all fours, and back on her back. She asked me to look and see if there was a stethoscope. I found one in our medic's bag and used it to listen to the baby's heart. It said thump, thump, thump, the way it should, but apparently it was beating more slowly than Eva was comfortable with. We were told to lay the woman on her back and that each of us should hold one of her feet, so she could kick against us. Her chin had to be all the way down against her chest, and I had to instruct the woman on how to fill her lungs with air and push."

"Goodness," I say.

"Yeah, it was surreal. The interpreter had his work cut out for him. There we stood, each of us holding a foot against our sides. She could have easily broken a rib or two, but it was worth the risk. The woman pushed and screamed, suddenly, water gushed into my face, it tasted sweet, and I understood that it had to be amniotic fluid. We listened again; the heartbeat was now even slower, thump, thump. 'Push,' I said. 'Push.' And she pushed, breathed, and screamed. The head descended a little more each time, she had cracked the code now and managed to push without screaming. Slowly, the head emerged between her legs. We got worried, it appeared to be a big baby. But then . . ."

He stops, his eyes shiny.

"Yes?" I say. Now I am also completely engrossed in his story.

"It all just sort of stopped. She started screaming again, even louder than before. Eva said we had to turn her over, so she was on all fours, and we did. 'Tell her to sway her behind back and forth,' Eva said. The interpreter translated, she swayed. And suddenly, the child was there! It was incredible."

"Wow," I say, his enthusiasm making me smile.

"It was a sweet, big boy, with soft black hair, pale skin, but limp and weak. He just emitted soft whimpers. Eva told us to hold him upside down and give him a slap on his behind. When I did, the entire room was filled with his screams. Since then, I've attended the births of my own children, but this was the first. I felt important in a wholly different way than when mine were born. It was fantastic, Clara."

"How nice," I say, and have to swallow.

"Yes," he says, taking out his wallet. "There's a photo of him in there."

I shine the light from my phone on it. The wallet has one of those old-fashioned transparent plastic pockets for photographs.

On the left is a photo of a blond and blue-eyed trio, who must be Stian's children. To the right, I see a younger Stian. His face is smoother than it is now and bears the world's largest and proudest grin, as if he were holding his own son in his arms.

"You have to do what's right, also when what's right is not necessarily legal. Do you understand what I mean?"

"Yes," I say. "I do."

CHAPTER 46

CLARA

Although there are no lights on in the windows, I walk up to the front door and ring the doorbell. Once. Twice. Inside, the sound of the bell resonates angrily. A third ring. A white electric car is parked in the driveway next to the somewhat neglected garden.

It is only 7:00 a.m. He cannot have left for work yet.

Finally, the light goes on in the hallway, and a figure can be seen behind the frosted yellow glass window, typical of the 1970s, in the front door.

Then he is standing in the doorway, a guy wearing plaid pajama pants and a dirty grayish T-shirt, with tousled hair and slitted eyes. I would never have recognized him, that's how much he's changed. Older, of course, but to my surprise, no longer fat. On the contrary, he looks strong and fit. On his chin is one of those silly goatees that I've never liked, on his forearms some huge tattoos.

I read a few of his articles in the car on the way over here. He writes well enough, especially considering he works for a local paper.

Now I've decided to be smart, behave as if I don't suspect him of anything, at least to begin with.

If it *is* true that this guy has my children, I mustn't frighten him, mustn't make him do something stupid, just trick him into giving himself away.

"Sorry to disturb you," I say, and hold out my hand. "Clara Lofthus."

"I know who you are," he says. His handshake is amazingly forceful. "I've been trying to get a word with you since you were appointed minister."

"So I understand," I say. "Can I come in for a bit?"

"Now?" he says, surprised.

I nod. He lets me into the hallway, the walls of which are covered in yellowed pine. All the rooms behind him appear to be the same.

"Just let me change," he says. He disappears and comes back a few minutes later wearing jeans and a wool sweater. I am shown into an overfurnished living room, where I take a seat on one of the leather chairs there. He sits on one of the others.

"You live here with your mother now?" I say, even though I know better, from the research I did on the way here.

He shakes his head.

"She's dead," he says. "But let's talk about you. I was recently at Storagjelet to watch the recovery of that old wrecked car, you know."

"What?" I say sharply.

Storagjelet? Wrecked car? What is this all about?

"So you didn't know they dredged Magne's car out of the fjord?"

I shake my head. I should say something but can't manage it.

"Yeah, it was more than a month ago. But the reason I've been trying to reach you, in addition to the fact that you've been appointed minister of justice, is that I would like to hear your version of what happened back then."

"What happened?" I say.

"Yes, when the car landed in the fjord."

Fucking hell. I hadn't heard anything about any dredging and am not prepared to talk or think about that now. "It was an accident. Magne died, I survived." Either way, it has no relevance now.

"Yeah, you're the kind who survives, aren't you?" he says. His gaze is hard, it's like staring into the eyes of a predator. The polite tone is gone.

"Is this how you interview people?" I ask, my voice as sharp as his. We sit there staring at each other, and then I understand.

I'm perhaps not adept at remembering faces, but now I see a face emerging from Halvor's that I remember only too well, and with the same clarity as when I can see my mother in the reflection of my own face in the mirror late at night.

A large mole beside his nose. A mole with a black hair in it, an identical mole, in the exact same place. There's no way that can be a coincidence. And now I see everything else. The close-set eyes. The jaw. Everything that is the same.

Halvor Haugo is Magne Lia's son. What does that mean? Is that why he has taken the boys?

Until yesterday, I believed it was Sabiya who wanted revenge. Maybe I suspected the wrong person but the right motive?

"Had I known you were planning to kill him, I would have done something," he interrupts me. "But I was a child, and you were a child. I didn't understand what I saw, much less what you did."

"Wait," I say, my armpits suddenly slick with sweat. "Are you saying that *I* supposedly killed Magne?"

"Of course," he says.

"Good God," I scoff. "We were going to visit my mother at the hospital. I was twelve years old, and he was driving drunk. I barely managed to survive. How can you claim that it was my fault?"

I am there again now, the car flying over the cliff, the car hitting the water, the water pouring in. And I am swimming and swimming, can feel the fear that he will grab my feet, pull me down with him, the way he pulled my brother under.

"Thank you very much," Halvor says. "I remember your official explanation."

"That man was rotten to the core," I say.

I am about to ask about my boys, whether this is the reason he has kidnapped somebody else's children. But before I get that far, before I realize what is happening, he stands up.

"How can you talk like that?"

"I knew the man much better than you did," I say. "He was a bastard, a psychopath who battered a defenseless little boy to death."

"That's not true," he says, standing there trembling.

Maybe it's just as well if he gets angry. If he loses control, it might be easier to find out something about the boys.

"What a shame you're related to him," I say. "You should at least refrain from having children of your own. Speaking of children . . ."

Before I can finish the sentence, he takes three steps toward me and punches me hard in the jaw. I don't see it coming, and it hurts so much that I see stars.

"What the hell," I hiss through clenched teeth, frightened and angry at the same time.

He raises his arm as if to hit me again, and I back away. At that moment, the front door opens.

Stian walks in, crossing the room in a few long strides. It happens so fast and I have been knocked so senseless that I don't actually see what he's doing, until Halvor Haugo is lying on his wall-to-wall carpeting.

"There," Stian says, with a coldness in his voice that I've never heard before. "You'll do time for this. Attacking a cabinet minister is considered a felony, section 115 of the penal code."

I walk over to the window as if by instinct and close the curtains. Now it won't be possible to see inside.

Stian leans forward, putting more weight on the knee he is resting on Halvor's chest.

"Neither the minister of justice nor I have the time or patience for more foolishness from you," he says. "I can have you locked up, here and now, and you will be in more trouble than you can even imagine. Or we can make a deal if you like."

Halvor stares at him, his eyes full of both fear and hatred. Stian moves his knee to Halvor's throat and applies pressure.

"What do you want?" Halvor croaks.

"My sons are missing," I say. "I want them back. Now. Understand?"

No response. A glimmer of doubt flickers inside me. Haugo is a pompous, bitter ass and Magne's son, but does he have my children?

"Tell me where they are, or I'll kill you with my own hands," I say. Now it's Stian's turn to clear his throat beside me.

"I don't know," Halvor croaks.

"You don't know?" I say. "You don't know?"

"We have compelling evidence that you are lying," Stian says. "You've been in Oslo recently, haven't you?"

He nods.

"You've been in the area where the children disappeared, when they disappeared. We know that you contacted them. Their smartwatches have been traced to this village. In other words, it doesn't look good for you."

"I don't know where they are, I swear," Halvor says. "But Clara can talk to her mother."

"My mother?" I say, all the blood draining out of my head. "What do you mean?"

"Yeah, Agnes Lofthus. Isn't she your mother?"

I nod, feeling completely stiff and paralyzed.

"She's . . . in the hospital," I say, my voice thin.

"Not anymore," he says, and seems childishly pleased to be able to tell me this, despite how frightened he clearly is.

Agnes. Out in the world? An unbearable thought.

"Where is she now?" Stian says.

"In a boathouse by the fjord," Halvor mumbles. "Buzz's place."

"Fine," Stian says.

Halvor Haugo remains lying on the floor as we leave.

"So," Stian says when we are back in the car. "Walking in there alone was perhaps not such a smart move?"

"No," I say. "How did you know I needed help?"

I expected him to say that, by chance, he looked up toward the house and saw what was happening and then ran up.

"I listened via your telephone," he says instead, smiling slyly.

"What?" I say, surprised. "Is that legal?"

"You received a personal data request to approve such measures," he says. "When a cabinet minister signs, it's not a problem."

"Did I sign it?" I ask.

"Presumably," Stian says, still smiling.

It makes no difference that he's heard me now, but does that mean there are other PSS people listening to me?

"How much did you hear?" I ask.

He hesitates for a second or two before answering.

"Enough to understand I was needed in there."

"Did you hear what he said about Magne? Apparently, he thinks it's my fault . . ."

"A psychopath, like his father," Stian says, and that is the least politically correct thing I've ever heard him say. On the way to the car, I told him what I'd discovered about Halvor's parentage.

Now I'm glad that I mentioned Magne to him earlier, gave him my version of the story.

"Actually, I feel sorry for him," Stian says. "He can't process the twice-over grief of having lost a father he never had . . . No wonder he's completely obsessed with you. Halvor could have been your step-brother, but you rejected him. And as if that weren't enough, he is convinced that you killed his father . . ."

"More than enough motive to come after me and the boys, you mean?" I ask, rubbing my sore jaw, which is burning, stinging, and throbbing. "Besides, he's bitter and horrible. Maybe it *is* him? Maybe he's just trying to deflect the attention over to my mother."

He shrugs. "It's not possible to say anything for certain just yet."

"Either way, we have to find Agnes," I say. "Can you call and ask if they have two rooms for us at the bed and breakfast in the center of town?"

"Yes," he says, wrinkling his brow. "But I thought you were planning to surprise your father first thing this morning?"

"We'll save time staying down here in the village, not having to drive up and down."

That's true, of course, but I also can't bring myself to sit there and lie to Dad, pretend that nothing is wrong. Besides, there's so much that I should have known about that he has kept from me. I am sure he knows that my mother is out in the world, and that the wrecked car is out of the fjord. News travels fast in this town. What has happened to us? Why doesn't he tell me anything anymore?

CHAPTER 47

HALVOR

I see their car drive away and rub my aching shoulder. Knocked onto the ground before breakfast in my own home.

What should I do? What is going to happen to me?

For thirty years, I've been thinking about Clara, but the last twenty-five of those, I haven't seen her, except in pictures. Then suddenly, she's standing on my doorstep before I've even gotten up, wearing jeans and a dark-blue jacket with a hood, looking just like she did in the old days.

That driver of hers was clearly no ordinary driver. He pressed his knee against my throat until I thought my final hour had come. His movements were strong and confident, that man knew what he was doing. Yes, I could report him to the police, but that would be stupid of me. In return, they would definitely report me for attacking the minister of justice. It's true, what he said about the maximum penalty. I would not have a good case. Nobody would believe me or stand by me, just like that time thirty years ago.

I was eleven years old, standing at the edge of the forest behind some ferns as tall as I was, watching Magne's yard. I had been there several times before, sneaking around outside the house, trying to build up the nerve to knock on the door and introduce myself.

"Hi, Dad," I would say, and then his face would break into a big smile.

He didn't know that I knew about him, but he knew about me and who I was. I understood that when I was going through my mother's papers and found the letter she'd hidden, where he confirmed that he could be my father.

On that day, I had already been standing behind the ferns for a long time, putting it off, waiting, and was just about to walk up and knock on the door, but I changed my mind again.

Then I saw her: Clara Lofthus.

She was one year older than me, old enough that we had never spoken, even though we went to the same school. Of course, I still knew who she was. Our school was so small that everybody knew everybody else. I knew her parents were separated, that her brother was dead, and that her mother was together with Magne, the teacher, who was my father.

Now I watched Clara open the door of his car, and it was as if my feet had been sucked down into the mossy ground beneath me. I stood there, watching, trying to understand as Clara filed away at something on the inside of the door of Magne's car. She kept at it for a long time. Finally, apparently finished, she left.

I wondered whether I should go in and say something to Magne, but I didn't dare. It would be too much if I told him both that *and* that I knew he was my father. What if he thought I had something to do with whatever she was up to? What if he didn't believe me when I said it was Clara? What if everything I had planned was ruined?

I didn't do anything, just slunk home again to the housing development where we lived, with a plan to go back soon. That never happened.

Just a few days later, Magne was dead. I understood that there had to be a connection between what I had seen Clara do and the accident but had no idea what I should do about it.

Magne's body was gone. The car had sunk to such depths in the fjord that it wasn't possible to recover it. I lay in my room at home, staring at the ceiling and wondering whether I should say something to my mother, but I knew that she would get angry with me for having gone through her things and for reading the letter and because I had gone up to his place and spied on them. Besides, she wouldn't know what to do about it either.

Should I talk to the police? Could I? No. They wouldn't believe me, maybe they would even believe I'd had something to do with it. That was my biggest fear. I couldn't even show them the window crank since the car was at the bottom of the fjord.

For thirty years, I didn't know what to do about it.

In high school, I had tried several times to befriend Clara. I hoped that if we became friends, I would find some way or other to prove her guilt. Soon I understood that she wasn't interested in having anything to do with me, had nothing but contempt for me.

Ever since then, for years and years, I've pondered how I could get revenge. Then all this happened. Henrik's death, the car being dredged up, Clara becoming a cabinet minister, the window crank. Then I knew that my moment had arrived. It was logical, to avenge my father, blow the whistle on Clara and punish her, and, on top of it, deliver a career-making scoop to the newspaper.

After a few days, I realized it wasn't enough. It wasn't sufficient revenge, not really.

Had my father not died just when I was supposed to get to know him, my life would have been completely different. Maybe I would have friends, wouldn't have been shoved around the schoolyard, bullied, and mocked, and Yvonne wouldn't have taken Lisa with her to the end of the fucking earth.

No scoop in the world can make up for everything I've lost.

It serves Clara right that her children are missing, even though she still has her father. That old goat up there on the farm irritates me, not just because it seems impossible to get him to talk to me. That he is still alive only drives home the fact that my own father, whom I never had the chance to know, is gone.

His farm has been abandoned for thirty years. Up there, I do find a kind of peace; no matter how much it hurts that he's not there and the place isn't mine, I feel nonetheless closer to everything I've lost.

It's dark, cold, and gloomy there. I've never lived there, never been in the house with my father. All the same, I feel more at home there, in his chair, than in this house where I've lived every day of my life.

I am stiff and sore and beaten black and blue. My throat is throbbing and pounding where that damned driver guy pressed his knee against it, but I collect a few things, throw them into a bag, and walk to my car.

First, I have to go to work for a few hours, but this afternoon, I'm going up there, to my place. I can hardly wait.

CHAPTER 48

CLARA

We are the only guests at the bed and breakfast. Now I'm sitting on the bed and waiting for it to be 8:30. That was what we agreed, Stian and I. Drop off our things, change, brush our teeth. Then head out again, even though neither of us have slept.

A ringtone sounds from the depths of my bag. In theory, it could be any of my three telephones. I still haven't got their ringtones down, but it turns out to be the encrypted number. The prime minister's office. I answer it, am told to enter a code, try to do it, am interrupted, become flustered and agitated.

What does the prime minister's office want? Now? I become frustrated with this procedure that I can't get right, don't have time for, but after a few failed attempts, finally a voice speaks to me.

"Hi, Clara," she says in a clipped tone.

It takes me a second or two to figure out whom I am speaking to; it is the prime minister herself. The last time I spoke with her was at that embarrassing cabinet meeting.

"Is this a bad time?" she asks.

"Well," I stammer, trying to think.

I have not called Mona yet to request a leave of absence. She must have tried to cover for me.

"I wondered if you would take a walk around Lake Sognsvann with me later today," she says. "There's some internal party business I want to discuss with you in person."

"Yes, I would be happy to," I say.

"Great," she says.

I curse inwardly. "But unfortunately, I can't today. I'm in Western Norway. I have a family emergency."

"Ah, I see," she says. "Well, we'll have to take a rain check, then."

"It's not something you can talk about over the phone?"

"No," she says, a sharpness entering her voice. "But since I have you on the line . . . We're in the final stretch of the fiscal budget process. Finance didn't accept your proposal for more resources for emergency preparedness. I am in doubt myself. We have a greater need for visible, political initiatives than the kind of preventive measure you've proposed. And since you're so busy, we'll let Finance get what they want this time around."

"But," I begin, before she interrupts me.

"We'll talk, Clara. Good luck with . . . whatever it is you're up to out there."

Then she's gone.

"Fuck," I say, striking the phone against my thigh. "Fuck, fuck, fuck."

I have made a fool of myself again, in a new way this time. A burning and stinging sensation invades my cheeks, my throat, behind my eyelids.

The last month, I have had a constant taste of blood in my mouth, I have neglected the boys, ignored Dad, all of it in an attempt to get off on the right foot, prove myself worthy of the trust placed in me, make the most of my time, get something accomplished.

Then Friday came and everything changed.

213

Yesterday, I went to the office, briefly, before and after my meeting with Sabiya in the underworld. Otherwise, here I am on Tuesday, and for four days, I have tried to suppress everything work related, all the things I'm usually passionate about, the things I live and breathe for. I have no choice, I have to save my children. Now I feel it anyway, like a whip burn on my skin, that I actually want to save this, too.

A walk around Lake Sognsvann. Can I use that in some way? I would have liked to have had some one-on-one time with her; it's not an offer one receives every day. This business with the party is something I need to deal with, work my way into. Besides, I must prepare her for the fact that I want to submit my bill again.

The worst part is still that the Ministry of Finance is tripping up my emergency preparedness proposals. The field is already underfunded because there is so little pomp and circumstance associated with it. Nobody has ever made emergency preparedness a priority. My proposal was more modest than it should have been, and now it has been squashed. I should have been there, arguing, fighting. I can't get anything done from here.

I would so have liked to have confided in her, gotten her to understand that I truly care, want to accomplish something, am willing to sacrifice virtually everything for my position, that I just have to save my sons first, that she just needs to give me a little time. When the children are home again, I will have to call her and explain why, despite being a newly appointed cabinet minister, I suddenly ran off to Western Norway.

I just have to find the boys first. And to find them, I must find Agnes.

My mother, my own flesh and blood. Is she the one I've been searching for all along? Or is this another dead end?

I've been so certain, first that it was Sabiya, then Halvor.

Now all my certainty is gone, along with my determination. The mere thought that my mother could have something to do with this makes me feel powerless.

We still haven't heard from the kidnappers. Almost four days have passed without so much as a word.

What does it mean? What do they want? Are the boys alive?

"There are two places we have to go," Stian says once we are back in the car. "The boathouse where your mother lives, at his place . . . Buzz? And then the farm where she was living before she was committed."

"Yes to the first," I say. "The second, you can forget about. I'm not going up there, no matter what. Really."

"Clara," he says. "I understand that you have bad memories there . . ."

"It's not about *that*," I say.

"That's what that lady at the diner said yesterday, too," he says with a smile. "So I'll say what you said: What *is* it about, then?"

"Go to hell," I say, but I can't help smiling.

"We can start with the boathouse," he says. "That is, after all, where she lives."

Ten minutes later, he is easing the car down the short hill leading to the boathouse. It's a kind of dollhouse, close to the water. He turns the car around while I run to the door and pound on it.

Nothing.

A pair of rubber boots sit outside the house. Some gloves are lying on top of them. I shudder and grasp the door handle. Locked. Then I walk around to the other side, knock on the window of what appears to be the kitchen. Nothing. It's dark in there, too. How naive of me to think that she would be sitting here with my boys, waiting for me. I circle the little house a few more times, peeking in the windows. There's no sign of life, but on the table inside, I can see a dosette box.

Medication. Kleivhøgda. The psychiatric hospital. Committed.

Of course, I have to go where she spent the better part of her adult life, talk with some of the people who know her there, like the busybody I met there last spring. What was her name again? Berit? Brita? She kept calling me for a period of time afterward. She even sent me flowers when I was appointed state secretary. I just ignored all of it.

"Ready for a trip to the farm?" Stian asks when I get back into the car.

"Not yet," I say. "First, to Kleivhøgda. I'll give you directions."

CHAPTER 49

ANDREAS

Now that we're here and have nobody to talk to and no school and no soccer practice and no games and no appointments, I have way too much time to think about all the things I miss.

There's a lot that has nothing to do with soccer.

I liked that Daddy was always the same, that I didn't have to figure out what kind of mood he was in. Daddy was always cheerful and lighthearted, like a nice summer day. Mommy tries to be summer but is winter.

I liked that he explained my math homework in a way that I understood, and that Nikolai understood, which got him to do it without crying.

I liked that he managed to make dinner as soon as we got home, without starting to do all kinds of other things first, that almost everything he made was good and that he made so much that we could take the leftovers to school in our lunch boxes the next day.

I liked the way he tickled us.

I liked the music he played full blast in the car.

I liked the way he drummed his fingers against the steering wheel.

CHAPTER 50

CLARA

"An hour and a half, according to my GPS. Is that right?"

"Yes, something like that," I say. "If we coincide with the ferry."

We drive along the fjord from the center of the village, in the opposite direction of our farm. I have always been glad that Kleivhøgda was located in another town, some nineteen miles and a ferry trip away, so there was no risk of running into Agnes when I went out for a walk.

That was before. Now she's out wandering around, without any health-care supervision. But where is she?

Neither of us says anything. Stian looks like he's concentrating on his driving. The roads here are different from what he is used to. Here and there, the road widens, but for the most part, it is narrow, with room for just one car at a time. A rock face on one side, the fjord on the other.

On the ferry, I stand by the railing and stare down into the white, churning fjord, as I always do. I like the thought that it can be one or two or three hundred yards deep, that we can't know what's down there, that there could be anything. The fjord is deep, inscrutable, unwieldy, his own master: he is invincible. The fjord is the most powerful and the most dangerous, but the fjord took care of Magne for me, and that has always made me feel that we are sort of allies.

I look up, gaze across at the mountain on the other side. At this time of year, there is often a light powdering of snow on the mountaintops.

Not now. Today, the mountain is dark, bluish black, with small specks of gold here and there.

The parking lot at the psychiatric hospital is almost empty.

The last time I was here, it was spring, one of those clear days with a lustrous blue sky. I stayed in the car for a long time, didn't want to go inside, didn't really want to see her, to remove the distance between us, which helped me believe that she didn't exist.

Visiting her made me feel like I was resuscitating her, but I didn't have any choice. Dad heard that she was talking again after many years of silence. It worried both of us. At that time, primal instincts started stirring inside me, and I did things I never imagined I would have to do again. I needed to know if she was a potential threat, how much she remembered, how lucid she was. So I mustered up my courage and went to see her.

It was a strange experience.

At first, I was surprised to see that she wasn't overweight and scruffy, an obese blob with food stains on her clothes, the kind of white-trash creature I imagined. On the contrary, she turned out to be the same slim woman with long hair, dressed in clothes that were either the same garments she wore thirty years ago or an almost-identical set.

She looked like a slightly paler, slightly older version of her former self.

At first, she spoke normally. In other words, she seemed astonishingly lucid. When I tried to say that it had been a long time, she commented that it had been thirty years, two weeks, and three days. She asked how old the twins were, said that now they must be around eight years old. That scared me, I hoped that she didn't even know they existed.

She remembered everything, she said, with a dazzling and terrifying smile.

Then she changed completely. All of a sudden, she was transformed, reverting back to the person I understood her to have been all these years: remote, lost.

I was relieved. Despite how upsetting it was to see her again, to hear her speak of my children as if she knew them, I came to the conclusion that she was, first and foremost, a kind of vegetable. A person destroyed by too many years filled with a potent cocktail of mental disorders, powerful medications, electric shock treatments, and isolation.

Just a few months later, she was discharged.

It was incomprehensible. Have the people at the psychiatric hospital lost their minds? They seemed so responsible, at least based on what little contact I had with them. Did she manage to fool them? Or did she simply make a dramatic recovery?

That spring day was one of the bluest of blues and greenest of greens, the way spring days can be only in this place at that time of year. Apple blossoms, dandelions, green hillsides, bleating lambs, and white mountaintops.

At this time of year, on the other hand, it is dark, wet, and raw. Despite the never-ending grayness, I have several times in the past twenty-four hours thought that we should move here, the boys and I. When this is over, we must move here. We must take care of Dad and the farm, protect them from everything evil and especially from my mother.

In the reception area is a young girl with long bleached-blonde hair. Her skin is covered with an excessively thick coat of foundation. It makes me want to scrape my nails down her cheek.

"I'm Clara Lofthus, Agnes Lofthus's daughter," I say. "My mother was discharged from here a few weeks ago . . ."

"Yes?" she says, winding a lock of hair around her finger.

"I need to talk to someone who knew her. Bodil, is she here?"

The girl's face brightens at the chance to dump the situation in someone else's lap. "Bodil Solvang," she says. "Yes, she has a shift now, I think. Wait a minute."

She picks up the phone, makes contact after a few seconds.

"Bodil, there's somebody here who wants to talk to you. Your name . . . ?"

"Clara Lofthus," I say, with demonstrative slowness and clarity.

The girl repeats my name.

"She's coming," she says after hanging up, and nods in the direction of a couch and a coffee table with magazines spread across it. "You can wait there."

"Thanks," I say, and take a seat, staring at the aquarium in the corner.

A pair of fish are swimming around. They have plenty of room. Maybe I should have given the boys an aquarium instead of hamsters.

Dammit. The hamsters.

I realize suddenly that I didn't give them any extra food, and neither did I arrange for somebody to feed them. They won't survive without food until I get home, and the boys will never forgive me. I'll have to send Axel a message later, ask him to go over to the house before I forget. He will take care of it, probably just be happy that I asked.

I try to unearth an image of this Bodil from the last time I saw her. The woman was big and sturdy, tanning-salon dark, with black hair, earrings. Extremely enthusiastic about our family reunion. Effusive. Curious.

The woman who now appears looks exactly like the woman of that clear blue spring day. Less tan, perhaps, otherwise pretty much the same. Her behavior, on the other hand, is quite different, as if she has been turned inside out, now showing her less agreeable side.

She can barely bring herself to accept my outstretched hand and manages to produce a forced smile.

"Well now," she says in a caustic tone of voice. "What do we have here? The cabinet minister in person. Your mother isn't here, if that's who you're looking for."

"I'm aware of that," I say as calmly as I can manage.

This woman is the best bridge to my mother I have. I must try to get her on my side.

"Thank you for taking the time to see me, by the way," I say.

"I usually make time for next of kin," she says coolly. "Including for those who are no longer my patients."

"How long has it been since she left?"

"Six weeks," Bodil says.

"Well, now she's missing," I say.

"Missing?" Bodil says, suddenly sounding afraid.

"Yes, I met her yesterday," I say. "We had a chat. She invited me down to her place today, and when I got there, it was locked up."

"She must have changed her mind, then," Bodil says with a shrug. "Maybe because of how you've been treating her all this time."

"What do you mean?" I say, my jaw tensing.

"That you've neglected and ignored her, even though we've tried to reach you, over and over again?"

I vowed not to get angry or let her get to me, but I'm already struggling.

"It's possible you know my mother well, but what do you really know about what she did to us?" I reply. "My brother hadn't even started school when—"

"It wasn't her fault that Lars died," Bodil says. "I don't think *you* know a thing about it, about what she's been through. Thirty years here, can you imagine? Maybe it looks like this is a nice place now, it *is* nice here now, but it hasn't always been this way. Your mother was grief stricken. Then she was hidden away, no visitors, no contact with her family. Maybe it's not so strange that after that she hasn't been well?"

"She has never really been well," I scoff.

"Well, you know what," Bodil says angrily. "Her first years here were horrible. Anyone would have been affected by what happened to her. If I hadn't come along and taken pity on her, God only knows how things would have turned out."

Ah, I see now. A savior story with herself in the starring role.

"Do you know of any other places she's fond of, where she might go?"

"Good God," Bodil says with a snort. "Agnes has been here for thirty years. She hasn't been on expeditions or camping trips or shopping excursions. She's just been here, with me."

She crosses her arms. Fleshy upper arms like hers are the ugliest thing I know. Her heavily drawn eyebrows are too close together. She hasn't bothered to address her facial hair. Her fake-tan skin has large pores. Now she exhales, a gurgling sound, the result of many cigarettes smoked over the course of many years.

"I wish I knew something," she says. "Your mother was my responsibility for a long time. I don't like it that she's out there all by herself without me, but it's been weeks since I've been able to reach her."

I sigh. This is a waste of time.

"One thing you should know," Bodil says, not as aggressively now, more resigned. "Agnes always longed for the life she had with Leif and you children . . . And she always talked a lot about the farm and the mountain. She was in her element there."

I stare at her for a few seconds, without actually seeing her, before I turn on my heel and almost break into a run, shouting a kind of thanks over my shoulder on my way out the door.

CHAPTER 51

ANDREAS

I liked that he always put down his phone when I went to his side.

I liked that he went on the roller coaster with us again and again and again.

I liked how he wrapped us up in towels after we showered, the way he tucked the duvet in around us when we went to bed, the way he kissed us and told us he loved us, even though we said we thought it was stupid.

I even liked how happy he looked when he went out to watch soccer and drink beer with Axel, and his stinky breath when he woke us up the next morning.

One thing that's awful to think about now is that I actually liked that he wasn't as good a swimmer as Mommy and wasn't embarrassed about it. He was a good swimmer, too, but she's really good, and I thought that was cool.

That part in particular has become completely impossible to think about right now because then it's like everything inside me deflates. And now, when we're here, all the sadness comes even closer.

CHAPTER 52

CLARA

"Clara," Stian says, in a quite insistent tone of voice when I have relayed my conversation with Bodil. "I know you don't feel like going up to your stepfather's farm. But if your mother has your children and needs to hide them somewhere, the farm is an obvious choice. It would be irresponsible of us not to check it out. It won't take long either, compared to this expedition to Kleivhøgda."

"Fine," I say as I pull out my phone and text a quick message to Axel, asking if he can feed the hamsters. Best to do it before I forget again.

As we drive up the steep hills where the car is constantly at risk of getting stuck in the almost overgrown dirt road, I start shaking uncontrollably. I never thought I would come back here.

Stian glances over at me but fortunately doesn't say anything. It's only when we drive into the yard and I have to close my eyes that he speaks.

"A medieval farm?" he says, staring at the dark building in disbelief.

"A *fake* medieval farm," I say, sighing. "Magne was hung up on things like that. He bought old houses and had them moved here. But listen, I have to go inside alone, I need to do this by myself. I know it sounds strange . . ."

"Whatever you say," he says. He's probably used to my quirks by now. "I'll take a walk in the meantime, have a look around, okay?"

I nod, get out of the car. He can't possibly think they're actually here since he's letting me go inside alone.

I stand there, looking around. I would never have imagined things could have fallen into such disrepair over the past few decades. It's as if the farm has been abandoned for hundreds of years instead of thirty.

The woodshed is falling down, the roof sagging along one of the walls. A birch tree is growing through the roof of the barn. The house is surrounded by wild grass a few feet tall, which has now lain down to die. The windows are broken, roof shingles missing. The stain Magne had brushed onto the wood siding is flaking horribly.

How awful it is here and how vehemently Magne would have hated this, he who took such meticulous care of this place. There is a kind of comfort in that.

I walk over to the barn door, open it, grope at the inside wall. The key is still there, even after all these years.

I walk toward the house—I actually do it, I manage it—walk up to the door, and am almost surprised that the key works.

The front hall is full of debris, old trash, some of it gnawed by mice, mingled with the droppings they left behind. I walk into the living room, which is pretty much unchanged, except everything is faded, gnawed at, covered in dust.

In the corner behind the door, I see a mousetrap with a dead mouse in it, or more precisely, the remains of a mouse. Only the skull is left, the rest of the body is gone. Did it run away, or have other mice eaten the corpse?

I turn around, walk back through the living room, and look in the kitchen, where the counters are filled with dirty dishes. Somebody has been here. I walk over and look in one of the bowls. Milk, a kind of light-brown muck, like milk that has been poured over Cocoa Puffs, the kind of junk the children love. It doesn't look many days old.

There is a door leading from the kitchen into a room I can't remember ever noticing before. Was it locked the few times I was here? I push down the handle, and the door creaks as I open it. It's a small room with a big fireplace, a strange combination. I lean forward, squinting. The fireplace was lit not long ago.

On a small, smudged teak table in front of the fireplace is a large picture in a frame. I pick it up. Magne, wearing dungarees and a blue shirt and suit jacket, classic local-government attire. He has his arm around a woman. I recognize her long floral-print summer dress.

It's Agnes, but there's something wrong with her.

She has no head. It has been cut out of the picture.

Beside the table is an old, battered armchair upholstered in brown leather with decorative metal studs. On the armrest lies Magne's knife. His initials, *ML*, have been burned into the handle.

Who has been sitting here decapitating my mother? Magne? Halvor? Somebody else? I shudder, even though I would have liked to decapitate her myself. Then I back out of the room; I've seen more than enough.

Instead, I walk toward the stairs. I have to go upstairs, no matter how difficult it is. I need to check all the rooms, look into cupboards, leave no stone unturned. My knees are trembling. Running up the stairs and still thinking that I can save Lars, that there's hope, only to find him lying motionless on the floor. What sight will greet me this time?

At the top of the stairs, I find a dead bird. I cringe, remembering the song I used to sing to Lars over and over.

> *Through the window a little bluebird flew, a blue-*
> *bird flew, a bluebird flew,*
> *through the window a little bluebird flew, a little*
> *bluebird flew on a day in May.*
> *Found a little boy with eyes of blue, dippedy-doo,*
> *dippedy-doo.*

I walk into the biggest bedroom, the one Magne and my mother shared. A wrinkled duvet, a newspaper on the nightstand. Three days old. A half-full cup of coffee, still not moldy.

I look under the bed, where there are huge mounds of dust and dirt, including a flattened dead mouse.

In Lars's old room, there's both a bed and a mattress on the floor, with bedding on it as well. I lift up one of the duvets, sniff it, but it has no odor. On the nightstand lie some crumpled paper napkins. Otherwise, it is every bit as dusty and dirty and disgusting here as everywhere else. Somebody has been here, but it wasn't necessarily the boys. It wouldn't exactly be difficult to break into this house.

I am about to leave when something causes me to pick up the pillow.

Lying on the mattress beneath it is a key ring with a Liverpool emblem and a tiny soccer ball. It's a unique little treasure, the key ring from a historical Liverpool moment, 1984 or something.

This means that my boys have been here, in Lars's room, in Magne's house. One of them has left their prized European League champion possession under the pillow. Now they are no longer here.

The shaking invades my entire body. Even my teeth are chattering.

On the way out, I see Lars. He is lying on his stomach on the floor and reading his bird book, concentrating, with his hands under his chin.

I see my mother standing by the stove and cooking something or other. She turns toward me and says something, but it's impossible to hear what.

I see Magne, sitting, holding his coffee cup in his chair in front of the television and shouting something to her. Nobody ever sees that he drinks, only that he goes back and forth to his bedroom and becomes increasingly wasted over the course of the evening.

I see the paramedics; they are carrying a stretcher between them and struggle to get it up the steep, narrow stairway. Finally, they have to carry Lars in their arms, without the stretcher.

I try to talk to all of them, one by one: Lars, my mother, Magne, even the paramedics.

Nobody can hear me, and it seems like they don't even see me.

That's when I see the note. A red heart, cut out of colored paper, nailed to the inside of the front door, the message written with a thick black marker. It must have been hung up by someone who was sure not only that I would show up here, but certain that I would see the inside of the door.

> Clara! By 6:00 p.m., October 9, Leif Lofthus must die if your sons are going to live. This is a nonnegotiable demand.

PART 3

The Mountain

CHAPTER 53

CLARA

I can't kill my father. I can't let the boys die. I must find them, and I must find them now.

The deadline is only four short hours away.

Kidnapping two young children is madness in its own right. Who makes this kind of demand as well? Who would ask me to make such a choice? Does my mother hate me or Dad or both of us so much that she's doing this?

"I need to see my dad," I say, hearing how childish the sentence sounds, but I say it again anyway. "I need to see my dad now."

"I thought you wanted to keep him out of this," Stian says.

After I came back shaking and showed him the note I found tacked on the inside of the door, another kind of gravity has come over him.

I also gave him the key ring the boys left behind, proof that they must have been in this awful place, slept here.

"After having seen the note, I am wholly convinced that this is Agnes, and if there's anyone who knows how she thinks, where she could have taken them, it's him. He knows her much better than I do. I should have been up to see him a long time ago anyway."

"We don't have much time before the deadline, Clara," Stian says.

"I know, but I'll be quick, I promise."

That foolish ultimatum has reminded me of how much I miss Dad. He is the only source of security I have in my life. I never imagined myself running around here without his even knowing I was in town.

Visiting Magne's farm was the final straw; things were bad enough before I found that note.

Everything that I erased from my mind comes back.

Now I'm twelve years old again, my leg muscles stiffening and the blood simmering in my lungs after pedaling up the hills to Magne's property. Over and over again, I hear Lars's faltering voice begging for help on the other end of the line, the voice that says he thinks they're going to beat him, that he's afraid, that I must come, that I must hurry.

I hurried, but it wasn't enough.

I was too late. I will forever be the one who failed him when it mattered.

All the days, weeks, months when we let him stay at that farm, Dad and I, when we understood that it wasn't good for him, but we let him stay there anyway, because we didn't know how to stand up to Magne and the others with power in the village, because we were too slow.

"Sorry for keeping you on the outside of things, Stian, but it's better if you don't come in with me right now, not at first," I say. "Dad is fragile. And one of us has to talk to Halvor again. I guarantee he's talked with my mother. Maybe he has some idea where she could be? He might have been at Magne's farm, seen something there, he might even be involved? You'll get more out of him than I will, that's just common sense . . ."

He nods, and I direct him to the turnaround a couple hundred yards from the farm, where he stops and lets me out. As I walk down the road alone, he turns the car around, and I raise one arm to wave. It looks like he smiles, in spite of everything.

Stian. Serious. Stoic. Strong. So handsome that it hurts to look at him, like looking directly at the sun.

What am I going to do about that? Nothing, at least not right now.

The farm, the house, Dad. This is the heart of the matter, the origin of all of it. This is the soil that I came from, the soil I will return to. Being here makes me think that things have to work out. And when it's over, I am not only going to spend more time with the boys, but also with Dad, more time here, in harmony with nature and the seasons and the whole thing. Besides, I have to do something about the impending disrepair. There are broken shingles on the roof, a leak on the second floor, the paint is peeling, and it has all snowballed in the past year. I noticed it last summer but then forgot about it again, because of Henrik and the ministerial appointment. Soon, I will take care of it, once all of this is over.

I knock on the door; the doorbell hasn't worked for years. After a little while, I hear the familiar sound of feet padding toward the door, of Dad's worn-out slippers against equally worn linoleum. He opens the door, looks at me, wrinkles his brow.

"Clara, are you here?" he says, a shaky smile spreading across his face as he opens his arms and pulls me toward him.

CHAPTER 54

ANDREAS

It feels like a big man is lying on my chest or like I'm wearing armor that's too small. It's impossible to breathe normally.

Now it's even worse than before, but it's been like this ever since Dad died.

I was so happy when autumn came because that meant the summer was over. The summer only reminded me of Daddy now, in the same way that Liverpool did. Maybe that means I've lost the summer, too.

What I'm going to talk about now was a little like the wild, yellow, awesome autumn, the one that lasts just a week or two, before suddenly everything is brown, slippery, and dead.

One day she was just standing there, on the far side of the upper soccer pitch, the one we played on at recess. She was watching us play soccer.

Who's that lady? Olav asked. She's been standing there staring at us for a long time.

You're right, I said.

The lady almost didn't look real; it was like she'd been taken out of a Christmas movie from New York. Her hair, the coat, the pocketbook, the glasses, everything. She was wearing a dress with a kind of pattern that looked old fashioned and weird. Over it, she was wearing a long brown coat. Everything about her sort of looked like a flea market.

What was she doing here? And why was she standing there watching us? She reminded me of something or someone, but I couldn't figure out what it was. Mostly, she was different. She had long, almost blonde hair that went down to the middle of her back even though she was old. Grandmother has hair that stops just below her ears, all the old ladies do. Besides, Grandmother's hair is gray, and this lady's was not.

Hi, boys, she said, and smiled.

Hi, I said.

Hi. Who are you? Nikolai said.

I will tell you, she said. But are you Andreas and Nikolai?

We nodded.

Who are you, then? she asked, looking at Olav.

I'm Olav, Olav said.

He's our friend, I said.

Olav, she said. I would very much like to have a word with just Andreas and Nikolai. Is that okay?

Sure, Olav said. He took the ball with him and disappeared.

We looked at her in excitement. I was also a little skeptical; we'd learned that we weren't supposed to talk to strangers who approach us.

This lady didn't look shady, but she was strange. Maybe she was going to sell us something? Or ask us if we had accepted Jesus as our savior? Maybe she was a Jehovah's Witness? But how did she know our names?

Yes, the lady said. Maybe I should just tell it like it is.

Tell us what? I asked impatiently.

CHAPTER 55

CLARA

Dad puts his arm around me as he leads me into the front hallway. Then he pads ahead of me into the kitchen and crosses the room to put on a pot of coffee.

I am struck by the abrupt familiarity of everything, the humming of the refrigerator, the water dripping from the faucet and hitting the bottom of the sink, the way the coffee maker inhales and gurgles, the sharpish light from the fluorescent bulb on the ceiling, the plastic table-cloth with nicks in it. And Dad, Dad who is standing there, a little droopier in the knees and shoulders than the last time I saw him, wearing dungarees and a shirt and suspenders. Dad who is standing there and certainly suspects that something is amiss but still has no idea what's going on.

How have I managed without him the whole autumn?

Everything that has happened since the last time we were together feels like an entire lifetime ago. The days have come and gone, and I have become a minister, my mother has been discharged, the boys have disappeared, and Sabiya has died; meanwhile, he has been here, listening to the radio, making coffee, frying bacon, feeding the hens, gathering eggs.

This autumn, I cut the cord, the daily phone calls, those that have joined us across mountain passes throughout all the years when I have been living elsewhere. This chunk of time has been scissored out, and we will never get it back again.

I receive a message, grab my phone. Now I am on top of the phone at all times, an expression of a kind of desperate hope that the boys, or whoever it is that has them, will contact me by phone even though they haven't done so yet. As it turns out, it's just Mona, who wants to let me know that Munch has accepted a job at the PR agency Flying Fish and will not cause any problems for me moving forward.

Good riddance, Munch.

Dad comes over, places a hand on my shoulder.

"Clara, tell me what's going on," he says, and now I am not the minister of justice at the king's table. Nor am I the girl who had to take charge back then when it was only the two of us and he lay on the couch, shaking, unable to do anything.

Now I am a little girl again and he is the adult, the one I always loved to follow around.

He sits down across the table from me, holding his cup of coffee.

"Why didn't you tell me that Agnes was released from Kleivhøgda?" I say, feeling a surge of despair inside me as I speak the words.

I shouldn't spend time on these things now, but it's as if the situation with the boys is stuck in my throat, as if I need to warm up to it with something else first.

"And this wrecked car that's been recovered?" I continue. "You must have known about both these things, and you didn't say a word to me?"

"Ah," he says, sighing. "I'm sorry, Clara. Yes, I knew about both, but I didn't want to worry you. I know I should have said something, but I just couldn't do it, I—"

"It's fine," I say, sighing. There isn't time. "It doesn't matter anymore."

"It doesn't?" he says, wrinkling his brow. "Has something happened?"

"The boys are missing."

"What?" he says. All the color drains from his face. "What does that mean?"

"Someone has taken them."

He stares at me, as pale as a corpse.

"We don't know very much," I say. "Just that the clues have led us here, to the village . . ."

"But," he says, his voice husky. "Wh-why . . . Who?"

"I thought that journalist Haugo had something to do with it. That's why we came here. I went by Magne's farm. The boys have actually been there. Besides, Halvor is Magne's son, but I think maybe he's not involved after all. On the other hand . . ."

Again, I have to stop, as if to summon my courage.

"Now I don't understand a thing," Dad says.

"Agnes," I say. "I think she's the one who took them."

"Your mother?" he says, incredulous. He thinks about it, shaking his head. "No. She hates me, yes. She's crazy enough, but she isn't capable of carrying out something like this. You said yourself last spring that she was completely out of . . ."

He is shaking, I can see it. His hands are trembling, and he has to put down his coffee cup.

I am doing this to him. Maybe I shouldn't have said anything. What can he do about it, really?

"Tell me everything," he says. "Start at the beginning."

So I tell him about what happened when I came home from work on Friday, about Stian, about what led us to understand that we had to come here.

When I finish, he is silent at first. I don't dare say a word, have to give him a chance to digest this, even though I don't have time. It's as if I can hear the clock that isn't here anymore ticking loudly on the wall.

"We have to put our heads together," he says finally. "You and I and that driver of yours, then we'll manage to figure this out, together . . ."

"Yes," I say. "But we're almost out of time. I found something, on the inside of the front door of Magne's house. Somebody hung it there, so they must have felt pretty certain we would show up there."

I take the note out of my bag, hand it to him.

He takes it, holds it at arm's length, squints, and his face turns even whiter than before. White and then red and then white again.

"But . . . me?" he stammers. "What have I done?"

I lean across the table toward him. "I already suspected Agnes, for various reasons, but that note at the very least convinces me that she *must* be involved in some way . . ."

Now he doesn't reply, sinks deep into himself, as if he is trying to see inward, find an explanation there somewhere. I feel overwhelmed by a huge black sense of grief about everything that has gone wrong.

And then, although I can't fully explain why, I sit on the floor, resting my forehead on Dad's knee. I haven't sat like that for many years, and I sit there sniffling while he strokes my hair.

"There, there, little girl," he whispers. "Everything will be fine, you'll see."

After a while, I straighten up and look at my watch. Good God, only three hours left.

Something that has been fermenting inside me since I heard Bodil speak about my mother and the mountain has now mushroomed. I remember how Agnes would pull us and drag us with her when she was in a manic period, when she had to go up to the summer farm, to climb all the mountains.

"I'm going to take a quick trip up to the summer farm," I say. "I just have to check and see if she's hiding them there."

"Alone?" he says. "Is that a good idea? What about this bodyguard of yours? Shouldn't you at least take him with you?"

"He's on a mission down in the village," I say. "It's fine, Dad, I don't really think they're there."

"I should go with you," he says, his voice tremulous.

"That's no good," I say, stroking his chin. "You know it. It will be much quicker if I just walk up there alone. I'll be back in an hour, an hour and a half."

I go into my room and find some old, worn running clothes in the closet, put on the white Air Max shoes I came in. They're really city shoes, I never wear them for running, but it doesn't make any difference now.

"Clara, wait," he says, coming out of the kitchen.

For a second or two, he stands in the doorway, his eyes glistening. Then he comes over to me with the same expression on his face that Nikolai has sometimes. He puts his arms around me, gives me a stiff, tentative hug.

He smells like an old man. Not bad or disgusting, just a little dusty.

"Be careful now, Clara," he says. "I don't often ask anything of you, but now you have to promise me."

"I promise," I say, giving him another hug.

He looks old. What a year it's been, for him as well.

"Bye," I say, and run out the door.

I should perhaps have called Stian, discussed it with him, gotten him to come, accompany me. The sausage factory should have taught me that it's idiotic to try and take matters into my own hands, alone, but the note upset me.

I don't have time to wait. I have personally sent Stian to find Halvor. Now I must take care of this by myself.

Before, I always thought that whatever I possessed in the way of soldierlike qualities, I got from my father, the Lebanon soldier, the man with the beret and the splinter. But when I think about it now, it strikes me that Dad was always a modest farmer who ended up in a war involuntarily. Maybe I actually get all of that from my mother? Now Agnes is my adversary, and I know so little about her. Sabiya, yes, even Halvor, I felt I understood them, in a way. When it comes to my own mother, I haven't a clue. I don't know her, have never known her.

As a little girl, I always considered her weak. Lying there in bed day after day must have been intolerable. How boring, I thought.

When Dad was in Lebanon, she stayed in bed, too. I had to take care of Lars and the animals and the house and the food and the shopping. I managed it for quite a while, but by the time Dad came home, everything was coming apart at the seams.

I never thought that I was weak. I thought that she was.

Last spring, she seemed to be just an empty shell, but I realize now that she must be much more than that. Maybe she was just pretending? To trick me?

She is scheming, sly, smart, and cunning. In the past few hours, I have tried to move past all the hate and think about who she really is, what she does, how she behaves and thinks.

What places does she like; where does she feel safe?

She is no longer at Kleivhøgda, not at Magne's farm, not in her boathouse, and not at our house.

She always liked being at the summer farm, far away from people and traffic. She used to lie in bed inside the summer farmhouse in the dark, silent and useless, but in her own mind, she was still a mountain person, who gave pompous speeches about the value of breathing in the sky.

She had come here because of the mountains, she said. So that's where I have to look for her, in the mountains.

CHAPTER 56

LEIF

Clara runs out the door. When she was younger, I thought I knew what was good for her, regardless of the condition I was in. She went with me everywhere. First, she sat on my shoulders. Then she ran after me across the yard, the hills, through the barn. No matter where I went, she was right on my heels. I explained to her everything I did and why I did it. She started asking questions of her own, too. About the trees on the hills, about the water in the brook, about the ants in the soil, and about the stars and clouds and everything that existed.

After Lebanon, I told her about the olive tree and the cave in the mountain, the goats, and the crickets; about the grenades that shattered the enormous silence; and about the splinter I pulled out of my hip and brought home with me. She was so obsessed with that splinter, even made herself a necklace out of it. The splinter and the beret, she never grew tired of looking at those things.

Then I was older, Clara was more of an adult and more independent, and I became increasingly uncertain about whether I knew what was best for her. Now I don't know anything anymore. I sit and stare into the distance. Reading is, of course, impossible. Doing anything else is impossible.

How happy it made me to see her at the door. I understood that something had to be wrong since she was here now, but not in my wildest nightmares could I have imagined what she told me. If somebody else came here and told me such a thing, I wouldn't have believed them.

I believed her not because she's my daughter or because she never lies, but because I *know* when she is lying. She's not lying now.

I should go after her, help her, but I don't have the strength. I haven't been up to the summer farm in years, and it would take me many hours to walk up there. Now it is also slippery and will soon be dark.

Damn Agnes. If only I'd thrown her into the ocean the day I met her at the boathouse, but I wasn't even man enough to give her a good scare.

I look into the distance. The same mountains, the same fjord. The hills have been green, white, brown, turned green again. The leaves on the trees around here have also changed, again and again. Now the trees have discarded their reddish-yellow frocks, dropped them onto the ground around them. There they stand, stark naked, stretching their fingers toward the grayish-white sky, waiting for winter.

Summer and autumn, winter and spring, again and again.

It has done me good to have this view of the landscape for all these years. Now looking at it doesn't help anymore. Something was ruined when that journalist bastard started showing up here, invading my little sanctuary, and suddenly Agnes was out again.

According to what Clara just told me, there's nothing I can do.

It flickers through my mind like a film, the way films sometimes move quickly, the seasons changing and changing, at high speed, until it's all over.

It's Clara who will inherit the farm, and after her, Andreas, or Nikolai.

That was the point of it all, of hanging on by the skin of my teeth, preserving the legacy of my father and his father and his father before him, to do as well as they did. To safeguard all the toil they sowed into this soil, to be able to pass it on to the next generation, to my daughter and her sons, and to all the sons and daughters who come after them. This is how life moves on.

The film of the changing seasons cannot be stopped. Now the faces of Andreas and Nikolai are part of it. Their pure, innocent faces, that I've seen on a regular basis since they lay side by side in the baby carriage just outside the house here. Andreas, so much like Clara at that age that it was comical, the same precocious way of being. Nikolai, more like their father.

Those two boys followed on my heels ever since they learned to walk, the way Clara used to. Up the barn bridge and down the barn bridge, across the hills, into the barn, into the forest, everywhere. They filled the hole in my heart left by Lars, yes, but in so doing, a new fear was born that something would happen to them, a fear that has just kept growing since Henrik died.

The thin threads of everything I have so painstakingly knitted together over the years, it's all unraveling now.

CHAPTER 57

CLARA

The landscape on the walk up is more overgrown than it was when I was little, the vegetation denser, taller, but we have pruned and chopped and preserved the trail, it is clear enough to follow. A gnarled birch with a white trunk here, a rock jutting out there, all of it is familiar to me. Now I run through my favorite part of the trail. I am so close to the falls here that I can hear them roaring, see them foaming white.

The trail curves through a fragrant pine forest. Brown pine needles cover the trail. Dark-green moss grows along the sides, regardless of the season. In some sections I can see far across the fjord, see the ferry crossing back and forth. For once, I don't stop.

The landscape gradually opens up as I climb. The forest is less dense, the trees less tall. The air is different, everything quieter.

Finally, I make it up to the brow, where the trail I am walking on plateaus, while the freshwater lake before me abruptly drops into the waterfall I have followed as I ascended. He, the waterfall, is huge now; there has been a lot of rain here.

This is our mountain, our place. Coming here has always reminded me of what happened to Lars. Now it will forever also remind me of something else, of what happened this past summer.

I sit down on a rock at the water's edge.

Here I breathed life into my little brother, many years ago. Here I saved his life, only to let it slip through my fingers a few years later.

Here I crawled onto land last summer, after watching Henrik be whirled away, over the white strip at the far edge of the smooth surface of the lake, which marked the boundary between still water and the thundering falls, between life and death, the point where everything came to an end, the thin, white line. I carry that moment inside me like a kind of tumor.

I did it and I shouldn't have.

I failed to save Lars, too, when it mattered, and I should have let Henrik live. I have made so many mistakes, and it has taken me such a long time to accomplish anything.

Now I am getting closer. I am closing in on them, I think, but still, I'm not with them, and it is getting late. It's cold, and the clothing I am wearing is suited for running, not for sitting still. I can't sit here; I have to find the boys.

"Lars," I whisper. "Lars, are you there?"

I went running up here last spring, after visiting Agnes. Then I managed to make contact with him. Actually, it has always happened here beside the water. That's what I am hoping for now, that he will talk to me, guide me. Since the boys disappeared, I have tried to make contact with him several times without success.

At first, it is completely silent. Then I hear him.

"Yes, Clara," he whispers. "I'm here."

"Are the boys here?" I ask.

"The boys . . . ," he says. Then he is gone.

"Lars?" I say, desperately. "Lars?"

Not a sound to be heard, and I know he's not coming back now.

I turn around, look up toward the summer farmhouse above me. The windows are dark. I fish the keys out of my bra, where I put them after taking them off the hook in the kitchen at home, squeezing them in my hand as I run the last stretch up to the farmhouse. I stand on the step and am about to unlock the door, only to find that the padlock is gone.

I lean my shoulder against the door and push. The door opens, I look inside, and my heart skips a few beats.

CHAPTER 58

ANDREAS

What? I said when the lady told us who she was.

That couldn't be right, even though she knew our names.

Our grandmother is dead, I said. She died long before we were born.

Did your mother tell you that? she said with a big smile. Yes, she probably wants you to believe that. Maybe she's ashamed of me. I've been in the hospital for many years. Some people think that kind of thing is embarrassing.

Nikolai and I looked at each other, not really sure what to think.

How can we know that's true? I asked.

She smiled again, as if we'd said something really nice to her. And then she started describing the farm and Grandpa's house and all the rooms there, the kinds of things that people couldn't know unless they had been there.

Hmm, I said finally. But you don't talk like Grandpa.

No, she said, and laughed, displaying all her white teeth. She looked almost like a fashion model in commercials for old people.

That's because I don't come from the same village, she said. I've lived there since I was young. I came on the bus and met Leif and never left again. I'm actually from Drøbak, a town just an hour away from here. Have you been there?

No, Nikolai said. But Olav and them have a cottage nearby. We heard there's a cool mini aquarium there, and a swim park and Santa's workshop, but Mommy never wants to go there.

I glanced at him in irritation. Nikolai talks too much, has no filter.

Exactly, the lady said. Yes, that doesn't really surprise me.

Do you have ID or something? I asked, the way they do on television.

It seemed like she was thinking about it; then she nodded.

After rummaging through her purse for a while, she took out something made of brown leather that looked really old fashioned, a strange oblong thing with a kind of clip made of something like gold in the middle. It didn't look like any wallet I'd ever seen before, but she had money in it, I could see, a wad of five-hundred- and two-hundred- and one-hundred-krone bills. Then she took out a little green plastic folder with a card inside.

My driver's license, she said. It's old, but here you can at least see my name.

We leaned over and looked. Agnes Lofthus.

Wow, Nikolai said. I didn't say anything.

Look at this, the lady added, and showed us some faded old photographs tucked inside the plastic windows in the old wallet.

There were two children in the photograph. A little boy and a blonde-haired girl who was a little bigger.

Both serious with huge eyes.

Mommy? I asked, and swallowed.

She nodded. And her little brother. Uncle Lars. You've heard about him?

She says he's dead, I said.

That's true, unfortunately, she said, looking sad. He died a very long time ago, when he was younger than you two are now. Anyway, you can call me Grandma if you want.

Yes! We want to, Nikolai said.

How nice, she said. Then there's one thing that's important now . . .

Yes? Nikolai said eagerly.

He was bouncing up and down on the balls of his feet; clearly, he thought this was exciting. So did I, but we didn't have to make it so obvious.

Besides, my insides had gone all cold, and I had a prickling sensation in my head. I didn't understand how Nikolai could seem so normal and so happy. There was something nuts about this, that we had a dead grandmother who was suddenly alive and standing in front of us and showing us a picture of Mommy when she was little. It was, like, too Christmas-movie-ish. Alarms were going off in my head, ringing like jingle bells.

Yes, the lady said. You must promise me something. Don't tell your mother that we met, okay? I don't think she would be happy about it. Then it would be impossible for us to meet, and I would so like to see you again.

So would we, Nikolai said.

I elbowed him. He had to calm down a little.

Perfect, Grandma said.

We walked away through the rustling yellow and orange leaves, and the lady asked us about all kinds of things, what we liked to do and eat, and what our favorite English soccer team was and what kind of sports we played.

Pretty crazy, I said when we got home. Our other grandmother, my dad's mother, hadn't arrived yet. Just think, we have a grandmother we didn't know about. Only, Mommy can't find out . . .

When I think about this now, it was strange that we weren't more distrustful of this new grandmother who suddenly appeared. It was perfect timing that she arrived at exactly that moment.

CHAPTER 59

Clara

Lying on the benches and the beds are bags and clothing that I recognize. There's food on the kitchen counter. Water in the bucket. I open the woodstove. Embers. They were just here. My mother must have seen me and taken them somewhere else. They can't be far away.

I try looking through the mess, to see if I can find something that might give me a hint as to where they've gone, but I don't find anything.

The past few days, I've been so sad, so desperate, so afraid. I have blamed myself. Now I'm only furious. This is so unbelievably outrageous. What a damn useless cunt she is.

I leave, pulling the door shut behind me. If there were snow, as there often is in the late autumn, I would be able to see their footprints. Now there is only this velvety darkness, bluer and bluer with each passing minute.

Within a half hour, it will swallow everything around me.

I look upward, toward the blue-black scree. There are millions of stones there. From those that are so small you can carry a handful of them in your pocket, to those as big as our house. Between the stones are hollows and crevices and caves. If you enter one such cave, chances are you will be the first human ever inside it. Last summer, I entered a narrow crevice, a kind of funnel that widened into a big room with a green floor and stone walls, where the sky itself formed a blue ceiling. A tiny, gurgling brook flowed down one of the mountain walls, like in the forest of *Ronia, the Robber's Daughter*.

Henrik and the boys went up in the scree without me. This was before I understood that he had to die, while we were still having a harmonious summer vacation, at least, considering that I'd become a state secretary and Henrik was having an affair and had just been released from police custody.

Afterward, the boys talked about the caves and the hollows. They interrogated their father about the scree. He got them all fired up with tall tales of what supposedly happened there over the years, tales of magic and wizardry and wood nymphs and robbers running away from the sheriff. After Henrik died, we didn't return to the summer farm. The boys haven't talked about the scree, and I haven't mentioned it, but I'm sure they remember it.

Agnes may have hidden the boys, yes, but they might also have run away from her. They could hide up there, alone, to escape her.

It looks like they left their jackets in the farmhouse when they ran away. That's bad news. In this temperature and with this wind, my own teeth are chattering, and I am shivering.

The shore lies below, and the water is dark gray, blue gray, steel gray with small crests of foam. It occurs to me as I run up the hill that the scree is huge, enormous. Big, menacing, and, up close, not as blue, but more a charcoal gray. Somewhere up there, in an area spanning many hundreds of yards of jagged, inhospitable terrain, they might be hidden, my boys.

They could have fallen down into one of the deep chasms you don't see until it's right in front of you, cracks that can be twenty or thirty yards deep. If so, I will never find them, dead or alive.

There is one more alternative, which I don't like thinking about.

My mother may have understood that the web is tightening around her and pushed them over a cliff somewhere, tried to get rid of them, in an attempt to cover her tracks and get away.

That would be ridiculous since their clothing is in the farmhouse. She wouldn't get away with it. But my mother is not rational, not well. The thought of that is perhaps the most frightening thing of all.

CHAPTER 60

ANDREAS

Every day, there was something new. She bought us sweets and magazines and little toys. We were happy about it, sure, but the best part was that she did things with us. Usually, we could only spend time with her in the afternoons, after school, before Axel or our other grandmother came to our house to make dinner and make sure we did our homework and all that. Luckily, we had time to do quite a bit in those hours.

She told us she hadn't driven a car for over thirty years, but now she drove around in a hybrid car with an automatic gear shift. She'd bought a smartphone and downloaded tons of apps. Nobody would have believed she'd never been on the internet before this autumn. We raced around in that cool rental car while the GPS lady told Grandma where to drive. Turn left. Turn right. It was awesome.

One day, we actually drove to Drøbak. It was too cold to go swimming, but we went to Santa's workshop and had pancakes.

We visited something called the International Museum of Children's Art that wasn't far from home, a gigantic haunted castle chock-full of tons of art.

We went to the reptile zoo and got to hold snakes, and we went to the movies. Grandma sat between us, holding the box of popcorn and smiling from ear to ear.

One time, she actually came and watched us play a home soccer game. She said we mustn't run over to her, that it was important that people didn't understand that she was there to see us. She was very nervous that Mommy would find out about her. So she stood there alone, cheering, and the other parents all stared at her because she looked completely different from everyone else.

And on that particular day of all days, Mommy showed up. Mommy who almost never made it to our games, who didn't even notice when we had a game. I saw the black car pull up in the parking lot. Then she stepped out, tall and blonde. Mommy could not be invisible, and neither could Grandma. As Mommy came walking up from the parking lot, I ran as fast as I could over to Grandma, who was standing on the sidelines along with the others.

"What's going on, Andreas?" Hans Marius called out to me, since I'd left the pitch without being told. I acted like I didn't hear him.

"You're not supposed to come over here," Grandma whispered sternly.

"Mommy's here," I whispered back. "You have to leave, but don't go toward the parking lot, she's walking over here from there right now."

Her eyes sort of widened; then she turned and walked away in the opposite direction.

That's how close we were to getting caught. None of us knew what would happen if she was really discovered. Mommy could have her put back in the hospital, maybe. Grandma said that the only thing she was scared of was that she wouldn't get to see us again. That would be the worst thing that could happen to her.

Her life so far had been empty and sad, she said. Everything had felt meaningless and lonely. Now that she'd found us, though, it felt like everything had meaning again, as if the lights had been turned on. I didn't really understand all that, but it didn't matter. We thought it was cool she was so interested in us, especially since Mommy had less and less time every day.

When Mommy told us about the new job, I understood right away how things would turn out. She said that we wouldn't notice any difference, but we did. It seemed like she was picked up earlier and earlier and dropped off later and later all the time and like her head was at work more and more. It reminded me of when she was working on that bill, the "draft," that irritated Daddy so much.

Grandma asked a lot of questions about Mommy, about when she left and when she came home, about her interests and what she liked and didn't like to do. She wanted to get to know her daughter through us, she said, since that was the only way she could. I got a little sick of all her pestering about Mommy. I liked it best when we could talk about something else.

Luckily, she was most interested in us and Grandpa. In fact, she seemed even more curious about him than about Mommy. She asked questions and bugged us about his health and if he seemed depressed and if he liked to drink beer and lots of other things. They had been married once, so maybe she was still in love with him?

Grandmother, Dad's mom, had only been sad since Daddy died, and that wasn't so strange, so were we, but it was tiresome anyway. Compared to Grandma, who was so happy, she seemed even sadder and grayer; it was almost like I couldn't stand being around her anymore. She sighed all the time, and tears were always streaming down her cheeks, while we ate, while we watched television, while she read to us. Grandma had lost a son, too, and she didn't carry on like that.

She told us many times that not only was it very important that Mommy not find out about her, but we also couldn't say anything to Grandmother, Grandfather, Uncle Axel, or our friends, because then Mommy might find out about it from them. This had to be our secret. That was fine with us. We liked having secrets with her.

CHAPTER 61

CLARA

Finally, I make it through the densest vegetation and enter a pasture, which is basically just grass, which I have to walk through to reach the scree. I jog up the hill. The grass that was green in the summertime is now brown, rotting and wet, flattened against the ground. My running shoes keep losing traction, slipping.

I am tired; getting up to the summer farmhouse took everything out of me, but finally I am up on the right side of the scree. We hiked up here, all four of us, after the boys and Henrik were here without me the first time. Now I'm by the one cave we looked inside of back then. Here there was soft green grass on the floor and a trickling brook. In the summer, an oasis, the Norwegian version of a secret Mediterranean paradise.

Now it's all different. Gray. Barren. Empty.

"Boys?" I call, but hear only the echo of my own voice.

I run out again, pass two ponds where we stopped last summer to skip stones. Into the next cave, which we also explored. It, too, is empty.

I have to try and call them instead. They'll hear me and come out when they understand who it is.

"Andreas? Nikolai?" I call.

Not loud enough. I try again. I can picture them, how they will jump out, their faces joyful, how they will run toward me, throw their arms around my neck. Their cold, flushed cheeks against my face.

I love you, I will say, and embrace them.

It was Henrik who used to say such things. I thought it was soppy and pathetic. Now I'm going to start doing it, every day.

I reach the upper-right corner of the scree. We walked along the edge up here to look down at all the rocks. In a state of delight mixed with dread, the boys examined the huge cracks in the mountainside. I warned them not to go too close, to stand on solid ground and look.

"Andreas? Nikolai?" I call. Not a sound.

I taught them that they shouldn't walk in the scree itself, since the cracks are so easy to miss. They nodded, but I saw that they were itching to try it. They had a greater understanding of danger than when they were two, three, four, yes, but they were still children, fearless, hardy children.

Oh, my boys. If Agnes has dragged you up here and something has happened to you, I will kill her, just as I've always longed to do.

I walk out onto a kind of plateau where we also went last summer. From here, I have a direct view of the summer farm and the lake and the landscape below. When the light is good, in the daytime, you can see the fjord, the green fjord, and mountain after mountain, far, far away, into the distance. Now the light is dwindling more and more with every passing minute.

I look over at a heap of rock slabs lying several feet away from me, an aberration in the otherwise pristine landscape. I once stood here and told the boys and Henrik about the quarrying that had long ago been attempted and which we could still see the remains of.

My heart sinks as I scan the enormous quantity of stones, from huge boulders five times taller than me to pebbles the size of peas. Even if I had a year, I wouldn't have time to search through all of it, and I have perhaps only an hour before it is completely dark.

I call again, get no answer, call out one more time. My voice breaks, my throat burns.

"Andreas? Nikolai?"

They must be here. If they were in the summer farmhouse, I would have seen them. Unless they're lying at the bottom of the lake, they must be up here. And then they would hear me and come out. They should be able to distinguish between me and my mother, even though both our voices are husky and sound quite similar. But what if they're lying in here somewhere and hear me but don't dare come out because they think I'm Agnes? The thought is unbearable.

I start climbing across and have just called out to them one more time when my feet slip out from under me and I fall backward, three feet, six, maybe ten. All the air is knocked out of me when I land on my back. Then the last of the light disappears and everything goes dark.

CHAPTER 62

ANDREAS

We were together pretty much every single afternoon, out somewhere or in her hotel room. Yes, once or twice, Grandma even came home with us. That made me a little nervous. Even though we just did it when we thought Mommy wouldn't come home, we could never be absolutely sure. So mostly we went other places.

Two or three times, she picked us up and drove us to school, even though it was just a ten-minute walk. She was very different in the morning; we understood that she wasn't a morning person.

Then one afternoon, she said she had something to tell us. Nikolai acted as if he thought she was just going to tell us about something fun we were going to do. I knew right away that it was bad news.

Boys, she said. It's been so nice spending time with you, but now I've spent all my money, so I have to go back home to my boathouse . . .

We had wondered about that, actually, whether she was rich. She was staying in a big, beautiful room at the Bristol hotel in the city, and she had been there for many days now. The rental car must have cost a lot of money, too, and she'd told us that she often ate at the Theater Café. We had been there a few times with Grandfather and Grandmother and knew it was expensive.

I'll be back, she said. You can visit me, too. I'll make a plan, just wait and see.

That was the kind of thing people said, and it never came true.

She seemed frenzied and weird, as if she had already left.

We should have known she was going to leave again, she didn't live here, after all, but neither of us had thought about it. Now she was suddenly going away again, just as abruptly as she'd come.

When she left, it was as if all the sadness came and washed over us like a gigantic wave of seawater. Everything that happened that summer was awful, but then Grandma came. She made everything so much more fun that we almost forgot to be sad for a little while.

Now everything was lousy again. I missed Daddy so much that my whole body hurt. I was angry with Mommy and with Grandma, too, actually.

Why had she come to see us, only to leave again? What was her plan? What did she really want from us?

CHAPTER 63

AXEL

Today, all of a sudden, I heard from her. I was so happy when I saw that she sent me a message. Finally, she was thinking about me, wanted something from me. I put the phone to one side, just to revel in the taste of that treat for a bit, daydream about what the message could be about before I read it.

I held out for five minutes. Then I couldn't stand it anymore, picked up the phone, and opened the message. Clara was in Western Norway, she wrote, and there was a minor emergency. Would I mind going to the house and feeding the hamsters? I had the code to the door. Thank you.

All this silence and this was the best she could cough up? I tossed the phone away, across the couch. I couldn't even be bothered to respond to the message. Who did she think I was? Her slave? Demoted from babysitter to hamster feeder? She could ask somebody else. Like her driver, for example.

After a few minutes, I picked up the phone again, opened her message, and sent her a thumbs-up. That was the rudest, coldest, most boring reply I could think of. When she saw it, she would have to realize she'd crossed the line.

After a while, she sent a short and sweet "thanks." That was it. Was she making fun of me? Did she think I was an idiot? Either way, now I actually had to go feed those animals. I couldn't just let them die.

I used to always enjoy the walk over to Clara's house. Now I drag my feet every step of the way. I stop in front of the door, tap in the usual code, the same code they've used for years, God only knows how many other people have it besides me.

There is a sour smell in the hallway. The smell grows stronger as I walk into the kitchen. I sniff my way to the trash can under the sink, open the door, and back away. Holding my breath, I tie up the bag containing whatever it is that smells so awful and hold it at arm's length as I walk outside to the garbage bins. I lift the lid and drop it inside, as if it were a dead rat. Judging from the stench, it could be just that. Probably it was fish or shrimp or something like that, there aren't many other things that give off such a foul stench.

It is only when I enter the kitchen the second time that I notice the rest of the chaos. I am a single father with three children, so my house isn't exactly spic and span. Henrik was quite tidy.

Clara is not a housekeeper. If she lived alone, she probably wouldn't have a single stick of furniture. This is one of the many things that fascinates me about her, makes her so different from Caro and all the other women I know.

Sometimes, though, I wonder whether Clara is, more than anything, a curse that has afflicted me, powerfully and brutally. Why am I so hung up on her when I'm not even sure whether I actually like her? Yes, she's beautiful. Sexy, too, though some people might find her too androgynous. Smart. Honest. Funny, if you like sarcasm. At the same time, she can be grouchy, caustic, petty, self-centered, and socially awkward. She is not empathetic, not warm, not especially interested in me, not attentive. Absolutely not flexible, open, patient, generous, or caring. Actually, she is none of the things I look for in a woman, embodies none of the values that I so esteem. Still, she is the only one I want, the only one who interests me, and the more she rejects me, the worse it gets.

What does that say about me, actually? Is it because I, who know so much about everyone, don't really know anything about her? Is that where the attraction lies? Or am I just a masochistic jerk who wants what I can't have, what isn't good for me?

People's impression of me is that I'm a guy who is reasonably chill and on top of things, or so I understand. I am, too, or I used to be.

Most people are, I guess, more sensitive and less cocky when you get past initial appearances, but I actually feel like I've changed over the past half year. The combination of losing Henrik and this Clara thing bursting into full bloom has turned me into a bitter, peevish old man.

I stand in the middle of the still-stinking kitchen, looking at a counter full of dirty dishes. I turn around and look at the big dining room table, where, not long ago, I served Clara pizza and drank red wine with her. It feels unreal now, in the dismal, gray autumn light and after the silence of the past week. It becomes even more unreal when I take in the sight of the table. A half-eaten bar of chocolate, plates, dirty cups and glasses, an overflowing ashtray.

The most remarkable thing is all the papers everywhere. Crumpled-up balls lie strewn across the table and floor, but there are also a few flat sheets of paper here and there. I bend over to look at one of them, which is covered with densely scribbled handwriting and arrows and names and catch phrases. *Andreas + Nikolai* is written inside a circle in the middle. In small clouds around them are lots of other names. *Munch. Sabiya. Unknown.* What is all this?

It seems as if she has been out of it, off kilter. An irrational hope flames up inside me. Is that why I haven't heard from her? Because she's had some type of breakdown? Has she not written me off after all? Is she not involved with this Stian fellow?

Regardless, what this strange tableau makes clear is that something is wrong. Clara is in Western Norway, the boys are there or somewhere else; at any rate, they're not here. Things were chaotic here before they left, it must have happened quickly, and Clara cannot possibly have been feeling well.

This table does not look like the table of a minister of justice. It doesn't even look like the table of a respectable single mother in Vinderen. The mess must be the explanation for why she has asked me, and not Åsa, to come over here. Better to have me see this than her mother-in-law.

Henrik's mother, Åsa, and Clara's mother, Agnes. A stab of guilt pierces my body at the thought.

It was Olav who came home from school and let it slip that a strange old lady had turned up at school who wanted to talk to Andreas and Nikolai. She had apparently told them that she was their grandma who, I had been told, died a long time ago.

Of course, I was shocked and skeptical. I knew that Clara's mother was dead. This is a scam, I said. The lady has to be someone pretending to be their grandmother, as a means to some kind of end. Maybe it could be connected to the minister of justice position? Maybe it was dangerous in some way? I almost called Clara to let her know, but then Olav started crying, he was so afraid that the boys would get in trouble with Clara and get mad at him for telling on them.

Fine, I said, I want at least to talk to Andreas and Nikolai myself. So I did and was surprised by how sure they were that this was really their grandma, and all the proof they claimed to have, like how she could describe Leif's house in detail and had a photograph of Clara as a little girl in her wallet. Based on what they told me, I started to believe that maybe this was Clara's mother and that Clara must have lied to me and Henrik and everyone else about her being dead.

Of course, I should have confronted her about it, asked her to tell me the truth, or looked into it, but I was a coward. Nobody wanted to get on Clara's bad side, and I just wanted her to like me, appreciate me, be closer to me. At the same time, I had this disturbing feeling that she was up to something behind my back, something that possibly involved her driver. That was confirmed when I saw them sitting together on the bench in the garden the other day.

The most inappropriate thing perhaps was that I went looking for Agnes at the Bristol hotel. I had the receptionist call up to her room and ask her to come down to the Bibliotek Bar. Then we sat there, in the chesterfield chairs, and I explained who I was and what I knew, and she listened and answered and explained. It was intense, hearing about all the years she had spent in an institution and how Clara and Leif had supposedly manipulated her so she ended up in a psychiatric hospital and let her rot there, without checking on her or visiting her. She had longed to get to know her grandchildren but had never had the opportunity.

I promised her that I wouldn't say anything, and I kept that promise. Yes, I even let her see the boys a few times on "my watch" without telling Clara. The darker side of me hoped that if I met Agnes again, I would learn more about Clara, something that would help me reach her. It didn't work out that way; I met Agnes only on that one occasion.

It is only now, after the fact, that it occurs to me that this was a gigantic betrayal of Clara's trust, the woman I so wanted to protect and help. Besides, it would have been dangerously simple for her to find out. Could it be that Clara *did* find out in some way, and that's the explanation for her silence?

When Olav told me that Andreas and Nikolai's grandma had left suddenly and that they seemed very sad, it made my stomach hurt. What had I done? Had I actually bungled all of this miserably?

I wanted to help Clara, make her happy. Instead, I had unwittingly ended up doing the exact opposite.

Can the filthy, abandoned state of this house have any connection to this Agnes story?

I walk over to the window, draw the curtains, empty the ashtray in the toilet in the hallway, collect all the papers in an empty bag, and put the dirty dishes in the sink. Then I go upstairs to feed the boys' furry little pets. After having seen the state of the kitchen, I just hope they're still alive.

CHAPTER 64

CLARA

I am alive, but I have no idea how long I have been unconscious. It could be hours. Most likely it was only a minute, maybe seconds.

I try to sit up, but knives of pain stab my body. I must have broken something. My ribs? My collarbone? A punctured lung? I try moving one arm first, then the other, it feels like only a sprain. I lift one knee, then the other. So far so good. I open my mouth. Something cold hits my tongue, my lips. So I'm alive at least.

For a few seconds, all I do is lie there, looking up into the grayness, afraid to lift my head and see where I've landed and how improbable it is that I will be able to climb out of here.

Finally, I raise my head, look in front of me, a little to the side. I am lying in a kind of boat-shaped ravine, and I landed on the widest part. My head has luckily not hit any of the stones lying on the ground around me, like black clumps of sugar, but something in the middle of my body feels like it's broken.

Even if I were in a functional state, physically speaking, even if I were a rock climber, which I am not, there is apparently no way out of this pit.

I can hear water dripping to the right of my head. Long before I die of hunger or thirst, I will have frozen to death. There's some consolation in that, but what is going to happen to my boys?

I count to three inside my head; then I sit up. It hurts only as much as you want it to, Daddy said to me once. I think he said it just that one time, and it wasn't like him, but since then, I have always remembered it, said it to myself, over and over. It hurts only as much as you want it to.

Now I *must* get out of here, must find them, save them. I roll over until I am kneeling on all fours. Then I stand up and look toward the end of the ravine that wasn't visible while I was lying on the ground.

The rock face leading up to the light is steep and consists of porous black stone. It is impossible to climb up there. I look around me. All the other surfaces are even more impossible, out of the question.

I take out my phone, call Stian. The phone battery shows that 20 percent remains. Stian will answer, he's always on duty, he will be able to help me.

The phone rings, once, twice, three times, four. I try again, with the same result. Fuck. Why doesn't he answer? Did Halvor beat him senseless? Has something else happened? I swallow, close my eyes, open them again, call Daddy. He at the very least answers immediately.

"Daddy," I say.

"Everything okay?" he asks, and I can hear how worried he is.

"No," I say, and swallow. The line crackles.

"Clara, I can't hear you very well," he says. "Is it the boys? Did you find them? Are they alive?"

"Yes," I say, and then my voice breaks. "But, Daddy . . ."

I am about to tell him where I am, that I am trapped down here and that he must find someone who can help, that he must call Stian or someone else, the local police, anyone, just send someone to help me. Then I hear a click and the connection is broken. The reception must be poor.

I take the phone away from my ear, stare at it. Shit. The screen is dark. I press the button on the side and think I can see the outline of an empty battery symbol in the semidarkness. How is that possible? I just had 20 percent. It must be the temperature that has done it. Now I am also so cold that I'm shaking. I have to try to find a way out of here, can't give up, not yet, I can't die down here without trying everything.

I kick at the rock face a few feet above the ground, confirming that it is loose, porous. Then I reach my other arm a bit farther up and take hold. One more hold and another and another, all the while ignoring the pain throbbing and pounding in my body.

With only three feet to go, I lose my grip and tumble all the way down again, skidding downward while my fingers desperately struggle to clutch at something, anything, until I land back where I started. At the bottom. I squat down, feeling the tears springing into my eyes.

According to my watch, I have two more hours. Stian will perhaps start looking for me eventually if he sees that I tried to call. If he comes up to the summer farm, he will find the farmhouse door open, go inside, understand something, but he won't manage to find me up here in the scree, at least not before I freeze to death. I tried calling him. I tried calling Daddy, but it didn't work. Only I can save me now.

Up the rock face. I have to make it this time. My adrenaline has numbed the pain for a little while, but it won't last. With every attempt, I will lose more strength. I look around me and spot an eight-inch-long stone shaped like a kind of chisel. I pick it up, reach under my sweater, and slide it under my bra strap.

Do it now, Clara. Find a good foothold, find a solid ridge for your fingers. Ignore the chest pains. Ignore the fact that your thighs and arms and your whole body are quivering. One more foot. One more hand. Then all of a sudden, I am stuck.

CHAPTER 65

LEIF

Again and again, I try calling her back. Each time, the call goes to voice mail.

We were cut off suddenly in the middle of a sentence. It must be her mother, or whoever Agnes is collaborating with, who discovered she was on the phone and took it away from her. I can picture it far too clearly, after hearing the desperation in her voice.

I should never have let her go up there all alone, should have insisted on going with her, managed it in one way or another, or at least convinced her to wait for this Stian. The idea that she should run up there alone, that was sheer madness. I was so dazed by what she told me, wasn't thinking properly. Now I see everything clearly. For once, my daughter doesn't have everything under control, she came to me for help, and I let her down.

I failed to help her, the way I failed to help my son back then. All the images, the seasons, the boys, Henrik, Lars. They spin around and around, faster and faster.

Clara has clearly been outsmarted by Agnes, in one way or another. Time is almost up. And Clara called me, most likely with a knife at her throat.

I sit down with my head in my hands. Bella jumps up onto my lap; I push her down again. Then I get up, walk toward the hallway, put on a hat, jacket, shoes.

I have to go out. I have to do something. That is always how the movie ends, with white letters flashing against a black background: *Do something, do something, do something.*

Agnes has inflicted so much pain, on Lars, on Clara, on me. Enough is enough.

CHAPTER 66

ANDREAS

The days we've been out here, in the village, Grandma has been changing her plans for us constantly.

She knew about a place, a farm, where she wanted to hide us. We
would have to walk a mile or two, but we would manage that just fine,
being as fit as we are, she said. She'd returned the rental car, and she
hadn't dared ask the landlord if she could borrow his car, because he
would be suspicious. We would have to carry whatever we had room
for in our knapsacks, and she would take a big bag.

It was wonderful to get out of the boathouse. It had stopped raining, and there were loads of stars in the sky.

Whose farm is it, really? Nikolai asked as we walked up a steep dirt
road. It reminded me of the road up to Grandpa's farm, but this was
even steeper and pretty overgrown. In the middle, there were lots of
tufts of grass and stuff.

Actually, nobody owns it now, Grandma said. It's empty, but I used
to live there. That was after I moved out of Grandpa's house, before I
got sick. I lived there with my boyfriend, Magne, it was his farm. Clara
was there sometimes, and Lars.

Is this farm where Lars died? Nikolai asked.

Grandma nodded so you almost couldn't see it, but it didn't look
like she liked that we mentioned Lars. We kept walking without saying

anything else. It was a long walk. My body felt all tired out when we finally reached the farm.

The barn was starting to fall down. A kind of shed had already collapsed. The house looked pretty nice, actually, from a distance. It was one of those big old-fashioned, long, brown fairy-tale houses, but when we got closer, it just looked all ugly and awful.

Grandma patted her pockets and pulled out a key to open the door. I guess she had made a copy. The door was a little newer than the rest of the house, but the lock had started to rust.

When she leaned her shoulder against the door and pushed it open, it was like the house sighed heavily. There was a thick layer of dust mixed with mouse droppings on the floor of the hallway. I had to swallow. Was this really where she was planning for us to stay?

Why doesn't anyone own this farm? I asked.

Ah, Grandma said, and sighed. Some of Magne's nieces and nephews are fighting over who should have it. They've been doing that for thirty years. They all live far away, and nobody takes care of the place. Wait and see, the whole place will fall down before they reach an agreement. But somebody else must have been here.

What do you mean? I asked.

I saw footprints in the dust. Cigarette butts. And somebody used the kitchen not long ago.

But . . . then somebody could come while we're here, couldn't they? I said, and shivered. It felt even colder inside than it did outdoors.

No, Grandma said. Maybe somebody was here this autumn, but nobody will come here now. Besides, it's safer to have you here than in the boathouse. The power was shut off many years ago, but I brought lots of candles. We can light the stove. There's a little firewood in the barn, and we can also burn some old things. And we must dress warmly, not light the stove so much during the day. Even though nobody lives around here, someone might see the smoke from the road, and we don't want that.

Where will we sleep, then? Nikolai asked.

I will sleep in my old bedroom, Grandma said. The two of you can sleep in your uncle's old room. There's just one bed in there, but I can move a mattress in from one of the other rooms. There are duvets and pillows and bedding in a closet.

I wanted to ask if he had died in there and how he died, but I didn't dare.

Grandma was sort of like a decaying hanging bridge, where some of the planks were safe and others rotten, and it was impossible to know for sure in advance which were safe to step on and which absolutely were not. You had to be super careful on all the planks, actually. The best plan would, of course, be not to walk out onto the bridge at all, but we were sort of past the point where that was an option.

Come on upstairs and help me out, Grandma said, and we walked up the creaky old staircase.

When we reached the top, we found a dead bird lying there. We could see it in the light from Grandma's headlamp.

Oh, yuck . . . , Nikolai said, backing away and almost falling down.

Nothing to worry about, Grandma said, kicking the bird away.

She took out duvets, pillows, and bedding. When I took hold of one of the duvet covers, it tore.

Yeah, everything's a bit shabby, Grandma said. And damp.

As we walked across the floor, it crunched beneath our feet. Dead flies, wasps, other things—it was hard to tell what was making the sound. Actually, this reminded me of the house of horrors we used to visit when we were at the zoo with Daddy. Here there was no howling or screaming or lights flashing, but this was worse, because it was real—the mice and the birds and the bedding that fell apart.

When Nikolai and I went into the little room behind the kitchen, everything got a thousand times crazier.

CHAPTER 67

CLARA

I pull out the stone chisel I found on the ground and pound with all the force I don't have at what appears to be a soft spot in the rock wall.

It holds, but both the chisel and the rock face are of porous material. I don't know how long this will hold. My legs are trembling beneath me.

I must keep moving upward. Five feet remain, maybe seven, up to the top. I stretch my right arm up as far as I can and reach a point where I can just barely dig in three fingers. I then lift my left foot, find a notch, place my foot there. I pluck out the chisel, drive it in solidly above my head.

Now I've made it much farther than the last time, am almost at the top. If I fall now, it's all over. I close my eyes, take a few deep breaths, and regret it immediately because it hurts like hell.

Then I lift my right leg. Left arm. Right arm. Left leg. I can reach the edge above me but realize that I'm not in the clear yet. Because now I have to pull the entire weight of my battered body up onto a ridge without knowing what it's like up there.

I start by moving the other hand up, digging my fingers into what feels like a thin layer of soil.

For my entire life, I have run outdoors. I am tough, have endurance, and am in good physical condition. But I have never done any weight lifting or rock climbing, am not especially strong, and now I am exhausted and beaten black and blue. In one way or another, I manage, nonetheless, to force my left elbow up onto the ridge, and then my right, so I am hanging by my arms.

Nothing could have prepared me for the insane pain that ensues.

I am hanging on by only two shaking elbows and seeing stars. If I pass out now, I'm done for.

The only possible solution lies in defying gravity, performing a kind of improbable lift that will flip me up over the edge and to safety. The flickering of stars before my eyes intensifies.

If only Stian were standing in front of me now, reaching out his hands to pull me up. Or Axel. I see Henrik and Daddy before me. Finally, I see Lars, as clear as day. That has never happened before.

"Clara," he whispers. "Don't let me down now, or it will all be in vain."

And then I drag myself up over the edge, onto solid ground.

At first, I lie there flat on my stomach, with my arms stretched out on the ground above my head, my body burning and throbbing. I just lie there, breathing. For a good long while. Then I get up onto my knees, and finally, I am standing upright.

I'm alive and I climbed out of the ravine. It's unbelievable. I was absolutely sure that I wouldn't be able to do it.

A tiny burst of adrenaline bubbles joyfully inside me, it's like champagne bubbles, soap bubbles, for a few seconds, until I remember that I still don't know where the boys are, my cell phone is dead, and I am injured. As the adrenaline starts to ebb, I can feel how much pain I'm really in. I must have broken several ribs, and there's something wrong with my foot.

I start moving out of the scree toward safety. After a few minutes, I reach the place where I entered and start limping down.

Here and there, I stop, call out. It hurts so much that I double over. I try to make contact with Lars again, but it's no use. My teeth are chattering. I am shivering and shaking. Should I just give up? Lie down to die? Trudge home again and call for help? That would be the sensible thing to do now, but by then, it will probably be too late.

Then I have a thought: What about the stone hut?

I have only thought about the caves, where I've been with the boys myself, but they were in the hut last summer with Henrik. Afterward, they talked about how they wanted to have a sleepover there. The hut apparently has a roof and walls and is easy to find inside the scree, if you know where to look, which I don't.

How did Henrik and the boys find the hut? Did they use a map?

I limp and hobble down to the farmhouse, walk in, light a candle, shine the light on a shelf above the counter where there is a stack of old Donald Duck books. Finally, I find the map Daddy made. I stare at it for a little while, until I am sure I have memorized it, fold it up, and stuff it into the back pocket of my leggings. Then I take a headlamp off the shelf, check that it's working, and attach it to my head. Finally, I put on an old down jacket hanging there on a hook.

The last time I wore a headlamp was in the sausage factory. At this moment, it feels like it was many days ago, but it must have been yesterday.

The headlamp is my only weapon as I start walking up the bumpy terrain leading to the scree again. I glance at my watch.

One more hour.

CHAPTER 68

ANDREAS

Although being with Grandma was stressful for us, we didn't get really scared until we were left alone on the farm, when suddenly she was gone for one night.

We put a dresser in front of the door, and neither of us got much sleep. When Grandma came back, she said she was going to move us again. I'd started to understand that Grandma's ideas about what was smart changed a lot. She seemed to have many personalities she could put on and take off, like the old Halloween costumes hanging in our closet that have long since become too small for us, but that nobody has put away. I also feel that there's more than one Andreas fighting over who is going to be the real me, but I am maybe more like one of those Russian dolls, with many different dolls inside one big one.

This time, I was happy Grandma changed her mind. There was something really wrong with that farm.

We were going to go to our summer farm, it was safer there, Grandma said. Nobody will show up there at least. Besides, wouldn't it be nice for us to be in a place we had a close, loving relationship to? A familiar place, she said. It felt like I had a black stone in my tummy. I didn't want to go to the summer farm. Maybe I would never want to go there again.

Of course, we couldn't take the usual route, through Grandpa's farm. That would be too dangerous, even at night, Grandma said, but she had another plan. As the crow flies, it wasn't far from Magne's farm to our summer farm. Just a mile or two, she said.

I said the f-word in my head. If we walked through the farm, we could escape into Grandpa's house. Now that would be impossible.

As it turned out, the walk to the summer farm was quite a few miles long, and it was both wet and steep. Grandma acted like she knew where we were, but we understood that, really, she didn't have a clue.

We thought we would finally get warm again when we arrived, because the summer cottage was much smaller than Magne's house, and here we could keep the stove burning all day long. Actually, it was the opposite; it was even harder to keep warm here, no matter how much we fed the fire. The cottage was all leaky.

And the flies that were hibernating in the ceiling started to wake up because of the heat from the woodstove. They buzzed and hummed in a creepy way. Then they started raining down on us. Mouse droppings we could sweep up and throw out, the spiderwebs, too, but we couldn't stop the flies from falling. Finally, I lay down under a duvet and pulled it over my head, while the flies dropped onto it from above and the films from last summer went berserk on the inside of my eyes.

Staying inside that cold, dark room with nothing to do was the pits. So I was happy when Grandma said we could go outside for a while if we wanted to.

After we'd been outside for just a little while, Nikolai grabbed my arm.

Look, he whispered, pointing toward the cottage and the water.

Right at the place where the waterfall descended, where you could follow the path either downward or upward, we now saw a person running toward us. It was starting to get dark, but we could still see who it was.

Mommy, Nikolai whispered.

He was going to run toward her when Grandma stopped him.

Stop, she hissed, taking a firm hold of his neck. We have to hide.

I knew that when she opened the door to the cottage and saw our things, Mommy would understand we were here anyway. We could maybe have called out to her, too, in hopes that she would help us, but it didn't feel that easy. Grandma seemed completely out of control now. We had to hide, but where? My brain was boiling, I couldn't think, but then Nikolai took over.

The stone hut, he whispered. If we walk alongside the brook, then she won't see us.

So we hunched down and tiptoed over to the cover of darkness beside the brook. From there, we could walk up to the scree without her seeing us. We stumbled and fell, and Grandma swore and sputtered, and my legs and my chest burned, but even so, after a while, we made it up to the scree.

A few minutes later, Nikolai managed to find the stone hut. We opened the door, went inside, and sat down.

It was freezing cold, we were sweaty and breathing hard and fast. We wouldn't be able to stay here for long in this cold. I reached into my pocket to feel the Liverpool key ring. It wasn't there.

Had I lost it? When?

Then it was as if Daddy were here again; I could hear his voice loud and clear. He talked to me about spending the night in the stone hut. It was summer, it was warm, everything was nice, and it wasn't too late for anything.

CHAPTER 69

CLARA

It is surprisingly easy to find the hut, even though I've never been there before, and it's pitch dark. The hut is situated against a rock. It is small and dark and easy to miss, since it almost blends into the surrounding mountainside and the grayish mist that has appeared. A tiny little human element in the middle of the wilderness.

It is quiet inside. Could they be in there anyway?

I walk over, take hold of the door handle, and open the door. There, seated on a stone bench against the wall, just a few feet away from me, are my sons. They are sitting with my mother between them, looking straight at me.

"Oh my God," I say, and run over to them, hugging first one boy, then the other. Then I get down on my knees in front of my mother; at the moment, I don't care that she's sitting there. I take Nikolai's hand in my left hand, Andreas's in my right, and hold them over my mother's lap.

I am just so relieved; my knees and hands and my whole body are shaking. I have finally found them. Now they are safe, now everything will be all right.

"Oh, my boys," I say. "Good Lord, how wonderful to see you."

"Mommy," Nikolai says, his voice flat. He has tears in his eyes.

I stand up, looking down at her sitting between them. She still hasn't said a word. She is real, she exists, she is sitting here, she took them. I want to hit her. But I can't, not while the boys are watching.

"What were you trying to do?" I ask her. "What were you trying to accomplish?"

"Me?" she says in a sarcastic tone, and releases that laughter that I have never forgotten. "You think *I* was behind this?"

"I *know* it," I say.

"Mommy," Andreas says impassively.

"Yes, baby?" I say, smiling at him. No matter how awful it is to be here with her, it warms me to see the two of them.

"It wasn't Grandma," Andreas says. "It was us."

CHAPTER 70

ANDREAS

Meeting Sabiya, even though she was really sad, reminded us of how Mommy should be. Sabiya couldn't be our mommy. Mommy couldn't be our mommy. Grandma couldn't be our mommy either, maybe, but she was cool and funny and the best grandmother in the world and we missed her. Besides, we were afraid of what Mommy might do.

After we met Sabiya, we decided to leave.

When Nikolai and I decide to do something and work together to make it happen, we are a pretty good team. I think we're capable of a lot more than many other kids our age. Partly because there are two of us, partly because Clara is our mother. She has almost supernatural powers. So does Grandma, who traveled to Oslo alone in a car after being locked up for thirty years.

Besides, after what happened to Daddy, I had sort of stopped being afraid. The worst that could happen had already happened, so there wasn't much left to be afraid of.

We didn't tell anyone, that would ruin the plan. On Friday, we stayed home from school. We packed our soccer-camp knapsacks. Mommy wouldn't notice they were gone, and they just lay in the back of our closets anyway.

We decided that we should bring as little as possible in our knapsacks, a pair of underwear and some socks and a sweater each, no toothbrushes, or she would understand that we had packed ourselves. We would have to buy new toothbrushes. Our tablets and telephones we would have to leave behind; we wanted to bring them, but the police would be able to track us on them.

We argued about stuffed animals. I didn't think we should bring any, because that would be another sign to Mommy that we had packed for ourselves, but Nikolai refused to leave without his panda. He'd slept with it every night since he got it from Grandmother and Grandfather as a baby and was madly attached to it. I could tell that he meant it, and it was so messy in our room that anything could be lost there for good. The kidnappers maybe would have even allowed us to bring a stuffed animal. So in the end, Nikolai was allowed to bring the panda.

I took only the key ring.

To make sure she wouldn't understand that we had run away, we wrote a letter that we left in the house that would make it look like we'd been kidnapped. We read on the internet about how letters like this are supposed to be and wrote one we hoped she would believe was real.

We wrote the text in English and translated it first into Chinese using Google Translate, then into Norwegian. It was supposed to look like it was written by someone who wasn't Norwegian. We understood that she would be scared, but that served her right.

When we left home, we were happy and excited, more than we'd been in a long time, as if we had swallowed a whole lot of birthday balloons full of helium.

We didn't have much money, but we had some cash that Grandmother had given us and some we had found in one of Daddy's drawers. When we put it together, we figured it would be enough to get us to Western Norway.

We left the letter on the table. Then we pressed the star that locked the door and walked to the streetcar that would take us to the train station. It felt like we were going to start a whole new life, the way people sometimes did in the movies.

The conductor on the train smiled and was super cheerful and wondered whether we were out traveling alone. Yes, we said, we were going to visit our grandfather, and Daddy had taken us to the station, I said. I was sure it was a good idea to lie a little. Nikolai fell asleep on the train, which was kind of nice, but in the end, I had to wake him up.

Up to that point, everything had gone so well it was almost scary, but we knew the difficult part would come later.

The train would reach the last station late at night. From there, we would take a night bus to the village. We were more afraid that a bus driver would contact the police about two children traveling alone at night. Now we would have to be really careful.

We had actually made this exact same trip once before, with Mommy, when the car wasn't working. That's why we knew that the bus usually stopped for twenty minutes in our village and waited before driving on. To be on the safe side, we checked online that this hadn't changed.

We also knew that the luggage compartment on the bus would be open the whole time it was parked at the station where it started, while the driver sat in the front of the bus and sold tickets or surfed on his phone or whatever it was he did. This was also so easy it was almost scary. We just dashed around to the other side of the bus and made sure to be quick and do it in a way he wouldn't see us in his mirror.

As soon as we were inside the gigantic luggage compartment, we crawled to the back and hid in a corner all the way inside, on the same side as the openings. From there, nobody could see us, not those who put their luggage in nor the driver when he came to close the doors.

Then we huddled close together, sitting as still as mice. Later, when the bus started moving, we could whisper a bit. But at this moment, we couldn't make a single noise. We were real stowaways, like those we had read about in books.

After a long time, the doors closed, and the bus started moving. It was hard not to be thrown back and forth when the bus turned a corner.

We had to tense our bodies the whole time to stay put. It smelled of the motor and diesel oil, the air was bad, but this was the last leg of the trip now. We would have to just lie here with our knapsacks and bear it.

Andreas? Nikolai said.

I'm scared.

Of course he was. I was also scared about all the things that could go wrong, now that we were almost there, but I couldn't let him know that.

It will be fine, I said, and tried to talk in a daddy voice.

Are we going to die? he squeaked.

Yes, I said. But not now. In another eighty years or so.

We also had to manage to get off at the right stop without anybody seeing us. I was really nervous about that part. Imagine if the bus didn't stop? Then we would have to get off at the next stop, but that would be stupid. It would be even worse if we fell asleep, so we took turns standing guard and keeping track of the time on our watches, which glowed in the dark.

Along the way, I realized that maybe nobody was going to the same place we were, in the middle of the night. The bus would probably stop there anyway, but if nobody got off, the doors to the luggage compartment wouldn't be opened.

Actually, this was exactly what happened. The time glowing on our watches was 5:40 p.m. The bus arrived, stopped, but the luggage compartment didn't open. My heart pounded hard. Nikolai started sniffling beside me, but I whispered to him that he had to be quiet. Then I crawled over to the doors. It was dark, and I had to feel my way using my hands, but yes, there was a kind of handle.

Are you ready? I whispered to Nikolai, who was still sitting curled up in his corner.

He didn't reply, but he came crawling over at least.

We have to run fast if I can get it open, I said. The driver will see and come to investigate. Okay?

Nikolai nodded, and the door opened. We ran with our knapsacks on our backs, without looking over our shoulders, and we never saw whether the bus driver noticed. We didn't know exactly where we were either; we just ran across a field with some bales of hay in it and into a forest. The most important thing was to get far away from that bus.

When we finally stopped to catch our breath, so happy to have made it this far, Nikolai's face twisted into a horrible grimace.

What? I said, looking behind me to see if the bus driver was coming.

My panda, Nikolai said. Oh no, my panda, I left it in the bus. Oh no, oh no, oh no . . .

Good grief, I said, and now I sounded like Mommy without meaning to. Why didn't you put it into your knapsack?

I forgot it, Nikolai cried. I forgot it.

He cried more than I could remember ever seeing him cry before, and I'd heard a lot of crying from that one.

Nikolai, I said. Listen, now we have to find our way to Grandma's house. Then she can call the bus company, and they will find your panda, I said. Just stop crying, okay? Remember what Mommy usually says, it only hurts as much as you want it to.

Mommy usually says that when somebody hurts themselves or is in pain, which she hates, but it worked, he actually stopped.

At home, we had made a map on ordinary paper after looking it up on GPS. Supposedly, we would have to walk only a couple of hundred yards from the bus to Grandma's house. We would get there very early in the morning, but that was good, too, because then nobody would see us.

At a little after six, we found the steep dirt road that turned off the highway, walked about a hundred yards or so down it toward the water, and then we arrived at Grandma's boathouse. She had shown us photographs when she was in Oslo, a dark-brown boathouse with a grass roof.

It was still pitch dark out. Grandma lived just a few yards from the water, we couldn't see that either, there wasn't exactly moonlight, just rain trickling down, but we could hear the waves breaking against the pebbles on the shore.

We tried ringing the doorbell, and we tried knocking. Nothing happened. We had gotten wet along the way, and it was far too cold to sit outside and wait for morning. We also understood that Grandma liked to sleep late.

We sat down outside the door, side by side, listening to the waves. It was really, really cold, even though it was only October, so we had to huddle together. I put one arm around Nikolai so we could stay warm.

I looked at my watch and saw that I'd received a bunch of messages from Mommy. Where are you, What's going on, Call me, things like that. I felt a little guilty, but that wouldn't do now. That was when I realized that our glow-in-the-dark watches could also be tracked.

Nikolai, I whispered. Take off your watch.

He gave me an odd look, and then he did what I said.

Give it to me, I said softly.

No way, he said. It's mine.

Listen, I said. We have to get rid of them. Somebody could find us because of them.

I want someone to find me, he said. Now a stream of snot was dribbling from his nose.

No, you don't, I said. Give me your watch now and wipe your nose.

He gave me the watch. I stood up, walked over to the fence by the water, took position, and threw first one, then the other. I could just barely hear two faint plops amid the sound of the waves and the rain.

There, I said, and turned toward Nikolai again. Now I don't think they're transmitting much anymore.

I'm freezing, Nikolai said.

Yeah, yeah, I said. I went for a little stroll, looking around the boat-house in search of open windows but didn't find any. Nikolai's lower lip was trembling when I came back. I could tell that he was thinking about his panda.

Wait, I'm just going to check something, I whispered. Don't move.

I stood up, turned around, took hold of the door handle, and pulled it. The door opened, and the light in the hallway flooded toward me. I had to laugh. It wasn't very smart of Grandma to leave the door unlocked, but it was nice for us. We walked into the house, took off our shoes, and tiptoed into something that looked like the world's smallest and most crowded living room. A heat pump droned away under the roof. It was warm, thank heavens. Two small couches. A table.

We'll wait to wake her up, okay? I said. Get a little sleep first?

Nikolai nodded. We each lay down on one of the couches. It felt like the softest thing I'd ever lain on. I pulled a blanket that was lying on the couch over me and fell asleep. I slept until I was awakened a few hours later by somebody who was standing there looking at me.

I opened my eyes and looked straight at Grandma.

She no longer looked like she belonged in a Christmas film. Her lovely, soft hair looked unwashed and was plastered against her head. Her whole body looked unwashed, actually, and she was missing both her lipstick and eyeliner.

Boys, she said. How did you get here?

We ran away, I said, and then I told her everything.

Wow, what fun, she said when I finished my story, even though it didn't look like she thought it was much fun at all. So now your plan is . . . to stay here?

Yes, I said. If that's okay?

I tried to remind myself that we thought she was pretty cranky in the morning and, for that reason, not at her best right now.

Of course, Grandma said. We just have to make sure nobody discovers you. Stay away from all the windows. The landlord is a real busybody. But you can stay here today.

I was actually a little disappointed that she didn't seem happier to see us, and Nikolai just sat there looking sad.

There's a little cellar underneath here, Grandma said. You can go down there just to be on the safe side.

We sat down there all day. It was pretty dark and pretty boring, and Grandma went out and forgot to give us something to eat, so we got pretty hungry.

CHAPTER 71

CLARA

A loud noise starts ringing inside my head.

"*It was us?* What do you mean by that?" I say.

"We were scared," Nikolai says. "We wanted to get away from you. So we ran away."

Everything in front of me turns white. I hear Andreas say something as if from a great distance but am unable to grasp any of the words. Now I'm not just afraid of my own mother but also of my own children. Without thinking, I back out the door, manage to close it behind me, stand outside with my back against the door, and breathe.

All the whiteness dances and flashes before my eyes.

My mother got to her feet in there, with a strange smile on her face, before I backed out the door. Although she is an elderly lady and the other two are children, there are three of them, after all, and I am just one. My boys are tall, big and strong. Even if I were in a normal state, I wouldn't be able to take on all three alone, and I am banged up, battered, exhausted.

My boys have sought an ally in my mother, against me. It's not to be believed.

I sit down, still with my back against the door, pull up my knees, and rest my arms on top of them, my head in my hands.

Did they organize all of this themselves? Are they the ones who wrote the letter? And gave me the ultimatum about my father?

My own sons. My flesh and blood, whom I carried in my womb, gave birth to, breastfed, lulled to sleep. This is what they have done. They are only children, yes, but that just makes it worse. What kind of child does such a thing?

The answer hits me like a hard blow to the head. Children like me. They've done this because they are my children.

I should never have come up here without Stian. What was I thinking?

I am so damn stupid. I slap myself, first one cheek, then the other, as if to force myself to think clearly, find a solution, bear the unbearable. It doesn't help.

What am I going to do? And what was it that Andreas said as I backed out the door, which I didn't hear there and then, because I didn't want to hear it, because everything was already unbearable?

Now I am unable to ward it off any longer.

There is not a sound from inside the stone hut. Still, I hear the same words in my ears, over and over again:

"We know what you did to Daddy."

CHAPTER 72

ANDREAS

When we stay up at the summer farm, Nikolai and I always spend a night or two at Grandpa's without Mommy and Daddy. Before, Daddy always used to say that it was so he and Mommy could have a little girlfriend-and-boyfriend time, but I thought it was mostly so Grandpa could have some time alone with us.

This year, I didn't feel like it. I didn't want to be away from Daddy. Ever since he spent those days in jail when I thought maybe we would never see him again, I wanted us to be together all the time. I could feel happy only as long as I was near him and able to see him. I didn't say that, but I think he noticed it and felt a little bit that way, too. In the evenings, he sat in our room until we fell asleep; I couldn't remember whether he had ever done that before. At the summer farm, he sat on the shabby couch between our beds, wearing a headlamp and reading, until he fell asleep. Mommy sat outside on top of her favorite boulder.

So I'd gotten a little spoiled since Daddy was always there when I fell asleep and when I woke up, when before, I had been used to him often working in the evenings and at night.

Please, can't you just stay here, I said when he walked down to the farm with us and had coffee with Grandpa out by the stone table. It was so nice sitting there, but whenever I thought about how Daddy would soon be going back up to the summer farm again without us, I got a tummy ache.

Something was strange about that day, something about the rustling of the wind, the fog over the fjord, the way the birds sang.

Everything that was actually nice, just felt wrong.

Now, Andreas, Daddy said wearily, you're going to stay here with Grandpa. Mommy and I are going to climb Trollskavlen Peak or Witch Mountain.

Don't go, Daddy, I said. I had a horrible feeling in my whole body, but nobody would listen to me.

I stood there watching Daddy grow smaller and smaller as he walked along the river, until he disappeared into the forest. The whole time, I had that horrible feeling in my body.

Come on now, boys, Grandpa said after Daddy left. Let's go find some ice cream.

So we went and had ice cream and did all the usual things, and I almost managed to forget the horrible feeling, but after we went to bed, it returned with full force. I lay in the room with the slanted ceiling and rag rugs and old pictures on the wall, the nicest room in the world, but I couldn't sleep, I was so afraid.

Usually, it was Nikolai who was afraid, but now he was fast asleep. Grandpa was snoring on the other side of the wall, the way he always did. Everything seemed ordinary, but it wasn't.

After we ate breakfast the next morning, I told Grandpa that I wanted to go outside for a while. This time I didn't go into the barn to lie in the hay and stare into space or go out to the hens to see if there were any eggs or to visit the rabbits. I went to the river, across the little bridge, over to the other side, where I'd seen Daddy disappear the day before. Then I started walking on the trail leading upward. It meandered like a brown snake, and on both sides of it, everything was green except for the small carpets of white starflowers in some places, with the odd blue blossom here and there. I didn't have time now to stop and look, or listen, the way I often did when I was out in the forest.

I didn't think about whether it would frighten Grandpa if I stayed away for a long time, or whether Nikolai would be angry because I didn't take him with me. I didn't think about anything at all, just kept moving up, up, up, at a pace close to Mommy's when she was out running.

The whole time, I could hear the din of the waterfall roaring. The weather had been nice and dry while we were here, but because of the meltwater from the mountain, there was tons of water in the river anyway.

Where the waterfall becomes a lake, as you walk up, the path continues alongside it. But there is also a path that goes up the hill on the other side of the lake, and there you can look down over the lake and the farm. For some reason or other, I ran up there. I wanted to see if I could see Mommy and Daddy, see whether they were sitting outside and eating. We did that often at the summer farm because it was so dark inside the cottage.

When I reached the top of the hill and looked down, I saw something that turned me into an icicle. Both Mommy and Daddy were outside, in the water, but they weren't together. Mommy was swimming toward the shore on the side where I was. It looked like she was struggling to move forward. Mommy is a good swimmer, even underwater. Daddy was in another part of the lake, much closer to where the waterfall began to descend. He was struggling, too, but it didn't look like he was able to swim; it was as if the current snatched and pulled at him. He disappeared here, then there, would go under water for a bit, then surface again.

He's in control, I said to myself, he's in control.

Clara, help, he called. Clara, help.

Then I could hear that he wasn't in control, not at all. Mommy just kept swimming away. I understood that she heard him but didn't want to see him and didn't want to help him. Besides, she was too far away, there was a big distance between them, and Daddy was being spun, swirling faster and faster toward the edge.

I was about to run down to the lake and jump in, but I understood that I wouldn't be able to pull him out of the current anyway. I wanted to call out to her, but my voice got stuck in my throat. She hadn't seen me yet, I had time to see her collapse onto her knees in the sand on the shore, and then I started running back to the path I had just walked up on, in too much of a hurry to watch my step, so I stumbled and fell but kept running, while the tears sprang into my eyes.

The whole time, I tried to look toward the lake, and I could see him there, until suddenly I couldn't see him anymore. Daddy, Daddy. Please, God, help him.

As fast as I could, I ran off the path toward the waterfall, so close that a whole lot of drops hit my face. It was like standing in the shower. I almost couldn't see, I blinked, I called for Daddy, expecting to see him any minute, in the white, thundering water, an arm, a foot, but there was nothing to see.

I groped at rocks and underbrush and bushes and tree roots; apparently people weren't supposed to walk here, almost in the waterfall. I almost fell in, I almost jumped in to be with Daddy, but I didn't. I didn't do anything. I just ran, searched, cried.

Finally, I sat on a rock by the big hollow where the waterfall came down, stared into the white veil of water, and waited to see if I could spot him descending in the falls, even though I knew it was too late. I also looked down in the pool below where the waterfall ended, to see if maybe he was floating around in there. I called his name. I waited and waited, until finally I got up and ran the rest of the way down to Grandpa's farm.

There I found Grandpa, who was standing and holding Nikolai in his arms.

Andreas, Grandpa said. There's been an accident. Mommy called. I've called for help.

Daddy, Nikolai cried.

I just stood there in the sunlight, shaking and my teeth chattering. Grandpa put his arms around me, hugged me against him, didn't think it was strange that I didn't wonder what had happened. We were standing there like that, he and I and Nikolai, when an ambulance arrived, and then a police car came driving into the yard. The people ran over to Grandpa and started asking him about things. I didn't catch what they were saying, not until Grandpa took me by the shoulder and asked if I could run up with them and show them the way and I nodded.

I can barely remember running up to the farm with the frogmen and the police. I was so tired, had already run so much, and I was shaking and so sad. I don't remember seeing Mommy again either. Everything about that moment has disappeared from my head.

Afterward, Grandpa said many times that he regretted putting me through that, as he put it.

Finally, I said that he had to stop saying it, that it didn't make any difference. It was true. Daddy was gone and Mommy hadn't helped him, she wanted him to die.

Nothing can make it worse or better. Not now, not later. Nothing can stop the films inside my head either, the film of Daddy walking down the steps between the police officers with his head bowed and the film where he is thrashing around out in the water, being whirled farther and farther away. He should have listened to me, but I should have tried harder, too.

Ever since last summer, I've been trying to erase these films, but they won't disappear. Maybe they never will.

CHAPTER 73

CLARA

I am so tired, so battered, so confused. I am on my feet but unable to move or understand what I should do with the three of them in there.

Then I see a figure walking up the trail. Stian. I breathe, counting inside my head: 1,001, 1,002, 1,003. At 1,020, he has reached me.

"Stian," I say.

Then my knees buckle, and I fall forward. Stian stands there, holding me up, the way he did when I lost my balance on the Palace Square.

"There, there," he says, cupping the back of my head with one hand, pulling it beneath his chin. "There, there."

He wraps his other arm around my body.

"Ow" slips out of my mouth.

He releases me, inspects me.

"Are you injured? What happened?"

"I fell into a ravine," I say, sniffling. "Broke a few ribs, I think, and sprained an ankle, but I climbed out again. And I found them, finally. They're inside."

I nod toward the stone hut. He wrinkles his brow.

"It was your mother who took them?"

"Yes, in a way," I say. "It's a little complicated."

I give him a quick, abridged version of the events.

"Okay," he says. "Let's get them out of there."

I glance at my watch. Twenty minutes to spare. Somehow, we managed it, managed to find them. In spite of everything.

He grabs the door handle, opens the door. I don't dare look inside, because now I realize that I have left the three of them alone there for a long time without any supervision. There hasn't been a single peep from any of them. My mother could have done anything to the boys while I was gone.

CHAPTER 74

ANDREAS

After Daddy died, I thought I should tell Grandpa or the police what I saw, but I kept putting it off.

When I was finally able to think again, I discovered that it was impossible to say anything. Because if Mommy went to jail, what would happen to us? We didn't have any aunts or uncles. Grandpa was too old and lived too far away. Who would take care of us? Grandmother and Grandfather? The thought wasn't exactly appealing, and I didn't think they would be up for it either. Uncle Axel? He wasn't really our uncle, and he already had three children.

I thought I would have to try to say something to Mommy, at least. Had to tell her that I saw her, that I understood, but I couldn't manage to do that either.

It was like everything was contained inside a black, slimy, sticky lump in my chest. Besides, I was afraid. What would she do to us if we said something? Ever since I stood on top of that hill and watched Daddy being pulled toward the waterfall, it's like I'm outside myself all the time. Nothing seems completely real.

I didn't plan to say anything to Nikolai, but when we went to bed the night after Daddy's funeral, he was lying there sniffling and crying. I couldn't take any more of it, so I told him to shut up. Then he lost it, said that I was a jerk who didn't care about anything.

This made me so cross that I told him everything. Afterward, he didn't say a thing, the guy who's usually always whining and pestering me.

Nikolai? I said. Nikolai?

What, he said, finally, in a voice that didn't sound like his.

Then I understood that he wasn't the same person anymore either and never would be.

It was actually his idea that we should try to scare Mommy a little. One day we moved a paper that looked like it was top secret out of a drawer and up onto her desk. Another day we put one of Daddy's shirts on the mannequin in her bedroom. Just a few days before we left, we wrote a letter saying that we knew what she'd done. We didn't dare write "to Daddy" or "to Henrik." We thought that would give away who had written it.

All these things were just practice for the big event, for leaving her. Mommy had taken the best daddy in the world away from us. Now she would see how it was to have her children taken from her.

Eventually, I understood that Grandma was angry with both Grandpa and Mommy. It had something to do with the old days, when Mommy and Uncle Lars were little and Grandpa and Grandma split up. I tried asking Grandma about it, tried to find out what really happened, but I never got an answer. And I really started missing Grandpa, Grandmother, Grandfather, Axel, and even Mommy.

Now Mommy's outside the door and we're inside here with Grandma. It's like being trapped inside a kind of strange war where I have no idea what any of them will do.

CHAPTER 75

—

CLARA

When I open the door, all three of them are sitting there quite calmly, as if somebody let a bit of the air out of them. She hasn't strangled them, hasn't poisoned them, hasn't done anything else to them.

Stian takes control, ordering them out of the hut, while I stand there watching. It's as if all the blood has drained out of my head, down my body, out of my fingertips, and onto the ground.

Blood of my blood, bones of my bones, soul of my soul.

It's completely dark now, but both Stian and I have headlamps. The boys walk past me and out of the hut without looking at me. Maybe because they don't want the sharp light from the headlamp in their eyes, or maybe because they can't bring themselves to look at me. If so, the feeling is mutual.

My mother, on the other hand, looks straight at me as she walks past, with scorn and contempt in her eyes.

Stian runs back to the summer farmhouse and gets a couple of dish towels that he tears up and wraps around my ankle.

We start walking down, Stian and Agnes first. Then the boys, then me.

"It's dark, it could be slippery, and only Clara and I have headlamps," Stian says. "The rest of you have to try to walk in the beam of our lights. Walk carefully so we make it down safely."

Nobody replies. All I hear is the rushing of the river, the whistling wind, the hooting of a horned owl, the sounds of nature.

A loud pling sounds from my mother's cell phone. Elderly people always set the volume too high. Who's texting her now? Bodil? Buzz? Actually, I don't care.

The last time I saw her, she was sitting in a chair, in a daze, her head lolling from side to side. Now here she is walking in the darkness, having held my sons prisoner for days. It is not to be fathomed.

My own mother. I don't know what I'm going to do with her. Stian will have to take care of it, put her somewhere far away from me. I hope more than anything else that I will never see her again.

I must try to talk to the boys, find out what they know, what they've been thinking, what it was that caused them to do something like this.

Regardless, we'll soon be back down at the farm. Daddy and the cat and the crackling woodstove are there, and I can probably have a shot of something; there's comfort in that anyway.

Stian walks back to me, takes my arm over his shoulder, as if to support me as I walk on my injured ankle. I like the feeling of hanging on his shoulder, the way I like his fingers against my back, his hands on my neck, me, who usually doesn't like such things.

I don't know what it means, or if it means anything at all, but I walk along and look at my sons, who, in a few years, will be a head taller than me, and I think that we have to make this work. One way or another, we must make it work.

Then something hits my face, just as out of nowhere as the rain on the Palace Square a month ago. I lift my head, look up.

Large white flakes hit my forehead, my nose, my cheeks, my mouth, my eyelids, settle side by side on the ground, begin covering the dark soil with white, for the first time this year.

When I come around the corner of the hay barn and walk into the yard, I see that something is not right. The doors of the barn are wide open, which they never are, and the light is on in the hayloft.

Dangling in the opening to the hayloft is a body.

I see it, even though I don't want to see it. I understand, even though I don't want to, understand that nothing will ever be fine again.

EPILOGUE

STIAN

Daddy, she wailed. Daddy, Daddy . . .

Then she started to run up the barn bridge, toward the body hanging from the roof. Viewed from the outside of the barn, his body was a black silhouette against the bright light behind it. I ran after her, managed to catch her in my arms and get her down on the ground, more roughly than I intended. Then I ran over to Leif. Even though I could see that it was probably already too late, I had to try anyway.

Afterward, Clara lay on the barn bridge, curled up in a fetal position, not speaking or moving, as if she, too, were dead. Terror stricken, the boys looked back and forth from their mother to their grandfather hanging there. Agnes stood beside them, a strange, frozen expression on her face and an inappropriate half smile. I had her take the children inside with her. It wasn't ideal, but it felt like the lesser of two evils. I had to assume she wouldn't take off with them again.

When the local police arrived, I called the psychiatric hospital where Agnes had been living. A lady who works there came and got her; it seemed as if the two of them knew each other well. Agnes went peacefully. I still wonder whether or not we should press charges against her. It's complicated. Because how can we do that without disclosing everything else that happened?

It was impossible to get Clara to say anything or move. Her build is slight, but she's also tall, sturdy, no little girl. Finally, I somehow managed to slip my arms beneath that long-limbed body, lift her up, and carry her across the yard, into the house and up the stairs. Then she was at least a safe distance from Agnes and the boys.

In the living room was an old cardboard box. I only glanced inside it; it seemed to contain things related to Lars. I would have to look at it later. For the time being, I moved it up into one of the bedrooms, no need for the boys to be exposed to that.

Leif's cup was on the table, along with a thick book that lay open with his reading glasses on top of it. It was as if he was just there, and he was, in fact. Later, I managed to worm out of Clara that she'd told Leif everything before she went up to the summer farm. She had even shown him the idiotic note that turned out to have been written by Agnes and which demanded that Clara kill him if she wanted to see the boys again.

Clara had called her father from the scree when she couldn't get hold of me, those few minutes when I had been busy with Halvor. They'd had a brief and chaotic conversation, which was cut off when the battery on her phone died, and which must have made him think that he had to sacrifice himself to save her and the children. For my own part, when I saw the missed calls from her and was sent to voice mail when I tried to reach her, I tracked her on her phone. For us, that is possible, even though the battery was dead. In that way, I was able to find her at the stone hut.

Leif had sent a text to Agnes while we were walking down. When I found out about that, I remembered the sound of her cell phone plinging. You win, I will do what you want. Just spare Clara and the boys. Leif, the message read.

Then he hanged himself with the loading straps he used for mending fences.

Clara blames herself for this sacrifice. It's difficult to imagine her back at work, but I am betting that she will turn things around. A woman who is able to climb out of a deep ravine in the dark with broken ribs and a sprained ankle can manage just about anything.

Never in my life have I met anyone like her, and I have met and seen all kinds. The past week has, in a way, made up for many years of a sedate existence, compared to my years in Afghanistan and other places.

Somehow, I managed to get Clara on her feet for the funeral. I went to the shopping mall in the neighboring village and bought clothes for her and the boys, washed and ironed, laid out clothing for all three of them. Yes, I even washed her hair, brushed it, and blow-dried it, the way I do with my daughters' hair at home.

It was, in fact, the girls I thought about when I saw Clara standing there beside the open grave on the steep hillside in the cemetery. She stood alone; it was as if she was transmitting a message that nobody should approach her, which nobody did. I was perhaps the only one who could have actually gone over to her, but it felt inappropriate there and then.

Leif's grave is beside Lars's. The headstone with the bird on it was moved over to the wall for this occasion. Maybe Leif's name can be engraved on the same stone, that will be up to Clara to decide. I took care of the funeral arrangements, but sooner or later, she will have to take the reins.

I made sure that uniformed police officers kept the press and thrill seekers at a distance. They had their work cut out for them; there were lots of people standing outside the cemetery walls. The pallbearers lowered the coffin down into the big, open grave using a rope, the way they still do here. All six of the people from the community whom I called had agreed to take part.

Since Clara was not in any condition to help the pastor with the eulogy or anything else, I tried to find out who actually knew him. It turned out to be impossible. For the most part, people didn't know Leif. People definitely didn't know Clara. Clara knew Leif, and Leif knew Clara.

The bothersome guy who owned the boathouse where Agnes was staying, the guy they called Buzz, claimed he was Leif's eldest and best friend, although there was nothing to suggest they'd been especially close. I thought I saw Halvor the journalist amid all the people on the hill leading up to the church, but I couldn't be sure. Either way, I'll be watching him.

The secretary general, Mona, had wanted to attend the funeral, but I told her it wasn't a good idea. Clara's in-laws were present, however. They're staying at a bed and breakfast down in the village. I don't know how much they understood. I tried to say as little as possible.

Åsa suggested that I should get Clara's friend Axel to come. He's the one who is closest to the boys now that Henrik is no longer alive, she said, and sighed.

I called Axel, who was initially testy and then horrified when he heard what had happened, before he said that of course he wanted to help out. Now he is staying with us here on the farm, has been given a room that resembles a kind of old-fashioned hotel room, in the middle of this somewhat chaotic and overfilled house. It seems anyway like he is sleeping on a mattress on the floor in the boys' room. He is pleasant and polite but reserved. There's something about him I can't quite put my finger on, which I have made a note of and will get back to later.

Both of the boys clung to Axel as the coffin was lowered into the ground, and it is the three of them who feed the sheep and the hens together. The children still aren't talking much and are downcast and red eyed. They are pretty guilt stricken, which is understandable. Leif would be alive were it not for the two of them and Agnes.

My small contribution toward cheering them up has been that I've managed to track down and bring home Nikolai's panda. So at least they were reunited with both that and the key ring.

Clara doesn't appear to care that the panda has been recovered, that Axel is here, or about anything else. She just lies in bed, curled up, like a defenseless, abandoned child.

ABOUT THE AUTHOR

Photo © Ann Sissel Holthe / www.fatmonkey.no

Ruth Lillegraven was born in Hardanger, Norway, where she grew up on a small farm. She debuted as an author with a poetry collection in 2005. Since then she has written seventeen books, including children's books, several poetry collections, two plays, and the prize-winning, internationally bestselling novel *Everything Is Mine*, the first in her Clara series. Her work has been translated into Dutch, English, French, German, Spanish, and Polish. Among other prizes, Ruth has won both the Brage Prize and the Nynorsk Literature Prize for the poetry collections *Urd* and *Sickle*. For more information, visit www.ruthlillegraven.no.

ABOUT THE TRANSLATOR

Photo © 2020 Nuria Pizarro Sabadell

Diane Oatley is a writer, independent scholar, and translator. She began her undergraduate studies of English literature at the University of Maine and completed an MA in comparative literature at the University of Oslo. Her poetry has been published in anthologies and journals in England, Norway, Spain, and India, and she is the author of three poetry chapbooks. In 2014 Diane received NORLA's annual Translator's Award for nonfiction, and two of her literary translations have been long-listed for the International Dublin Literary Award. She is a member of the Norwegian Non-Fiction Writers and Translators Association and the Norwegian chapter of PEN International.